Upgrade U

Also by Ni-Ni Simone

SHORTIE LIKE MINE

IF I WAS YOUR GIRL

A GIRL LIKE ME

TEENAGE LOVE AFFAIR

Published by Dafina Books

Upgrade U

Ni-Ni Simone

KENSINGTON PUBLISHING CORP.
www.kensingtonbooks.com

DAFINA BOOKS are published by

Kensington Publishing Corp.
119 West 40th Street
New York, NY 10018

All Kensington titles, imprints, and distributed lines are available at special quantity discounts for bulk purchases for sales promotion, premiums, fund-raising, educational, or institutional use.

Special book excerpts or customized printings can also be created to fit specific needs. For details, write or phone the office of the Kensington Special Sales Manager: Attn.: Special Sales Department. Kensington Publishing Corp., 119 West 40th Street, New York, NY 10018. Phone: 1-800-221-2647.

Dafina Books and the Dafina logo Reg. U.S. Pat. & TM Off.

ISBN-13: 978-0-7582-4191-7
ISBN-10: 0-7582-4191-7

First Printing: March 2011
10 9 8 7 6 5 4 3 2 1

Printed in the United States of America

To my mom, my number-one cheerleader!

To Taylor, my thirteen-year-old sweetie,
who secretly thinks I'm cool!

To Sydney, my eight-year-old diva,
who thinks I'm the greatest mommy in the world!

To Zion, my three-year-old man,
who tells me he loves me twenty times a day!

To Korynn, who doesn't hesitate to call me up
and say, "You have to change this,
no one says that anymore!" LOL

To Keisha, the forever teenager who doesn't hesitate
to dream with me what it would be like
to be seventeen again!

To Ari, who appointed herself my fan club president and
then showed me how much she deserved it!

Love: Giving someone the ability to destroy your heart, but trusting them enough not to…

—A<small>NONYMOUS</small>

ACKNOWLEDGMENTS

First and foremost, I thank God for the gift, the determination to pursue the dream, and the opportunity to fulfill it.

To my parents, my family, church family, coworkers, and everyone who has ever supported me in my career—those seen and unseen—I thank you for all that you do and have done!

To my agent, Sara Camilli—thanks for being the best!

To Selena James and the Kensington family, thank you for this wonderful opportunity!

To the bookstores, online stores, libraries, and message boards, thank you, thank you, thank you for spreading the word and putting my books on the map!

To the schools that have included the Ni-Ni Simone series as a part of your reading programs, I thank you for your support and truly pray that my writings make a difference.

Saving the best for last, the fans! What author could ask for more? Thanks so much for being here to support my literary ventures and I sincerely hope to make you proud. Be sure to join the Ni-Ni Simone chat room at www.nini girlz.com, where we chat about books, Ni-Ni Girlz online magazine, and all sorts of hot topics!

By the way, I'd love to hear your thoughts on *Upgrade U*, so be sure to e-mail me at ninisimone@yahoo.com.

To become an official part of the Ni-Ni Simone fan club,

send an e-mail to fanclubpresident@ninisimone.com or visit ninisimone.com for details.

And to every teenager in the Big Easy, I wrote this one for you, bey-be!

Stay blessed!

Ni-Ni Simone

Upgrade U

1

What's higher than number one?

—Beyoncé ft. Jay-Z, "Upgrade U"

Stiles University, Big Easy, USA

"Seven, promise me you'll call home every week. Okay? You hear me?" my mother said, as the tears she held back caused her words to tremble. She palmed my face softly between her hands and kissed my forehead. "I'm never too far away—"

"To tap dat azz," Cousin Shake said as he walked into my dorm room, holding a stack of two cardboard boxes in his hands and nodding his head to the side for emphasis. "That's what's wrong witcha now, yo mama babies you too much. But see, I know your tricks, homie. And I know that you applied to a college far away from home, so you could get your hoochie off in peace"—he dropped the boxes on the floor—"but ain't gon' be no peace. 'Cause I'm gon' send somebody to keep a watch on you."

"All right, Cousin Shake," my mother said sternly.

"Grier, you know I love da kids," Cousin Shake said, and as he spoke, the seat of his metallic gold MC Hammer pants flapped with every word. And the taco meat on his chest—that he so proudly showcased by wearing no shirt beneath his matching gold vest—seemed to get tighter by the moment. Ugg, I just wanted him to leave!

"Why are you looking at me like that, Seven?" Cousin Shake said. "Huh? I'll tell you why, 'cause you know that I see right through you."

"Cousin Shake, behave" was my mother's failed attempt to get this sixty-year-old throwback to listen to someone besides himself.

"You don't tell me to behave, Grier," Cousin Shake admonished. "I raised you. Now, all I'm doing is making a point."

"And what's that?" I said with a little more edge than I should've.

"Watch your tone, Seven," my mother warned. "What's your point, Cousin Shake?"

"My point is"—he turned to me—"that just 'cause you in the Big Easy, Seven, don't mean you have to be the big easy. Feel me? I mean, you still big, but you don't have to be all easy, greasy, and handing over your goodies to every Tom, Raheem, and Josiah, just 'cause me and your mama's up in Brick City."

What?

"Cousin Shake," my mother snapped. "That's a bit much."

"See?" Cousin Shake snorted. "That's her problem—you spoil this girl too much."

"This is my baby." My mother hugged me tightly. "And she's never been this far away from home or me before."

"Ma, I'll be fine." After all, this wasn't my first time in college. I went to Spellman for half a semester, until my stepfather lost his job and we had to move from Atlanta back to Jersey. But that didn't last for too long, because I was seriously on my grind. I was turning eighteen and had big dreams. Dreams that only going to college would afford me. So while my twin sister, Toi, stayed close to home and attended NJIT, I applied to Stiles U, and courtesy of my good grades and perfect SAT scores I was awarded a full academic scholarship. So me, along with my BFF, Shae—who also transferred from Spellman—arrived in the Crescent City ready to roll.

"I'm here!" Shae screamed running into our dorm room. She ran over to me and said, "Girl, it's some cuties up in here, honey. Told you southern boys were the truth!"

Obviously Shae ran in here so fast she didn't realize we weren't alone. "Shae—"

"Seven," she said, not letting me get a word in, "I couldn't wait to shake my daddy at the gate. We got to the registration office and I was like, 'Dad, seriously I got it from here. I handed my stuff to Big Country and waved bye-bye to Samuel Parker. Whew!" She wiped invisible sweat from her brow. "How'd you ditch your blockers?"

"She didn't," my mother said, causing Shae to halt in her spot.

"Why didn't you warn me?" Shae mouthed, as she slowly turned around and gave my mother a small wave.

"I was trying to tell you to shut up," I mumbled.

"Told you," Cousin Shake said, wagging his finger at us. "From cute lil sweet Jersey girls to nasty Louisiana—"

"All right, Cousin Shake," my mother said, as Shae walked over and gave her a hug. "These are good girls and New Orleans is one of the greatest cultural cities in the world."

"Yawn," Cousin Shake said, as if he could not care less.

"Mama!" poured from down the hall and toward our room. "Could you please stop trippin'? You acting like I've moved to Arizona, Utah, or California somewhere, I'm back home, in N'awlins. And from the time we stayed in Houston until I applied to go away to college, we've talked about this...over and over again....Dang." Whoever this was, stopped in our doorway, looked up at the numbers on the door, and nodded her head like she was in the right place. The woman standing beside her wore the same look of sadness and worry that my mother did and the six-foot-tall man who stood behind them looked to be as bored as Cousin Shake.

"Wassup, round? How ya livin', yat? I'm Khya." She batted her extended lashes and flipped her one-sided Rihanna-esque bob, with blond streaks running through it, from over her left eye to behind her respective ear. She placed her hands on what looked to be about a size-sixteen hips, complimented by a small waist and a rump shaker that would put Nicki Minaj to shame.

Khya continued on with her spiel. "Seems we already got two things in common: late acceptance and registration. 'Cause according to the RA's Facebook status"—she looked at her BlackBerry for a quick moment and then back to us—"that's how they choose who was gon' be sharing the triple dorms."

Khya slammed her hot pink and floral Coach shoulder bag on top of a desk, and without missing a beat or taking a breath she continued, "It's 'bout to be crunk, ya heardz me? I can look at y'all and tell y'all good people. So since we 'bout to be roommates, ya might as well hit ya girl with some introductions."

True story: I didn't know what the heck just blew in

here. Even Cousin Shake looked confused. This chick's New Orleans accent was thicker than you could ever imagine or wrap your ears around hearing.

"Y'all must be from up north," Khya said, "'cause y'all lookin' at me like ya slow. Now what's good?"

Was that an insult? I stopped my eyes from blinking and did my best to wipe the confused look off of my face. I walked over to her, with Shae beside me, and said, "Hey girl, I'm Seven and this is Shae."

"Wassup, ma?" Shae said.

Khya blinked. "Oh my, y'all got some serious New York accents on y'all."

Did she just talk about somebody's accent? And she's standing here sounding like Lil Wayne's ex-wife, Toya.

"Actually, we're from Jersey," I said.

"Nawl," Cousin Shake interjected. "Actually, we're from Earth, where we speak English."

"Oh, you so funny and cute." Khya laughed. "You look just like 1982. Who is this, your great-granddaddy? He needed a walk or something, a day out of the home?"

"Yep," I said, laughing. "That's exactly who he is."

"Be quiet, Seven." My mother twisted her lips at me and then turned to Khya and her family and said, "I'm Grier, Seven's mother, and this is my cousin, Cousin Shake."

"I'm Toni." Khya's mother sniffed and dabbed the corners of her eyes. "Nice to meet you, and this is my husband, Kyle."

"It's hard, I know," my mother said, and I could tell she was swallowing tears. "But we have to let them go."

"I've been telling her this since forever," Kyle said.

"I know, Kyle," Toni said, with tears bubbling in her eyes. "But she's my baby."

"Oh, Toni," my mother joined in, "I said the same thing." She was now dabbing her eyes too.

"Looka here, Mama," Khya said. "Listen, you call me tomorrow, okay? 'Cause I really would like to get settled into my room."

"Give me kisses first."

"Mama!" Khya arched her eyebrows in embarrassment. "Would you stop?"

"Kisses," her mother insisted.

"Mama, I'm not—"

"Get yo behind over there and kiss your mama, girl," Cousin Shake growled. "And you too, Seven. Y'all better be lucky you got mamas, somebody that can tolerate you. 'Cause I'ma tell you the truth, I don't like kids, I fight 'em. Now give me a reason to handle you"—he looked at Khya—"and I'ma show you what 1982 was really about. Now try me. Go kiss yo mama, like I said. And do it now, 'cause I don't have much time. I need to go and meet my wife Minnie. She's at the hotel waiting for me, so we can get our flash on and get thrown some beads on Bourbon Street."

I don't know about anyone else, but the visual of Cousin Shake and Miss Minnie flashing anybody was about to make me throw up in my mouth.

Khya and I walked over to our mothers, hugged and kissed them, and as if they'd practiced it, they simultaneously said, "I love you. Call me if you need anything."

"Okay." Toni sniffed. "I'ma go now."

"Me too," my mother said. "Come on, Toni, we can walk out together."

Khya gave her father a hug. "Don't forget to get me some tickets for the basketball games, baby girl," he said.

"Okay, Daddy." Khya kissed her father on the cheek, and then he left. That's when we realized that Cousin Shake was still there.

"You can leave too." I tried my best not to snap, but the mere sight of him lingering around caused my blood pressure to rise.

"Who you talkin' to, Fat Mama?" he growled, calling me by my childhood nickname. "Girl, don't make me handle you. Now your mama may have ran outta here like she's crazy, but I'm not leaving until we pray."

Oh hell to da nawl! "Cousin Shake, that won't be necessary," I insisted.

"What?" He frowned. "Don't make me put my thang down on you. Since when you start refusing prayer?"

"You know how he is," Shae mumbled. "Now let's just bow our heads and get this over with."

I couldn't believe this was happening to me. I grabbed Khya's hand and said, "Come on, roommate, we in this together."

Reluctantly we bowed our heads and Cousin Shake began. "Our Father, Who art in Heaven, wassup, bruh? How's Julio, Mary, Margaret, Paul, Radio-Raheem, and er'-body? I know I ain't been to You in a minute, Lawd, but You know, like Fat Joe says, 'If it ain't about money why we wastin' time?' 'Cause moneeeeey's," Cousin Shake started to sing, "always on my mind. You can believe that I be where the G's at—"

"Cousin Shake!" I said sternly.

"Who you yelling at?" he said. "You know when I get to talking about Julio, I get a lil carried away—"

"Who is Julio?" Khya whispered to me.

"Jesus," I mumbled. "Just roll with it."

"Oh my…"

"Now, Father," Cousin Shake's prayer continued, "please look over these girls and remind them of what Your word says, remind them of Your seven commandos."

"It's commandments," Khya interjected, "and it's ten, not seven."

"You correcting me, Karate?"

"It's Khya." Khya attempted to enunciate her name for Cousin Shake, "K-Y, the *h* is silent, the *y* makes a long I sound, and then there's the sound of *ya*. Khya."

Cousin Shake moved his fingers as if he were speaking in sign language. "Are you cra-ay-zee, interrupting me during prayer time?" Cousin Shake snorted. "Let me tell you something, Cashew. Don't sleep on me. I might be sixty-two, but I will bring it to you. Ya heardz me? Now, as long as you rooming with these two, then you part of the family. I'ma send you care packages, just like I'ma send them. I'ma send you a ten-dollar allowance just like they gon' get.

" 'Cause in college I know y'all don't have no money. And I'ma be here for you when you need me and to mess you up when you get outta line, but don't try me. 'Cause I'm lookin' for a reason to unleash my aggression." He squinted. "Word to the mother-son-cousin. Now bow yo dam'yum heads."

"Just do it," I whispered to Khya. "Trust me he only gets worse."

We bowed our heads again.

"Like I said," Cousin Shake went on, "Lawd, remind them of the five comrades: Thou shalt not bear thou goodies for nobody. Thou shalt not steal time away from thou homework to get thou skeezin' on. Thou shalt not come home without calling first, because thou room will be turned into a love den for Big Daddy Shake and his Minnie. Thou shalt get a J-O-B. And lastly, thou shalt know that Cousin Shake loves you and he will never be too far away if you need him." He sniffed. "Hallelujah. Amen."

Was he crying? Ugg! Just when I couldn't stand him, he acts human. "Awwl, Cousin Shake, I love you too!" I said, giving him a hug.

"Me too!" Shae joined in.

"Me three!" Khya said, completing our group hug.

A few seconds later, Cousin Shake said, "All right, get up off me now. Minnie don't like too much perfume in my taco meat."

Yuck! I promise you I couldn't stand him. He walked toward the door and hit us with a two-finger peace sign. "Deuces," he said and a few minutes later he was gone.

2

He on some other sh*t.

—LUMIDEE FT. PITBULL, "CRAZY"

I have to stop calling him.

But I can't believe he hasn't returned my text.

So what? I don't give a damn.

Yes, I do.

Puhlease, two can play that game.

But he said he would be here to help me move in.

Where is he?

Maybe he didn't make it to campus yet.

He's a ball player. He's always on campus.

Maybe my text didn't go through.

Yeah, right, out of the five hundred I sent, not even one went through? He got 'em.

Prove it.

Fail.

Seriously, I was buggin'. I sat on the edge of my unmade twin-sized bed, in a sea of cardboard boxes, while Q 93.3 FM serenaded us during our pre-party preparation. Khya sorted through her makeup bag, picking out the right eye shadow. Shae laid True Religion jeans, a hot-pink ribbed tank top, and stilettos across the foot of her bed—all while I straight fronted like going to this party was the most pressing thing on my mind.

But it wasn't.

I hated that I played myself like this. I really wanted to enjoy this moment. I mean, seriously, my freshman year of freedom was just beginning, and the hottest Big Easy bounce party was about to go down. I needed to be practicing my booty bounce, not sitting here with a grip on my cell phone, praying it would ring or signal that I had a text message.

"So when are you going to get dressed?" Shae asked, sliding gloss across her lips.

"Yeah, really," Khya said as she applied mascara, " 'cause we fidda catch da wall, bey-be."

What did she say? "Khya." I laughed. "Catch a who?"

"Da wall, honey. It means—"

"Get your groove on," Shae interjected. "So get up and stop thinking about Josiah." She pointed to my cell phone.

"Who's Josiah?" Khya asked, while she looked in the mirror and blew kisses at herself. "I am so sexy." She turned away from the mirror and said, "Now tell me, who is Josiah?"

"Seven's boo," Shae volunteered.

"All right now." Khya snapped her fingers. "You miss him, Seven? Where's he at, in Jersey?" She sat on the edge of the dresser.

At this point I wish he was in Jersey. . . . Then at least I would understand not hearing from him.

"No, he's—"

"Right on campus, girl," Shae snapped.

Oh no, she didn't.

"Oh hell nawl!" Khya said. "What's his name again? Jamil?"

"No, Josiah," I said.

"Well, he sounds like Jamil."

"Who's Jamil?"

"My ex-boyfriend," Khya said. "Being on the same campus and not calling is something he would do."

"I never said I haven't heard from Josiah."

"Actions speak louder than words," Shae said, pointing to my phone.

If looks could kill Shae would be laid out on the floor. "You need to fall back, fa'real."

"Girl, please." Shae smiled at me. "You know I love you. Now, come on 'cause my baby, Big Country, is throwing a slammin' part'tay."

"Yes, he is!" Khya hopped off the dresser and turned up the radio where Sissy Nobby screamed about a spinning top. Khya placed her hands on the wall and proceeded to break down the art of a Big Easy bounce.

"Don't stop, get-it—get-it!" Shae jumped up and joined Khya, both of them shaking their bottoms as if their behinds were having multiple seizures.

Okay, so, despite how I really felt, I had to jump off the bed and join them. After all, attached to my size-fourteen hips was more than enough rump to spin. Not to mention Shae wasn't really doing the dance that well. And since she was my homegirl, I wanted to show her how it's supposed to go down.

"First of all," I said, half smiling and half smirking, "this is how it's done." I did a Beyoncé pop, swept the floor with it, and bounced my booty like I was a New Orleans native and not a transplant.

"Dang, girl!" Khya said, shocked. "No, but you killin' it. Put you on some super-tight-tight-glued-on jeans, a cleavage-busting tee, and we're sure to leave Big Country's party with so many numbers that you'll be like 'Josiah who?' Come on now, just for tonight, Josiah don't even matter."

Heck, maybe she was right. Josiah didn't matter...at least for tonight.

"All right." I picked out my gear for the party. "Time to get dressed," I said and headed into the bathroom.

Before I stepped into the shower I did all I could to ward off thoughts of calling Josiah again...but I couldn't fight it. I had to call him at least one more time. The problem was that one time turned into two...and two times turned into too many, especially when they were all met by his voice mail.

So, forget it. I showered quickly and headed back into the room with Shae and Khya.

As I dressed in a pair of tight jeans and a Ni-Ni Simone original T-shirt that read, DRAMA RULES EVERYTHING AROUND ME, Shae, Khya, and I talked about everything under the sun. From Khya's family remaining in Houston after Hurricane Katrina, to Shae saying how happy she was that her mother was in a drug treatment program, and me talking about how my relationship with my daddy was the best it's ever been.

We chatted away like old friends and yet there was only one problem I could see: the unsettling feeling that washed over me and forced me to think that maybe...I really needed to skip the party and stay in our room...just in case Josiah came knocking....

3

Don't even think about calling me crazy
You know you peeped that lady…

—BRANDY, "WHO IS SHE TO U"

I did my best to get my top model on as my stilettos clicked across the floor…but it was hard, especially since Big Country's tight dorm room was packed from the door to the walls. And the party didn't stop there. People lined the hallway and spilled into the adjacent dorm rooms. Actually the entire floor was crunk; and Melvin, a.k.a. Big Country "Da Stunna" was the DJ, and his soul mate, Shae, grooved right next to him.

I did all I could to curb my thoughts about Josiah, especially since Shae and Khya were taking 10th Ward Buck's advice on how to catch da wall.

A few minutes into me forcing myself to smile instead of rolling my eyes and slowly walking back toward depression, "Girl, what da hell you ovah here lookin' like a chap fo'?" floated over my shoulder.

That was Khya. She stopped her booty from bouncing long enough to step to me and say, "Looka here." She frowned. "Ain't no mishaps in dis crew." She paused, and as Big Country switched the music from 10th Ward Buck to Sissy Nobby, telling us to beat it out the frame, Khya took a few minutes to show er'body in the room exactly what that meant.

Five minutes after she was done and was fanning sweat from her face, she looked at me and resumed what she had to say. "You see me and Shae tearin' da wall down, fa'sho'. And you all ovah here bucked up, and *ya know* we too cute for that. Ya heardz me?"

What the . . . I did my best to stop my eyes from blinking. "What did you just say?"

"She said"—Shae popped her gum as she came over and stood in front of me, doing the Reject dance—"that you lookin' all shades of crazy standing here"—she twirled her neck—"everybody else is here having fun and you're doing what?" She pointed to my cell phone. "Holding out for Josiah? Now let's have some fun and stop sulking over that boy."

I can't believe she said that.

"You still sulking?" Khya said before I could respond to Shae. "Oh hell to da nawl, bey-be, we don't sweat no man." She wagged her finger. "This is our motto: He's act-ing shady, so we bust out crazy. Lump . . ." she said slowly. ". . . his . . . azz . . . up . . . and I'm not talking 'bout putting the hands up. I'm talkin' 'bout bustin' out all his windows, texting all his homies, and telling 'em he's the official inch-long minute man.

"I'm talkin' 'bout calling that Precious-lookin' chick who Jamil cheated on me with and telling her that Jamil was diagnosed with VD. I'm talkin' 'bout swearin' fo' God to my mama, my daddy, the po'lice, oh, and the judge, that I didn't mean for the bat to fly outta my hand when I was bashing dents in Jamil's car and hit that old lady. I'm talkin' 'bout teachin' that mofo not to play with my emotions! I'm talkin'—"

"A lil crazy." I patted Khya on the shoulder. "And I'm concerned."

"Something you wanna share?" Shae arched her brow.

"No, I'm good," Khya sniffed, while throwing one-two jabs in the air. "I'm calm. It's just, you know...he ain't have to do me like that. She had four kids, too. Now you know he was wrong. But anyway"—she batted her eyes—"forget Josiah if he's acting shady."

"He's not acting shady," I said a little too quickly to even sound believable.

"Girl, bye," Shae said. "You need to stop frontin'. He was supposed to help you move in and he's nowhere to be found."

Should I floor her now or later?

"What?" Khya said, shocked. "Oh, that sounds like he's messing with Shaka-Locka."

"Shaka-who?" Shae stopped in her tracks.

"Shaka-Locka. That's the heifer Jamil cheated on me with." Khya whipped out her cell phone. "Let me call this trick and see if she's struck again—"

"First of all you won't be able to hear a thing in the middle of a party, and second of all," I snapped, "Josiah's not cheating on me and especially not with somebody named Shaka-Locka!"

"I can hear very well, and besides, you don't know what Josiah's doing—you haven't heard from him in months," Khya said, dialing.

"It's only been two days."

"Two days?" Shae said, taken aback. "You didn't tell me that."

"Two days, two months," Khya said as she placed her phone to her ear. "Same difference. And you don't know if he's messing with Shaka-Locka or not, 'cause this here skeezer's a worldwide ho." She turned her attention toward her cell phone as the person on her receiver said hello.

"Looka here, Precious," Khya said, "are you back to being a trick again? Are you messin' with my homegirl's man?" Khya paused. "You know you look like Precious, Shaka-Locka, just live with it. Now, is Josiah over there?" Pause. "Oh you know what I'm talkin' 'bout." Pause. "You gon' do what?" Pause. "You know I'm 'bout-it, 'bout-it—you ain't said nothing but a word. Ring da alarm! You can bring the whole damn ward if you want to. Matter'fact bring the whole damyum parish!"

"That's enough!" Shae snatched Khya's phone out of her hand and hung up. "This isn't about you and Jamil!"

"You're right," Khya said with the look of a wild doe in her eyes. "You're right, I was just making a point."

"And what was that?" I said. " 'Cause you just scared the bejesus outta me."

"The point was," Khya said, "that we don't tolerate play-boys."

"Somebody call me?!" Big Country screamed into the microphone. "Somebody call for a playboy?"

Shae turned toward Big Country and shot him a long and cold evil eye.

"Dang Cornbread, I'm just playin'."

"Anywho"—Khya cracked her knuckles—"you need to sho' lil whoady that being played is not your color."

"Pause." I gave them the gas face, turned to Khya and gave her the warning eye. "Back up, for real, though. 'Cause, yes, I love my man, but if he was playing me, which he is not, then I would leave him alone. Puhlease, believe I am not on it like that, okay? So shut it down. And for your information, not that I owe you an explanation, but me and Josiah are fine and he doesn't toss me shade."

Khya wiggled her neck. "That's what I said about Jamil—"

"Fail." Shae frowned. "We are not going there again, Khya. It's not about you and Jamil."

"And it's not about me and Josiah either." I rolled my eyes. "Okay, so back up and go enjoy lil Ricky Ross over there." I pointed to Big Country.

"Dead," Khya snapped. "Now apologize to Shae for getting her all hyped up, 'cause Ricky Ross is a trade, ya heardz me? A hottie. So don't be comparing him to Big Country. We came here to pass a good time and y'all trippin'. Trippin' hard too. You don't need to be gettin' Shae all excited, like she about to be a rapper's wife. It ain't gon' happen, you will never be on one of those *Housewives* shows—"

"You can stop now, Khya," Shae said.

"I'm taking up for you, Shae, and I'm just sayin' that Big Country better stick to these lil dorm-room parties and playing the bass drum in the band. Trust."

"Whatever." I sucked my teeth. "All I'm saying, Shae, is that your rah-rah about Josiah is a dead issue."

Shae chuckled in disbelief. "The only reason I'ma let you live, Seven, is because we're best friends, but you don't have too many more chances to come out the side of your neck, 'cause the next time it's gon' be a problem."

"Whatever."

"Yeah, whatever." Shae turned and walked away.

Khya looked me over. "You know you're wrong."

"Oh, now it's all my fault?" I stabbed my index finger into my chest.

"Pretty much."

I twisted my lips to the side. *Dang.* I glanced over at Shae, who was a five-foot-three, size-six, mocha-colored human AK-47, who stayed loaded at all times. Disguised only by her big button brown eyes, full smile, and micro-braids, as sweet and innocent to those who didn't know her. But if you knew her, and especially if she was your bestie, you knew that Shae was the embodiment of keeping it real. Anything she had to say she said it to your face, whether you liked it or not. To love Shae was to know that she didn't play and that she would fight for you to the end.

But that didn't mean I always wanted or welcomed her opinion.

Ugg! I hated when she was mad with me.

I could tell that I really hurt Shae's feelings by the look on her face. *Dang, I hated apologizing.* I looked at Khya and frowned.

"You too cute for frowning. Now apologize to Shae, 'cause you Flava Flav stank-azz-ugly wrong."

"You being a lil extra."

Khya twisted her lips. "I'm not being extra. You so wrong you got yo mama twisted."

"What?"

"Seven, follow me here," she said slowly. "You are... Chris-beat-'em-down-Brown-before BET-gave-him-back-his-career wrong."

I hesitated. "Dang, was it that bad?" I said, feeling guilty as ever.

"Okay, maybe it wasn't that bad, but still." She pushed me slightly on the shoulder. "Now let's go. Apologize. So we can get this party poppin' again."

I walked over to Shae like a stray puppy with her tail tucked between her legs. "Shae." I chewed the corner of my lip and leaned from one foot to the next—something I used to do when I was five, after we had a fight on the playground. "I'm sorry." I pinched her cheek. "You forgive me? I was trippin'. My fault. I love you, you know that."

"Umm hmm," she said, still looking pissed. "And I guess I shoulda fell back when you asked me to." She seemed to be giving in.

"So you forgive me?" I whined.

"I didn't say that."

"I'll let you go first the next time we jump rope," I said jokingly.

She looked at me seriously and said, "You my homegirl, like my sister, and you know that. And you also know we're not in first grade and we're not in high school screamin' 'ballin.' We're in college—it's time to grow up and not let boyfriends, love, or anything else stop us from having a good time."

"True," I said, "and I'm sorry for trippin'." We started to hug.

"Sniff, sniff," Khya said as if she were crying. "Group hug."

"Awwl," we said, opening our embrace and letting Khya in. "We love you too, Snuckums," I said to Khya and we all fell out laughing.

After a few moments of hugging, I convinced myself

that I was straight buggin' because there was no way I needed to let Josiah's texts—or lack of—control my mood and stop my groove—so I started to get my party on.

"Hold it," Khya said in the middle of our dance, "is that—" She looked at Big Country. "Is that Baby Boy da Prince?" she said, excited. "Oh hell yeah!"

A moment later the entire party, including me and my crew, were going crazy over this jam. The dudes were holding their iced chains by the humongous iced-out charms and waving 'em in the air. All the girls were doing a soft bounce and everybody chanted, "I'm so fresh, I'm so clean...the bundle in my jeans and it's real homie...Naw meen..."

Finally, I was feeling this party. The music was hot and everybody in the place was straight. We continued our chant, "Naw meen...Naw meen..." until sweat formed streams of water over our faces and necks.

"Awwl, suckie-suckie now," Big Country shouted into the mic. "Y'all ready to get crunk?!"

"Yeah!" everyone screamed in unison.

"All right, let's bring it on, 'cause this is how we do it in the Boro!" Big Country cupped his hands around his mouth, leaned back, and shouted, "Mur...frees...boro, No'th Cacki-lackie, baby! The Dirty-Dirty. Here's to sharing a lil bit of what we got with you, Stiles U!"

The entire crowd was hyped as Big Country mixed one jam into another. We were all jamming and waving our arms in the air...and then it hit us all at the same time... this fool was straight-up playing country music. Not down-south rap or DC Go-Go, I mean the real deal: Kenny Rogers and Willie Nelson. Those dudes.

It was almost as if we were in a movie and someone put

us on pause, 'cause we were all standing still while Big Country was in his own zone singing, "Know when to hold 'em/Know when to fold 'em." The only thing that snapped him out of his place in space was Shae slapping him on the back of his neck.

"Have you lost yo mind!" she screamed as people filed toward the door, swearing that Big Country's first party was retarded.

"Oh my fault. My fault. Don't go nowhere," he said, slapping on Drake's CD, just in time to stop the crowd from leaving and save the party's rep. "Big Country 'Da Stunna' got this," he said into the mic, "See y'all was 'bout to leave and this pajama-jammy-jam is 'bout to turn into a fish fry!" He popped open the extra large cooler that sat beside his DJing table and said, "I got some dressed po-boys and Doritos y'all!"

The crowd went wild.

He continued, "I got some crawfish. We 'bout to break the heads off!"

"Yeah!" the crowd serenaded him.

"All silkie-silkie nah! I got some grilled chicken livers with pepper sauce and mustard greens straight outta my mama's care package. And fo' er'body from up north, my Jersey and New York crew, I got some Chinese chicken wings, some cat sticks, I mean crab sticks and whities! Oh yeah, baby. Ya smellin' me now, ain't you?" He turned the music up, the crowd was already amped, but now with the promise of food their excitement went through the roof.

"Cornbread." Big Country turned toward Shae, calling her by the nickname he'd given her when we were in high school. "Go fire up the deep fryer, baby! It's about to be on and sizzlin'!"

The deep fryer? All I could imagine was the fire depart-
ment and the campus police shuttin' this down—which
meant one thing: this was my cue to leave.

"Khya." I tapped her on the shoulder, 'cause there was
no way I wanted to hear Shae's mouth.

"Wassup?" She smiled a little too hard and that's when I
noticed she had some dude checking for her.

"I'm retiring for the night."

"You sure?" she asked, paying me little to no attention.

"Yeah. I'm sure."

"All right, I'll meet you back in the room." She looked at
the cutie she was kicking it to. "In the morning that is."

I shook my head. "Bye, girl."

"Bye," she said, never turning around.

I stepped into the hallway and felt like I was walking
through hell. It was hot, sweaty, and filled with a million
people.

I walked toward the exit and suddenly stopped dead in
my tracks.

I could've sworn that I saw... nah, that's not him...
but wait, let me just stand here and get a good look. After
all, nothing was worse than running up on somebody
and they turned out to be the wrong mofo.

I just knew my eyes had to be deceiving me. Students
passed back and forth before me, so I was doing my best
to see clearly.

I stood still and waited for a few seconds—that felt like
hours—until my view was clear. That's when I knew without a doubt exactly who I was seeing: Josiah. Boldly leaning against somebody's room door, showing every last
one of his thirty-twos; while some chick—who had every

ounce of her C cups spilling from the deep plunging neckline in her midriff—was all in his face.

Now we had a problem.

My first instinct was to straight trip, cuss, and go off. But then I thought about how that would only make me look stupid. I did all I could to fight off the tears I felt banging on the backs of my eyes.

"Seven." Shae ran up behind me. "Why are you"—her words started to drift—"leave . . . ing." She was silent for a moment. Long enough for me to clear my throat and get myself together. "Hold da hell up, is that Josiah?" she spat. "Yes, it is. Oh, I'm 'bout to tear him up!"

"Who we 'bout to give it to?" Khya said as she rummaged through her purse. "Where are my nunchucks? I could've sworn they were right here."

"You can chill," I said. "We don't need any weapons, and anyway where did you two come from?"

"I came to find you," Shae said.

"And I came behind her," Khya answered. "Now's what's going on?"

"We just found Seven's boyfriend." Shae pointed to Josiah.

"Awl right, now." Khya gave a sexy growl and snapped her fingers. "Ouwl, hey, lil tender—"

"Khya!" Shae spat.

"What had happened was ummm . . . what I meant to say was . . ." Khya pointed to the girl Josiah was standing next to. "Let's just get to the point—who is that chick? And is she the reason Josiah hasn't called you in a year?"

"It's been a two days," I corrected her. "And I don't know who she is."

"So you know what this means, right?" Khya said, answering her own question. "It's 'bout to go down, round!" She looked Josiah over. "I mean, he is fine. Looking like a straight Trey Songz. And yeah, he's all tall and big." She smiled. "Looking all strong like he can handle a girl with a lil meat on her bones… and yeah, he looks the exact way that I envisioned my baby daddy. But that doesn't mean, we just gon' take anything off of him. Oh hell nawl. We 'bout to shut Soulja Boy down!"

"Don't worry," I said, successfully putting my hurt feeling at bay. "I got this."

I arched my back, patted the sides of my fitted Juicy Couture jeans that were glued to my thick hips just right. My hair bounced to the small of my back as I stepped along side of Josiah and said, "Wow, you like what you see?" I looked the girl over. "I give her about a three."

Josiah was clearly in shock and caught so far off guard that he took a step back and then two steps forward toward me. "I thought you weren't coming until next week?"

"Oh really?" I batted my eyes. "Perhaps had you checked the zillion text messages I sent you, you would've seen that we were able to get housing a week before classes started."

"Who is this, Josiah?" the girl questioned him.

"I'm wifey and you are—"

"Some lil greasy Wing Shack ho." Khya looked the girl over. "Yup, I said it—and what?"

"Oh, I know y'all ain't bringing no smack to me?" The girl looked at each of us and rolled her eyes.

"Oh, word?" Shae smirked. "Let me put you on notice real quick. I don't do a buncha chitchattin', I straight pimp smack. Now look at me like that again!" She turned to Josiah and pointed into his face. "And when I'm done with her, you know I'm comin' for you!"

"Chill," Josiah said. "It ain't even like that." He reached for my hand and I snatched it back. "Seven, listen to me."

"Oh you don't owe me any explanation," I said. "It's cool. Your message is loud and clear, son."

"What?" He frowned. "What are you saying?"

"Listen, boo." I gave him a fake smile. "I gotta go, now."

"Seven—" Josiah called behind me. "Sev!"

I didn't even turn around; instead I kept walking down the hall and out of the building.

Shae and Khya walked in silence with me. Once we reached our dorm, Shae said, "I'm sorry that happened to you, Seven. Like, I don't even believe this."

"We shoulda just lumped him up, and then we would feel better," Khya said. "But you know what, Seven, don't even sweat that. Tomorrow, I'ma introduce you to somebody else."

"Okay, enough of the pity party. For real." I looked at them like they were losing it. "Do you see me sweatin' it? I don't care. I'm cool. I prefer to know the truth."

Shae looked at me strangely. "You can keep it funky with me, Seven."

I hated that she knew me so well.

"Shae—" I quickly looked her in the eyes and then looked away. "I'm fine. I wanted to chill in our room anyway. So listen, you and Khya go back to the party and have a good time. You got a boo that loves you to death; and Khya, you had a cutie who was all up on you. So for-real, for-real, I'm straight. I'm 'bout to wrap my doobie up, put on me some pajamas, and get some serious sleep on."

"You sure?" Khya asked, concerned. "'Cause cuties come a dime a dozen. And if I leave, trust and believe you won't be seeing ya girl 'til the morning." She laughed a little. "I'm just saying, one of us has to tour campus."

I laughed. "It's cool, Khya. Now you and Shae go back to the party. I promise you, I'm okay."

"All right." Shae looked at me with reluctance in her eyes. "Call me if you need anything."

"Okay, but I won't be calling you," I said as I watched them walk away.

By the time I stepped into our room I felt like I was going to break down at any moment. My eyes scanned the stacked boxes and for the first time since I'd arrived here this morning, I wanted my mother. I picked up the phone to call her and quickly changed my mind. The last thing I needed was to confess to her in my moment of hurt. Not a good move, especially since mothers forget nothing.

My sister, Toi. I'll call her. Fail. She'd just tell Mommy.

The iron fist in my throat beat like a drum and the pounding grew harder and more intense, forcing me to the point where I couldn't fight it anymore, so I laid across the foot of my bed and cried like I was in mourning.

That's when I realized that suddenly and without warning I'd become that chick. The stupid chick. The one we never set out to be and swear to all our friends we would never become.

You know the chick you laugh at, shake your head at, and admonish for being desperate, needy, dying for her boyfriend's attention. I was her and she was me. I'd called Josiah a million times a day, texted him over and over and over again. I knew it wasn't cool. And I knew I needed to stop. But if I knew all of that...why didn't I stop? Why did it have to come to this?

It's not like I didn't see that he'd been acting shady. Heck, I remember the exact moment when it happened: March 8th, 8 P.M. I called him and he spoke to me as if I were his boy. "Yeah, wassup? Let me get at you later," he'd said in one breath, and before I could even ask him why he was talking to me like that, I heard a girl's voice in the background as he hung up.

I wonder was it the same girl he was with tonight?

I confronted him on March 9th, the next morning when he called me back. And he said, "I can't believe you sweatin' me with this. Why would I have some random chick around when I'm your man and especially when I'm talking to you on the phone?"

"But you were talking to me in code."

"Code?" he said, as if I were stupid. "What code? You know what?" He sighed. "If you don't trust me, then maybe—"

Don't ask me what he was going to say after he'd said maybe, because for me the implication was enough, so I didn't let him finish. Instead my mouth said, "Of course I trust you." Even though my heart didn't.

I went on, "And I'm sorry for trippin'." Even though I felt my trippin' was warranted.

"I love you, Seven." I felt like he was saying that out of habit.

"I love you too."

"A'ight," he said. "I'll talk to you later."

"Later."

And from that day to this one, I'd been warring with thoughts of us growing apart. But we'd been together since high school. I was his shortie and he was my boo.

We were a fairytale.

A hood love story.

A Romeo-and-Juliet romance, but we were supposed to get married and have kids at the end.

He always told me I was number one.

And I always asked him what's higher than number one?

I guess tonight he gave me an answer.

We were supposed to last forever.

But why did forever have an expiration date...?

This had to be my fault.

But sometimes things just happen....

But us breaking up was never supposed to happen!

It was official: I was that chick and I didn't exactly know how to change it.

This was sooooo crazy. The overflowing river of tears left a bitter taste of salt on my lips. I always swore that I would be strong and not cry; snap my fingers and everything would be all right...but I tried that and all I came up with was a phony lecture to myself filled with more "forget hims," "I don't need hims," and "I got thises" than I could count....

I closed my eyes and hoped that when I awoke all of this would be a dream.

4

A part of me wants to leave
But the other side still believes...

—Melanie Fiona, "It Kills Me"

"**S**even!" I jumped out of my sleep; my heart pounded so hard and fast that I felt like it had dropped to my feet. My eyes scanned the room and nothing. All I saw were cardboard boxes and two empty twin beds. I ran my hand over my face and closed my eyes.

I have to be dreaming.

I turned over and snuggled deeper into my pillow.

"Seven, answer the door!"

That was Josiah. And I wasn't dreaming. My eyes roamed my room until I found a small alarm clock on top of a box that read 3 A.M.

"Seven, don't play with me, answer the door! It wasn't what you thought!"

He pounded again. "Why aren't you answering the door, Seven? What, you got somebody in there?"

Is he serious? Did he just come pounding randomly on my door...and now he's screaming like a fool about a what? A who? Another dude?

How about let's discuss that heifer you were giving the up-down to. I wish I would open this door. Puhlease!

"Oh, it's like that, Seven? You leaving me out here like this?" He paused. "I hope I'm not hearing another dude up in there."

I couldn't stop smiling long enough to process how ridiculous—scratch that—*how jealous* he sounded.

Good for him. Touché. Now he knows what it feels like. 'Cause he's got hella nerve pounding on my door questioning me. What about "I'm sorry, Seven?" "You been there for me before there were any groupies." What about that?

True story: Just hearing him pounding on the door, sweatin' me, felt like someone had intravenously given me energy. I felt like I could lie here all night, not cry, and make him wait.

I loved him, yeah. I wanted to see him, yeah, but did I want to continue being played? No.

He pounded again. "All right, so you playing games now?"

I turned over and closed my eyes. Now I knew for sure I would sleep without having crazy dreams of him being with that chick, because the reality was he was outside of my door doing his best to get in here with me.

"If I leave," he said through the door crack, "and find out that you ran into the arms of another man, it's gon' be a problem."

And?

"And," he stressed, "if I leave just know that I will never come back."

Do you. I know he didn't think that I would be moved. *Puhlease. Not me. Go kick that to the chick you were with. Hmph!*

I laid still, doing my best not to laugh out loud. A few minutes passed and Josiah's pounding stopped. A few seconds after that, an uneasiness came over me, forcing me to wonder what he meant when he said he wasn't coming back. Did he mean forever? Did he mean he would be gettin' with that other chick? Did he mean that I wouldn't be on his mind anymore...I wouldn't be his shortie...wifey? Was lying here being stubborn to prove a useless point worth giving away my man? I'm not sure....All I know is that his pounding was music to my ears and just like that it was gone.

I had to get up. Josiah was more than just some random dude—he was my high school boo. The present love of my life. The future Mister to my Misses. We had a history together....Our yesterday was beautiful. He deserved to have me listen to his explanation. I mean, it's not like I saw him tonguing the girl down or feeling her up. He was only leaning against the door...kicking it with her....

I hopped out of the bed and hoped like hell that yesterday wasn't all we had left.

My heart awakened the nervous butterflies in my stomach. I opened the door to find...nothing. I looked wildly from right to left and still nothing. Tears filled my eyes. This was too much. Why didn't I let him in?

I leaned against the back of the door, closed my eyes, and as tears covered my face, I felt soft lips pressed against mine.

"Looking for me?" he whispered.

My baby. I breathed a sigh of relief as a thousand pounds felt like they'd fallen off of me. We kissed, and a few minutes in, he broke the kiss and asked, "You got somebody in there?"

"What?" I frowned. "Please, no, heck no. You don't have to worry about me. But I can't say the same—now who was that chick? And why didn't you call me? You been cheating on me?"

"Seven, I swear on everything I am, I don't even know that chick."

Just when I was prepared to believe almost anything he had to say, he says something stupid like this. I twisted my lips. "You didn't know her? Sure," I said sarcastically.

"I didn't mean it like that."

"Seems you don't mean a lot of things."

"Listen, I know that chick from around campus. I was only speaking to her. That's it!"

"Why didn't you tell me that when I was standing there?"

"You didn't give a chance to explain."

True, I didn't. "You could've made me listen!"

"How? When you walked away and when I called you, over and over again, you wouldn't even look back."

He's right—I didn't look back. But what did he expect me to do? "Josiah, listen, maybe we just need to take a break."

"A break? Oh, so that's what this is really about? You wanna break up with me?"

"You're the one who hasn't been returning my calls. Ignoring my texts. Straight-up dissing me. I expected you to help me move in and where were you?"

"I thought you were coming next week!"

"You shoulda called me back instead of being in that trick's face, and then you would've found out that my housing came through early!"

"Damn, Seven." He sighed and pressed his forehead

against mine. "I can't do this with you. For the past few months I've had a million things go wrong—grades, practice, my coach is on me. For real, I'm tired and I'm not with anybody else but you. I didn't know you were here, and if I did, you think I would've straight-up played you like that?" He kissed me gently on the lips. "I'm in love with you." He kissed me again. "I wanna marry you someday. But if you feeling some kind of way"—he took a step back—"then I'll step off."

I was confused. My mind told me to cuss him out and tell him I really wasn't buying this. But my heart wasn't hearing it. "It's not that I'm feeling some kinda way—"

"Then what is it? 'Cause you slow walked to answer the door, so it's looking like you tryna be out."

"Excuse me for not being in a rush, especially since I've left you more than a thousand messages and you haven't returned not even one of them!"

"I just told you what I've been going through!"

"You should've talked to me!"

"You know I'm not good with expressing myself, Seven. I had game after game, and I've been running around campus like—"

"A playboy."

"You know what, Seven? I'm not about to beg you to be my girl."

"Then step then, 'cause I'm not about to beg you either." That's not what I meant to say. Really, it wasn't, but I wasn't about to be played like some lil high school dummy. Nah, he had me twisted.

"Are you serious?" he said as if he couldn't believe I just bucked.

"Hmph, you must not know 'bout me." I wiggled my neck from left to right for emphasis.

"A'ight, I'll step then," he said as he turned away and walked swiftly down the hall.

"Whatever." I flicked my hand as if I'd just performed a magic trick. I could feel tears rattling my throat. I walked into the room and slammed the door behind me.

I sat on the edge of my bed and just as I placed my face in the palm of my hands, my room door pushed open and, "You really weren't going to stop me?" came from the doorway.

It was Josiah. I felt the tears that I was about to let fall from my eyes instantly dry. "Nope." I gave him a could-care-less, Kanye shrug. "I sure wasn't."

"So what's really good—we're done? That's what you're saying?"

I hesitated. "No, that's not what I'm saying."

"So wassup, you don't love me anymore?"

I felt unwanted tears bubbling in my eyes, forcing me to give in. "Yeah, I love you. But I'm not about to be some dumb chick chasing after you and playing games with you. If you don't wanna be with me, then tell me. Trust me, I'll live."

"I never said that I didn't wanna be with you." He walked over to the edge of the bed and stood before me. "I love you." He pulled my hand to his chest. "So, let's just stop all this and chill like we used to." He spoke against my lips. "I missed you, Seven, and I know that I owe you an apology for not calling like I should've. And I'm sorry. You're my heart, Seven. Don't ever doubt that. I don't know what I would do if you weren't here with me."

"I just want you to keep it real with me." I responded to his kisses.

"I've always kept it real with you. You know I love you, right?"

"Yeah."

"So chill." He placed his hands on my waist and we began to kiss passionately. A few moments in and his hands were all over me. We fell onto the bed and he reached over my shoulder and flipped off the light switch that was closest to my headboard.

"You got condoms?" I said, flipping the lights back on.

"What?" He squinted, obviously caught off guard. "Condoms?"

"I can't...not without a condom."

"So, what are you saying? You don't trust me?"

No, I don't trust you. "Of course I trust you." I hesitated. "It's not about that. I just told you before I'm not going there without protection."

"You trippin' off that again?" he said, pissed. "You about to mess up the mood."

I don't care. "I'm not trying to mess up the mood, but I'm not about to be running scared because my period is late. I went through that already and you know how paranoid I was."

He reached in his back pocket and pulled out a Trojan. "Now can we hit the lights?" He waved the condom pack in my face.

Why was I still reluctant? "Yeah." I shot him a small smile. "Of course."

The room filled with darkness and the only light that streamed in came from the flickering street lamp. Lingering chatter from the courtyard and a few musicians blowing their horns in the air was our backdrop. It was romantic really, a way for me to pretend that what we were sharing was beautiful. An escape from my thoughts; the very thoughts that had me convinced—beyond a shadow of a doubt—that Josiah's being here with me . . . like this . . . had more to do with him wanting some becky than it had to do with him wanting to offer me an apology.

5

I'm all strung out...

—KE$HA, "YOUR LOVE IS MY DRUG"

"Waaaaaa! Snap-Snap, bey-be." Khya stood over my bed and shouted, "Time na roll! It's 'bout to be on and crackin'!" She snatched the curtains back. "We have to get dressed and head to the cafeteria. 'Cause according to some Twitter post, folks gon' be showin' dey azz!"

"For real, though?" Shae said, a little too excited.

I opened my eyes one at a time. The burning New Orleans sun gleamed through the window and blew into my face like a heat wave. Not to mention that Josiah didn't leave until five this morning, and I just went to sleep a few hours ago.

I sat up in bed, tossed the few strands of hair that slipped out of my doubie pins away from my face, looked at my friends, and said, "You are so inconsiderate. Just because you two were out all night, and now you're feeling all fresh and clean, doesn't mean that I feel the same way—"

"It's obvious you don't feel like that," Khya said. "You got cold all in your eyes—"

"Crust all around your mouth." Shae laughed.

"And that hair." Khya frowned. "Girl, you look like who shot Boom-Keke and left her body there."

"Dead." I fell back onto the bed.

"Would you get up!" Khya said, flipping through her phone. "Status alert!" she said, extremely hyped. "Groupie-4life just updated her status to say that the ballers will be arriving any minute."

"First of all who is Groupie4life?" I asked.

"Lil fake-behind bougie trick, wears pearls all the time. Always screaming about Jesus. Her daddy's a preacher. She's a few rooms down from us. Met her yesterday at the party."

"Oh no." I laughed. "That's a mess!"

"Now listen," Khya continued, "she says that the ballers will be in the caf in a few minutes."

"So what?" I said. "Who cares if the ballers are arriving at any minute? I'm so over athletes."

"Yeah, really," Shae interjected, "especially given what happened last night. If I see Josiah again, I can't be held responsible for my actions."

I stared at Shae, and as soon as we made eye contact I quickly turned away. For a split second, I forgot they didn't know that Josiah and I had made up last night. It completely slipped my mind that they were still pissed with him while I was over it.

I thought about coming clean and telling them the truth. But then again, Shae wasn't exactly the type to understand that sometimes a man...you know...does things

that are crazy—or he may not always make the best decision—or like, hell, things just happen.

And yeah, I was mad with Josiah...but when all was
said and done, we made up, and not because I'd exactly
forgiven him—but more because I didn't wanna be mad
anymore. Plain and simple. I more or less wanted to make
up for the sake of getting my life back on track...or something like that.

I tried to think of a million ways to tell them Josiah was
back in boo status, but I just couldn't bring myself to do it,
so I took the easy route. "Girl, please. I don't even wanna
talk about Josiah. I'm so over that. It's not even worth the
aggravation."

"Oh really?" Shae arched her brow.

"Yeah, really," I said. "He is the last thing on my mind."

Shae gave me a suspicious look. But I ignored it.

"Sure." Shae rolled her eyes. "If Josiah came knocking
on that door right now, and said, 'Seven, open up! I need
to hollah at you for a minute,' you know you would be
like, 'Okay, lil daddy.'"

"Whatever. You're crazy," I said, being a little too extra.
I looked over at Khya, who'd been extremely quiet, and
realized that she was sitting on the edge of her bed in
shock. "What the heck...is wrong with you?" I asked.

"I'm scared for you," she said, sounding concerned. "I
mean, really, really scared." She walked over to me and
pressed the back of her hand over my forehead.

"What are you doing, and why are you scared for me?"

"'Cause you're just as crazy as you wanna be!" She
shook her head. "What do you mean you're over athletes?
Do you realize that Stiles U is a Division One school?"

"And?"

"Girl, listen at me: round here you gots to get it how you live—or in this case how you wanna live—do you think I'm majoring in sports medicine simply for the degree? Not. I don't even like science and can't stand the sight of blood. But you got to do what you got to do, 'cause see, I need me a few thousand square feet in my mansion. The FEMA trailer never worked for me—that's how we ended up in Houston. I don't know about you, but when it gets cold I prefer blue sable furs to wool. And I may have a lil extra junk in my trunk, but I have no interest in cooking so I need a chef, a maid to clean, and a governess to keep er'body in check."

This chick was a hot mess in the flesh.

"And what are you going to give him in exchange, Khya?" Shae asked.

"Some kids, and if he behaves I'll name the oldest one after him. Ya heardz...me...?" Her voice drifted as she focused in on her phone. "That's my alert." She swiftly walked over and picked up her phone. "Honey, this chick is trippin' on Twitter." She jumped up and down like an excited five-year-old. "Dang, they goin' in. They goin' in! Would y'all put your clothes on?" Khya looked at us. "It's about to go down!"

"Why? Who posted something now?" Shae asked.

"Golddigger2damax, just posted." Khya read from her BlackBerry's screen, "She says, 'Josiah "Meal Ticket" Whitaker, number twenty-three, point guard on the basketball team, hood-rat-azz girlfriend has brought her big butt to campus and is a freshman here. Anybody know who this hoochie is?'" Khya screamed. "Oh, it's 'bout to be on and crackin' up in here! Oh, I got to know what hoodrat has locked down...wait a minute." Khya looked at me with one eye open and the other squinted. "Umm…hmmm… who was lil whoady that we were about to cut up last night? Was he, ahh—Meal Ticket?"

I arched my brow. "Yep, pretty much that's him."

"Oh, see"—Shae rolled her eyes and swerved her neck—"something tells me I'ma have to bring out the Newark ghetto-girl, you-don't-know-me-like-that side of my personality." She paced from one end of the room to the next, and if I'm not mistaken I think she was throwing up gang signs. "You got some Vaseline?" She turned to me.

"Shae," I said, "wait a minute before you start spittin' out blades."

"Ah hell nawl, they talkin' 'bout you, Seven?" Khya said amped. "Let me shut this down real quick. 'Cause I don't appreciate them calling you a hoodrat. They could've at least called your name or said you had hoodrat tendencies. But to straight-out call you a hoodrat, that's just wrong."

She started typing on her phone and speaking aloud what she was posting. "Public service announcement: The hoodrat is my friend and roommate, Seven McKnight. And if any of you have a problem, we 'bout to be in the cafeteria in the next twenty minutes, so if you got the balls bring 'em! And anyway, she dumped him last night!"

"You have lost your…freaking…mind," I said, tossing the sheet off of me and rising from the bed.

"So does this mean you're not going to the cafeteria?" Khya twisted her finger in her cheek.

"Oh, she's going," Shae said, answering for me. "And I wish somebody would come crazy."

This was nuts. Like, seriously I needed to tell the truth.

Yeah, that's it, be honest. "Shae, Khya, listen, about Josiah—"

"I know you're hurt, Seven," Shae interjected.

"No, that's not it." *Would she just let me finish? This is hard enough.*

"That's called denial, Shae," Khya said, looking at me as if she was a moment away from suggesting therapy. "Anybody can see that she's about to lose her mind."

"Would you two just let me finish? Dang!"

"You can calm down—" Khya said. "Wait a minute, is that my phone—" She paused and listened to the singing ring tone. "That's not my phone." As she said that I realized that it was *my* phone ringing.

"I got it." I reached for my clutch purse and looked at my phone's caller ID. Josiah. There was no way I could answer the phone here, but there was no way I could completely ignore his call either.

I pressed the talk button on the receiver but didn't say anything into it. I looked at Shae and Khya and said, "It's my dad and you know how he is. I'ma just take this in the bathroom and afterward I'll shower, and then we can leave."

"Okay," Shae said.

"All right," Khya remarked, "and hurry up, 'cause I don't wanna miss any of the action."

I walked into the bathroom, closed the door, and leaned against it. "Hello?" I said, placing the phone to my ear.

"Seven," Josiah said, "what took you so long to say something?"

"No reason...I just, you know," I said, looking for an excuse, "couldn't get the phone to work right." *Whatever the heck that means.*

"A'ight," he said. His voice was soothing to my ears. "Listen, ma, I called you because I felt like last night was one of the worst nights we've ever had since we've been together and I just wanted to apologize for my part. Had I known that you had arrived earlier you know I would've been with you every step of the way."

"I know."

"You know I love you, Seven, no matter what."

"I know. I love you too."

"A'ight." I could hear him smiling. "I'ma catch up with you later today, okay?"

"What time?" I know it was a nagging question, but I needed to know.

"Around two-thirty, I'll come check you."

I looked at the clock: 9 A.M. "Why so late? Can't we hook up before then?"

"Nah, I have practice."

I wanted to ask him more questions and demand that he explain what million things he really had to do, but there was no way I could risk him getting upset, so I simply said, "A'ight. I'll see you then."

"Love you," he said and then he hung up.

Instantly I felt high and confused at the same time. But I really couldn't deal with the confusion at this point, so I focused on being in love.

I turned on the shower, imagined my baby's face as I stepped in, and sang my heart out.

6

It's my decision to love…

—Jazmine Sullivan, "Season 2 Love"

"Shae," I said as gently as possible, "you may not realize this, but you're not going to grow anymore and five-foot-three is very short. So please stop ice grillin' every chick you see."

"Whatever, as long as they understand that we came ready to roll, it won't be a problem."

"And I got my nunchucks today," Khya said as we walked into the caf. "So if they bring it"—she rolled her eyes wildly around the room—"we gon' swing it."

"Would y'all stop? We are too cute for drama," I said as we walked into Famous Amos's Café also known as the caf—or better known as the campus hot spot—which, according to Khya, was nothing more than a crunked club that served three meals a day.

It was set up like a mom-and-pop diner, with framed black-and-white posters of accomplished and well-known African Americans along the walls, and a jukebox that belted nothing but old-school jazz and blues. The lone cashier, a heavyset black woman with coffee-colored skin and peeks of auburn hair beneath a black hairnet, rolled her neck and popped out food totals like an auctioneer with an attitude.

An L-shaped food court lined the walls along the right side of the double entrance/exit doors, and sporadically placed along the floor were soda machines. An even mixture of tables and booths were everywhere; and much like high school, cliques were definitely in the building.

Mostly everyone who sat in here and hung out had a clique; and those who were solo grabbed their grub and hurried on their way.

The Greeks were represented like crazy, making catcalls, shout-outs, waging battles, and some of them were straight-up showing off their newest steppin' routines in the middle of the floor.

The groupie chicks were planted by the door, making it obvious what they were here for; the athletes had a corner locked down—and no, Josiah wasn't there—with chicks all around them like the paparazzi.

And oh yes, since this was the south, the hand-clappin', foot-stompin', and award-winning band was in full effect.

Already, with the exception of what happened this morning, I was lovin' Stiles U. It was the embodiment of what the black college experience was all about. It had been in existence since 1910, started by Ernest Stiles, a farmer and musician, and his wife in an effort to teach blacks how to read, write, play music, and run their own businesses. The school began with nine students, seven of them the Stileses' children, and a hundred years later Stiles U had evolved into one of the finest higher-educational institutions with hundreds of disciples and thousands of students.

And yeah, all of that is what impressed my parents, but as for me and my crew it was simply the place to be. Period. Dot. Dot. Dot. And yeah we wanted a good education of course, but college was also about evolving into adulthood, living life, making important decisions, partying, and of course being on your game at all times, which is why since all the Internet groupies were gunning for me, we made sure our appearance was hot.

I wore a well-fitted hot-pink tube dress that outlined my size-fourteen hips perfectly, with the hem of it stopping midway my thighs. The boldness of my outfit clearly said, "Yes, I'm reppin' well for the big girls."

Khya—who swore that voluptuousness was a gift—rocked a pair of leggings and a fitted tee that read: IT WAS DEFINITELY ME WHO STOLE YOUR BOYFRIEND.

Shae threw on a pair of booty shorts and a white middriff halter.

Nevertheless, no matter how cute we looked it didn't stop me from being nervous, especially since I hadn't come clean with them about Josiah. After checking out the scene and nobody daring to step to us, we grabbed breakfast and found us a table near the door.

"Well, Seven," Shae said, sipping a bottle of orange juice. "I'm glad you're not sitting around crying over Josiah, looking like a sad puppy."

"I'm telling you, girl, I can't take a buncha crying and carrying on." Khya took a bite of her buttered baguette. "I mean, I am considerate, I'll slide you twenty-four hours to mourn. But after that, I'ma be like, oh, you 'bout to shut the hell up, cuz."

I laughed. "Are you serious?"

"It don' matter dough." Khya smacked her lips and took a sip of her iced coffee. "'Cause you dusted your shoulders off in like five minutes. Please put me down on yo secret."

I hesitated. "I just...ummm..." I paused. "You know... like I just figured that things happen."

"Like what?" Khya pressed.

"I don't know, it just works out. Now, would you two let it go?" I said, frustrated. "I really don't even wanna think about Josiah. So let's just hurry up and eat so we can leave. Matter fact," I said, looking around as more people walked in, "let's just go back to the dorm now."

"Why?" Shae took a bite of her bagel. "We ain't never scared."

"Fa'sho'!" Khya spat. "What, you see somebody, Seven?" She looked wildly from left to right. "Is there a problem up in here?" Khya said, raising her voice and pointing at a few people who turned our way. "What you wanna know if this is Seven McKnight? Huh? Well, it is, so what—you tryna bring it?"

"Khya, stop it," I said, tight-lipped. "Before something jumps off."

"Oh, I 'on't care. 'Cause I will handle er'body up in here!" She snapped her fingers in a Z motion. "Oh-kay."

When the few people who were staring quickly turned away Khya said, "I ain't think you wanted none."

"Forget them," Shae said. "Who we need to handle is Josiah."

"Seriously," I said, "we're not going to talk about Josiah again."

"You know what I'm thinking?" Khya said, completely

ignoring my last statement. "I think we might need to get a gris-gris for Meal Ticket, I mean Josiah. Do you have any strands of his hair?"

"Ill. No, I don't have any strands of his hair." I twisted my lips. "And put something on him like what?"

"Like what I put on Jamil. Girlie, I put something on Jamil so fierce that one day he was walking down the street and all of a sudden he broke out looking like Bobby Brown. Messed him up for months. I told him, 'I ain't the one, Jamil—messing with me ain't for you.' How he gon' cheat on me with Shaka-Locka of all people, this chick look just like Precious. Do you know how much of an insult that was to me? I mean he just straight-up played me for crazy." She pulled out her phone. "Know what, I need to check this mofo one mo' time for that crap."

"Girl, down," Shae said, taking Khya's phone. "Puh-lease, let it go."

"I've let it go," Khya snapped. "And really, do I sound like I care what Jamil does? Not. I don't care. But I tell you what, he bet'not"—she pointed her index finger—"be with Shaka-Locka or it's gon' be a problem. Other than that, I'm cool—plus that cutie I kicked it with last night just might be enough for me to forget Jamil and take back that gris-gris I had on 'im."

"A gris-who?" I asked.

"Gris-gris. Gun powder, red pepper, and a chicken bone. Blew it right in his face."

What kinda? "It's official—I'm scared." I threw my hands in the air. "Maybe, I need to see if there are any single rooms still available."

"Nope," Khya said with a mouth full of food. "That was the RA's status update last night. But chill, Seven, we don't have to do any real damage to homie, I mean there're different types of gris-gris."

"What..." Shae said slowly. "...are...you talking about? And why can't you ever speak in plain English."

"Voodoo." Khya nodded her head to the side for emphasis. "How's that for plain English?"

"Voodoo?" me and Shae said simultaneously. "What kinda...?"

"Put a spell on him." Khya twisted her lips. "That's what we need to do for Josiah. I promise you, Seven, we can go and see my grandmama, Maw-Maw Baptiste, and Josiah won't even know what hit 'im. All of a sudden he'll just be walking around and bust out looking like Lady Gaga or Gary Coleman reincarnated. Which one you want?"

"I'm 'bout to throw up in my mouth!" I said, gagging.

"Why you always wanna commit a crime?" Shae shook her head and laughed. "Khya, tell us now, will we need to call your parents for bail money?"

"Nawl, long as don't nobody bring it, they don't get it."

No matter how I'd felt, Khya definitely made me laugh. I was laughing so hard that tears poured from my eyes and the only thing that made me stop was this dude walking up to our table and smacking Doublemint gum, like he was popping hard plastic bubbles. "Pardon me," he said with a twang. "Ah'cuse me."

I blinked my eyes twice, because for a moment I thought I was seeing things. Why did this dude have green sponge rollers in his hair and a canary yellow boa wrapped around his neck? He slid his starch white oval shades off and said, "Two snaps up and a fruit loop. Honey, are you Seven?"

"Ummm," I stammered. "Yes, I'm Seven and you are?"

"Courtney, your fierce, fly, and fabulous, neighbor."

"Oule," Khya said, "aren't you lively?"

"And you know this." Courtney snapped his fingers. "But listen, girlfriend, I just came to thank you"—he shook my hand—"for keeping me entertained last night."

Entertained? I pointed to my chest. "Huh? Me? I kept you entertained? I didn't do anything."

"Girl, bye." He pulled up a seat. "You need to stop being shy, cause for-real, for-real if you're not majoring in theater, you're missing your calling."

Khya looked at me. "What did you do last night?"

"Nothing." Don't ask me why, but my heart was thundering in my chest.

"Well something went down," Shae said with a look of confusion.

"Maybe he was there when I went off on Josiah at the party."

"Oh, that was lil daddy's name?" Courtney said. "Jo-sigh-ya." He enunciated every syllable. "That's kinda hot."

This cat was working my last nerve. "I umm…really think you have the wrong person, sir," I said sarcastically.

"Something told me I shoulda recorded you and posted everything on YouTube."

Recorded me? YouTube? Oh, I might be punching him in the face.

"You made sure your neighbor knew your name," he carried on. "And I really appreciate that, 'cause my first night on campus I thought I was gon' die from boredom and this roommate they have dumped on me—oh, honey." He wiped his brow as if he were due to faint. "Say this with me: nasty! I swear all this fool does is pass gas. Air bubbles fallin' all out his behind."

"Oh my…" Khya said, sounding like a southern belle. "You gon' make me clutch my pearls."

"Clutch 'em, honey, clutch 'em. 'Cause I got right down in his face, and said, 'Let me tell you something, I will fight you. Fart again! Please, fart…again!"

"Well, it's official," I said, throwing a napkin over my food. "Breakfast is over."

"Don't let me stop you from eating your food," Court-ney said. "It's cool. Plus, you probably need to eat. I'm sur-prised you have any energy. Being as though, you didn't get to sleep until about six this morning."

"What?" Shae said, shocked. "Okay, please just tell us what you're talking about."

How in the heck does he know what time I went to bed? "Am I the only one who finds this a little freaky?" I looked at Shae and Khya, who paid me absolutely no at-tention.

"We think just alike, Seven," Courtney said, " 'cause that's the same thing I said about you last night."

"Excuse me?"

"Check it," Courtney said, extremely animated. "Picture this. I was talking to my friend, Asha, on the phone telling her how glad I am that I graduated early and was able to come to Stiles U. Because, you know, this is the place to be. And I spoke to her for a long time until she tried to ex-plain to me—why she had a boyfriend and I…well, was the king of single…so I ended up getting off the phone with that heifer."

"Where are we going with this?" I spat. "Really."

"Baby slow down," he said. "Bring it back, Seven, I'm getting to the point. Now listen: last night about three I was lying in my bed and all of a sudden I heard, BOOM! BOOM!" He pounded on the table. "Well, you know me; I walked over to my room door, blocked it, and said to my roommate, 'If an odor floats across this room get ready to die!'

"After ten minutes passed I ended up not smelling anything so I unblocked the door and laid back on the bed, but I kept hearing this pounding." Courtney slammed his fist onto the table again. "BOOM! BOOM! That's when I got up, opened the door, and saw our boo—I mean your boo—standing there begging you through the door crack to open up."

What?

"Oh really?" Shae said, twisting her lips. "Okay, and what else happened?"

Khya's mouth dropped open. "O...M...G!"

"Look, Shae," I said, "I was going to tell you and Khya, but I just couldn't—"

"No, it's cool," Shae said. "I'm glad you didn't tell us, because I'm sure his version is much more detailed than yours would've been. So what else happened, Courtney?"

"Okay, so"—Courtney popped his gum—"he pounded and he pounded, and he screamed, 'Seven, I love you! Help me, Seven! Help me to love you!'"

"He didn't do that!" I snapped.

"You were caught up in the moment, honey, you don't know. Now let me finish—after he begged and pleaded for me—I mean for Seven—to come save his life, she came out in the hallway and cried, 'Why-why-why?'"

"That is not the way it happened."

"Chile," Courtney continued on, "I thought fa'sho' you

were going to send cuteness away or bust out screaming, 'Don't make me cut you!' But you didn't, girl. You were on your grind. You killed that scene."

"That is soooo not true!" I chuckled in disbelief. "I swear none of that happened."

"Ain't no need to lie, Seven. If I can room with the connoisseur of farts certainly you can be honest."

"Look," I snapped, "what happened is that Josiah came by to apologize, we talked, he said he didn't know I was going to be here this week...and we...you know...made up."

"You certainly made up," Courtney carried on. "I mean I missed out on when exactly you two walked into the room because I went to make some popcorn—."

"Oh, he was in the room too?" Khya said. "No wonder you didn't want him looking like Gary Coleman."

"All I know," Courtney carried on, "is that once I put the glass to the wall, it was on. Chile, I felt just like a church lady in heat." He fanned his face. "So anywho now that I know you, Seven, and very well I may add"—he looked at Shae and Khya—"why don't you introduce me to your friends?"

I looked at Courtney and rolled my eyes so hard it's a wonder bullets didn't shoot from them.

"Dead!" Courtney screamed. "Courtney's dead."

Hands down, this was some bull. How did he get all in my business and I don't even know him? And I really wasn't ready to deal with Shae's judgment and Khya thinking that I just out and out accepted anything—because that is far from the truth. But what was true was me wanting to kick Courtney's behind.

"Don't be mad, Seven," Courtney said. "I admire you."

"And we admire you, Courtney," Shae said, "for telling us the truth. So anywho, my name is Shae."

"And I'm Khya, wassup, round? I think between my status alerts and your glass to the wall, we gon' make one hellva team. And I got something that's gon' fix your roommate and his lil nasty problem."

"Do share, honey, do share." Courtney popped his gum. "Is it a bullet made out of Imodium AD? 'Cause he can tear up a bathroom too, chile! Funk miser. Trust, I don't know where they got this jungle bunny from, but he got to go. And don't you know he's from Jersey. A resident of my home town, Newark," Courtney said in disbelief. "He's about four feet tall and he calls himself, Lil Bootsy—"

"You're from Newark?" I frowned. *I sure hope I don't run into this clown when I go home. . . . Wait a minute. . . . What did he say his roommate's name was?* "Who's your roommate again?"

"Percy Jenkins, but he calls himself Lil Bootsy."

Oh . . . my . . . God . . . Jesus must be pissed off with me—

Before I could finish my thought, Courtney screamed, "There go the lil freak right there!"

I turned to the right and in my sight was a nasty ghetto throwback of a mess: Percy a.k.a. Lil Bootsy, b.k.a. Miss Minnie's son and Cousin Shake's stepson, the one who always dressed in a sky blue velvet suit and a cape, and thought being called a pimp was the world's greatest compliment.

Now I know for sure I have arrived in hell with gasoline panties on.

Percy walked over to our table and said, " 'Sup, Shae? 'Sup, my beautiful plus-size queen." He looked at Khya and growled. "Your prince has arrived, and don't let my size fool ya, 'cause I like my women big and juicy. Ain't that right, Seven?"

"I don't know what you like."

"You need to stop frontin'," Lil Bootsy snorted. " 'Cause you know if I wasn't your cousin I woulda tapped that by now."

I completely ignored him.

"Seven, you don't see me talkin' to you?"

"Don't worry," Courtney said, "if they don't see you they will smell you in about five seconds. Five...four..."

"What are you doing here?" I snapped in disbelief, I swear I wanted to fight him. Real talk—I couldn't stand this dude.

" 'Cause this college was cheaper. They accepted me in the EEO program, and my stepdaddy, Cousin Shake, sent me to look after you...so here I am." He stretched his arms wide and smiled, showing his top grill of pink and yellow gold teeth. He snorted at Khya and said, "You like that, don't you, girl? I see you watching me. Look at it good now." He opened his mouth. "Spells, you need to get with me."

"Listen, lil avatar," Courtney said, "she clearly doesn't want to be bothered with you."

"You don't know what she wants!"

"Well, I do," Khya interjected, "and, Seven, I want you to get your lil cousin."

"I'm older than her," Percy said.

"Well," Khya continued, "get your lil big cousin."

I quickly spat, "He is not really my cousin."

"Oh, you just gon' disown me right in my face?"

"She probably don't see you." Courtney popped his gum. "She probably still looking for you, 'cause you so damn little that I'm sure all she hears is a voice."

"Oh, I see I'ma have to drop a silent killer for you."
Percy snorted.

Courtney slapped his hand over his mouth and said,
"Oh no!"

"What the heck are you talking about?" I frowned.
"Silent killer?"

Before he could answer the question I thought for sure
I was about to pass out. "What is that smell?" I looked
down at Percy, and before I could think of how I was going
to lay him to rest, the crowd in the caf started moving
swiftly out the door. *Oh...hell...no...*

As I went to clobber this weed for chasing everybody
out of here, someone yelled, "Parade, y'all!"

"Parade!" Khya jumped out of her seat. "Oh hell yes,
welcome home to me, Khya Baptiste! Welcome home,
bey-be! Second line in the hiz'zouse!" She looked at me
and Shae in excitement. "Listen, when we get back to the
room, Seven, then we'll discuss how you got lil nasty crea-
tures coming out the woodwork, neighbors all up in ya
business, and of course we'll save the lecture of how you
don't have to accept every apology that homeboy brings,
but until we get there, we need to get this parade poppin',
now come on!"

"Parade?" Percy said. "Let me go get my tambourine.
Later." And he ran out.

*Parade? Do I look as if I care about a parade when
someone has taken a bullet and shot my life away?* "I'm
not going. You go ahead."

"You trippin'," Khya said. "We all need to be on the second line groovin'!"

"Don't worry about her," Courtney said to Khya. "She's
just a lil upset with me right now. But she'll get over it.

Now, I'll go with you, I'm all for getting something pop-pin'. The only things I need to know are: if this second line thing is gon' sweat my hair out and what exactly is it?"

"Look," Khya said, "all you need to know is that cuties are everywhere! Now come on!"

"Got to go!" Courtney stood up.

"Why is there a parade?" Shae asked.

"'Cause it's hot outside," Khya said. "Hell, 'cause it's Monday and the breeze is blowin'. I don't know. This is N'awlins—we don't need a reason to party! Now come on, before they move off this street and we have to run behind them to catch up!"

"We're coming," Shae said to Khya and Courtney. "You two go ahead. We'll catch up to you."

I knew as soon as they disappeared from sight that Shae was going to start lecturing me, so I simply turned to her and said, "Josiah showing up at the door didn't even go down the way Courtney described it."

"You know, Seven, whatever you do with Josiah is on you. If you're cool with what went down last night, then who am I?"

"Shae, I'm trying to tell you that it wasn't as deep as Courtney tried to make it seem. I mean, come on, you can look at him and tell he's extra."

"Oh, he's extra?" she said, nodding her head. "Okay."

"Look, I'ma big girl and I told Josiah that if he wanted to do other things—see other girls—then I was out."

"Why does it have to be on his terms? You know what?" She sighed. "You're right, you're a big girl, so I guess we'll find out what big girls do."

"Would you two come on?!" Khya rushed back into the caf and over to the table.

"I thought you were gone already and in the parade?" I said, surprised.

"Looka here, round," Khya said, placing one hand on her hip. "We in this together. Ain't no, you go have a good time, while I sit back and figure out life. Nah, it don't even go down like that. We're roommates, we fixin' to be friends for life, so we gon' be 'bout-it, 'bout-it together. I don't care that you let Josiah in the room—'cause the truth is I'da let my boo in the room too. Ya heardz me? All I care about is him treating you right,'cause if he ain't—"

"Then Courtney will be all up in dat azz!" Courtney yelled from the door. "Now come on! Fa' real, 'cause it's so many cuties out here my mama might not never see me again. Geezus!"

I looked at my friends—even Courtney, who I had a feeling would be forcing his friendship on me—and pushed my lips into a smile. "A'ight, come on!"

7

Don't ever... wanna deal with this again
So... you better tell her...

—TEEDRA MOSES, "YOU BETTER TELL HER"

The beaming sun provided a spotlight for everyone who grooved down the center of the street. The campus was huge, and sat in the center of the hood. Only one side of the campus was gated, and the other side, where the parade jumped off, was smack-dab in the middle of the French Quarter—brightly painted row houses, jazz clubs with painted neon signs that hung above the doors and read COME AS YOU ARE.

People were everywhere: some bouncing and doing African-inspired dances on the sidewalks. There were dancing crowds on just about every other galley; but most people were either in front of or behind us, dancing, playing instruments, singing, chanting, and partying down the center of the street from one block to the next.

I couldn't help but drop off my self-doubt and sulking at the caf's exit, because there was no way, in an atmosphere like this, that I could feel anything more than joy, wonder, and excitement.

Like for real, the Big Easy amazed me. Now, don't get it twisted, I loved my city and would be a Brick City honey for life, but there was no way I could deny the beauty of this southern hood.

Every other parade I'd been to, I was a spectator, watching the club, group, or organization fly their flags, maybe play a few horns, and wave at the people as they walked down the street, but this was a straight-up party. We were dead in the mix and it was so many tenders I felt like I was going boy shopping. And these tenders weren't just standing around. These tenders were blowing horns, playing the drums, banging tambourines, singing, and chanting as practically everyone grooved down the street.

I whispered to Khya, while I moved my shoulders and feet to a natural rhythm, "What am I supposed to do?"

"Just what you're doing." She twirled beneath a lavender parasol that someone had just given to her. "And just remember," she screamed over the music, "to let yourself go!"

I took her advice and danced like crazy.

"When you're out here"—Khya grooved—"dancing in the street, on second line, nothing else exists—"

Except Josiah. I stood frozen as I spotted Josiah a few feet in front of me, entranced in a conversation with the girl I saw him kicking it with last night at Big Country's party.

Instantly, my heart sank. A tailspin of emotions crashed through my veins, causing me to feel a rush of panic, confusion, and uncertainty all at once. I didn't know whether to play it cool or to lose it.

But, I had to stay calm...but, for-real, for-real, I desperately wanted to flip out more than anything...but I couldn't.

Right?

I mean, like, flip out about what, though? Josiah's obvious lie to me? A strange feeling? Me not liking this chick because she's standing too close to my man? Huh? Does any of that make any sense? And I don't want to play myself by being the insane girlfriend who spazzed every time her boyfriend had a conversation with a female. But he lied to me.

You know what, I'm not about to sweat him. I'm good. I'ma act like I don't even see them, fall back, and peep the situation.

I stood silently in my spot—as Khya grooved and moved with the crowd—and waited for what felt like forever, but in reality was about ten seconds, and then I couldn't take it anymore. I had to say something....

I started walking toward Josiah so fast that I'm not certain how it all went down, but somehow I ended up on the ground and a dude dressed in a glittering green suit was doing his best not to trip over me. And just when I thought I'd left being clumsy in high school....

"You all right?" The guy managed to catch his balance. He extended his hand and helped me up.

"Thanks," I said as he walked away. I dusted myself off and looked back over to where Josiah had been standing only to see that he was gone, yet the chick was still standing there like she was homeless. I started to position my hands like guns, point them toward her, and pull the triggers...but I didn't. Instead, I felt a pair of unexpected arms wrap around my waist and a whisper in my ear. "Why didn't you tell me you were going to be here?"

It was Josiah. I closed my eyes, took in the seduction of his cologne, and then quickly broke the spell. I stepped out of his embrace, turned to face him, and said, "That's funny"—I batted my eyes—"especially since you told me you had practice, so maybe I should be asking you, why didn't you tell me you would be here?"

"Practice was cancelled," he said a little too quickly.

I stood silent and nothing would fall from my lips. I wondered when he started lying to me. Did it happen slowly or all at once? "Okay, Josiah." I tried like hell not to sigh, but I couldn't control it.

"What?" he said with a slight attitude. "You don't believe me?"

No, not at all. "Josiah, I'm not trying to argue with you. If you say practice was cancelled then it was cancelled—"

Before I could go on, some guy stepped slightly in front of Josiah and said, "Excuse me, bruh." He looked me over twice, stopped at my breasts for a moment, and I guess when he decided he'd had enough of that view he looked in my face and said, "I'm Devin, wassup, ma?"

What? I looked around because I knew for certain I had to be mistaken. Was he...ummm...trying to get with me, while my boyfriend was standing here? I mean, he was cute—six-foot-three, milk-chocolate skin, and he clearly had the potential for me to find out his name and hook him up with one of my homegirls. But him trying to get with me and doing it in Josiah's face was a whole other ball game.

I guess when I didn't answer he figured he needed to greet me again, so he did: "Wassup?"

"Friday night at seven, Red Fish Grill in the Quarter. Matter of fact, we can get this romance poppin' and head over there right now."

I didn't even have to turn around to know that was

Khya. Where there was a cute boy, Khya, her tight clothes, and her cleavage were always somewhere around. "I'm Khya." She smiled at Mr. Bold, whose eyes molested her breasts and then reached her face.

"A'ight, that's wassup," he said and then returned his attention back to me. "That sounds like a nice lil spot she mentioned, we can head on over there now."

"All right," Khya answered. "Give me a few minutes to get my purse."

"Khya," I said sternly, as I glanced at the thumping vein about to jump out of Josiah's neck. I turned to ole boy and said, "Look...what's your name again?"

"Devin," Khya interjected. "Devin 'Air Bender' Singleton. 2009 Graduate of Carter G. Woodson High School in Baton Rouge, one of the top basketball players with a high probability of getting drafted. And they call him Air Bender, because when he jumps he bends the air to let him through." She made a motion with her hand as if she were shooting a basketball and said, "Swoosh. Now, Seven, let's go so we can get our future crackin' with the up-and-coming LeBron James."

I didn't even have to look at Josiah again to know smoke was coming from his nose and ears. Can you say gettin' what his hand called for?

If I was shiesty I would take homeboy's number while standing right here...but nah, as tempting as it was I'll fly above. "Screech!" I held my hand up. "Bring it back, Khya. Bring it back."

"Seriously," Josiah said, finally speaking up, as if the cat had stolen his tongue and just returned it. "She has a boyfriend."

Devin gave me a one-sided grin and said, "What he doesn't know isn't my concern."

"Yo fa'real dawg, chill," Josiah said to Devin, as more of a warning than a statement. "Fall back, this is my girl."

Josiah wrapped his arms around my waist, and pulled my back to his chest. "This is Seven." Immediately my eyes wandered over to where homegirl was watching us from afar. I hated that I couldn't get a good read on whether she cared or not.

"Oh, damn, you're Seven?" Devin gave me the up-down. "My fault, my dude." He gave Josiah a pound. "You should've introduced me." He looked me dead in the eyes. "I keep telling my roommate to stop being rude. You wanna trade him in for a darker version who scores more points?"

"Well, you might be a lil darker," Khya said, "which happens to turn me on—but you don't score more points. Matter of fact your nickname changes when you get to the foul line; and it becomes Lil Whack. Just sayin'."

Devin smirked as he looked at Khya. "Your mouth is ridiculous."

Khya's face lit up like Christmas. "Don't worry 'cause when you realize that I'm the woman for you, you gon' love all this mouth. Now—" She walked over to him with her BlackBerry in her hand, snapped a quick picture, and said, "I need about five minutes before we leave, because I need to go and get my spare phone battery, update my status, and load this picture on the Internet."

"You might wanna ask my permission," Devin said.

"Permission?" Khya frowned. "Who do you know gets permission to put somebody on the Internet? Boy, please."

Devin laughed in disbelief and as he and Khya became involved in their own conversation, Josiah turned me around toward him and pressed his forehead against mine. "I promise you I was about to leave here and come check you."

"Okay." I arched my brow.

"Seven," he whispered, "I'm not feeling this new attitude."

I swallowed. "Me either."

"So whatchu saying?"

"Nothing. I'm not saying anything." I graced his lips with a kiss, desperately wanting to change the subject. "Now, since your groupie doesn't seem to be leaving"—I pointed to the girl—"do you want to walk over there and introduce me?"

"Behave." Josiah frowned. "I told you that was nothing."

"Then you better tell Ms. Nothing that I've been here for two days and already I'm sick of looking at her."

I think my jealousy turned Josiah on because his face lit up. "Believe me, she knows who my girl is."

"There y'all are." Courtney fanned his face as he walked over to us. "I was looking for you." He tapped me on the shoulder.

All I could do was shake my head. I swear I don't think I'll ever be able to shake this dude.

"'Cause the good Lawd knows," Courtney carried on, "I couldn't take another moment of Shae and Big Country." Courtney looked at Josiah and said to me, "What have I done for you to be so rude to me?" As he spoke his boa moved with the wind.

I swear I was so over this dude. "O...M...G...what the heck are you talking about?"

"Can I at least get a proper introduction?" Courtney insisted. "'Cause watching him beg at the door last night doesn't count as one."

"Beg at the door?" Devin laughed. "A'ight, I think that's my cue to leave. Later, Josiah, I'll catch up with you at the party tonight. Bye, Seven." He smiled. "Bye, Khya."

"Bye, Hubby—I mean Air Bender—I mean Devin, honey," Khya said as she blew Devin kisses.

Devin walked away and I turned to Josiah. "Party?" I frowned. "What party? I thought you were supposed to spend some time with me."

"Pause." Courtney held his hand up. "You don't nag him the day after y'all make up!" He hit me with the tail end of his boa. "You at least wait until tomorrow. Now, introduce me."

"Have you lost your damn mind?" I said tight-lipped to Courtney. "If you hit me again I'ma rip that thing to shreds."

"And you gon' have a problem too. This is Dolce and Gabbana—do you know how much this thing cost me? I should tackle you for the thought of it all. But I'ma let you have that. Now, introduce me, 'cause I'm not going away."

I sighed. *I think God really hates me.*

"Drama," I said to Courtney, "this is my boyfriend, Josiah. And Josiah this is Courtney—"

"Not just Courtney," Courtney interrupted while cheesin' extra hard. He shook Josiah's hand as if he were having a seizure. "But Courtney Lay'mar Piére. Boy, you so bad that you make me wanna lock you up."

What?

"That's a good one, Courtney," Khya said. "I'ma have to use that."

Courtney continued, "I'm trying to be the first male cheerleader for the basketball squad, you think you can hook that up? My mama always said it isn't always about what you can do, but more about who you know. And trust me, I would be good too," Courtney rambled. "Picture it: me in black leggings, skin-tight black wife beater, and Voguing...all over da place...all...night long. The people'll be like—'all hail to the king,' 'cause he runnin' the court—oh wait." Courtney turned his beady eyes toward me and stared. "Oh my..." He slapped his hand over his mouth. "I just figured out why you're so angry."

Where did that come from? "What?" I said. "Anybody else confused? What are you talking about?"

"Oh nothing."

"What do you mean nothing?" I spat. "What is it?"

"Forget it." He shook his head and tapped himself on the hand. "Bad Courtney, bad."

"Are you hearing voices or something? Would you just say it!"

Courtney shook his head. "I don't know if I should say it."

I wanted nothing more than to punch him in the face. "Just say it!"

He blinked. "You can calm down." He cleared his throat. "Maybe I should ask you instead of assuming: Are you the hoodrat they were talking about online this morning?"

"Hoodrat?" Josiah said, taken aback. "What?"

"Yup, that was her," Khya confirmed.

"Dang, girl, you all famous and everything." Courtney shot his sick smile at me. I promise you, this dude rode every last one of my nerves.

"And you know this," Khya said proudly, "ya heardz me. But I tell you what, we'll take a lil heat from the paparazzi, 'cause we're dying to be in the paper, get chased down the highway, and have helicopters flying over our heads—but trust and believe, nobody else bet'not come crazy."

"Fa'sho'," Courtney agreed. " 'Cause this yo goldmine, I mean this is your boyfriend, Seven." He smiled at me. "So don't worry..." His voice drifted as a group of cuties stood in the center of the parade and played a jazz tune.

"Oh, honey," Khya said as if she were in a trance. "I think that one there has a record deal. Hey, lil cutie." She waved.

I looked at Josiah, and he mumbled to me, "Where did you get these two?"

"Be quiet." I chuckled, as Khya and Courtney continued raving. "These are my new friends," I said.

"I see that." Josiah kissed me behind my ear and whispered, "I missed you, Seven. A lot. And I don't want you thinking about anything other than how much I care about you." He kissed me gently in the center of my head and sang as softly as his baritone voice would allow him, "Search around the world, but you will never find another shortie like mine."

I closed my eyes and listened to him sing alongside the jazz that played; and for the first time in a while I remembered how good it felt to be Josiah's girl. My dimples folded deeply into my cheeks and I couldn't stop smiling.

Josiah was the b-boy all the cats wanted to be and all

the girls wanted to love....And I had him. Me: Seven McKnight—an everyday around-da-way Brick City chick with thick hips and radiant pecan skin.

I had the hottest boyfriend and right now at this moment my life was sweet. Period. Forget all of the lingering thoughts floating around in my mind. I could push those aside, because as for right now, nothing else existed, except this moment. "I love you, Josiah." I turned to him and pressed my lips against his.

"I know you do," he said as we started to kiss. "I know you do."

"Awwwwl." Courtney's admiration created a choir behind us. "All I need now is a candy cigarette and an Al Green CD."

8

Tell me how you do it...?
First, you need...some cutthroat music...

—Soulja Slim, "U Bootin' Up"

B^{zzzzz}...*!*

"Oh, heck to da nawl, bey-be!" Khya said groggily as she sat up in bed with her silk scarf hanging halfway off of her head and loosely covering her left eye like a hood pirate. "Which one of y'all took an early-morning class?" She squinted her free eye and wildly looked around the room, until she spotted me slamming the palm of my hand on top of my buzzing alarm clock.

"Have you lost your mind, round?" she spat at me. "Oh, this 'bout to be a situation."

"It surely is," came out of nowhere. "So unless you want to be handled, you better heed to my public service announcement: Don't nobody say nothin' to me until after I have had my coffee and turned on my Aretha Franklin CD."

What'da... "Coffee?" I frowned. "Aretha Franklin? Shae, are you delusional?" I said as I fell back onto my pillow.

True story: We'd been able to rise and shine easily almost every morning with glee last week. And that was because…well…every day felt like we were headed to a party. But today was the first day of classes and it seemed that all of our energy had suddenly fled from our bodies and left us for dead.

I lay in complete silence for at least ten more minutes. My eyes were heavy and I wanted nothing more than to drift peacefully back to sleep, but I knew I needed to get up early—to put my gear together if for no other reason. After all, this may have been college, but the silent fashion show never ceased. Don't trip.

Suddenly a smile loomed on my face and I knew right away what I'd be throwing on today: tight-and-glove-fitted, destroyed-and-distressed-washed jeans with splashes of multicolored paint all over them, a black midriff halter, and four-inch strappy stilettos. For my accessories I would rock hoop earrings and multicolored jelly bracelets.

Can you say ka'yute?

I turned my head and looked at the clock: 6 A.M. *Maybe I could steal ten more minutes of sleep—*

"Come on, divas, time to get up, wash the night funk from ya butts, wipe the brown crust out ya eyes, get the phlegm out ya throat, and puhlease handle them wedgies, 'cause you had a big one the other day, Khya—"

"Shae," Khya snapped, "I don't need you calling me out about my wedgie. I told you my thong was twisted."

"Ill," I said as I shook my head. "Just gross."

"Hmph," Khya grunted. "Nothing is worse than that music you're playing. What happened to your Soulja Slim CD?"

"Y'all better learn to appreciate Ree-Ree" dropped into the air.

"Who, Shae?" Khya frowned.

"Why do y'all keep calling me out of my sleep?" Shae said, sounding as if she'd been in a coma for a million years. She rolled over on her back and placed her pillow over her face. "I need at least five more minutes of sleep before I'm able to move. Now stop calling me."

I was completely confused. "Weren't you just talking about Aretha—"

"That was me!" A series of pounds beat against the wall with every word, rattling my Trey Songz poster. "Courtney!"

Instantly I was pissed, especially since I almost fell out the bed from being scared to death. The last thing I expected this morning was a talking wall. I took my fist and beat against it like crazy.

"Owwwwl!" Courtney screamed, and the sound of a glass falling and rolling across the floor roared from behind the wall. "I'ma pray for you, Seven, because I know that was you. All I've been is nice to you and you over here tryna cut me! Banging on the wall and you know I got a glass to it! Keep it up and I'ma—"

"Courtney—"

"Wait a minute, Seven, hold that argument, 'cause I think..." His voice started to fade. "I smell something! Oh ...I'm 'bout to mess...him...up. You better come get your lil cousin, Seven!" And the next thing I heard was Courtney and Lil Bootsy threatening to beat down one another.

"We need to change rooms," I said to Shae and Khya.

"I heard you, Seven." Courtney pounded on the wall.

I looked at Khya and Shae and we cracked up laughing—actually we all fell out. This dude was way too much!

"It's Z 29.3 Stiles University's AM station!" Shae's alarm clock radio screamed suddenly. "It's ya boy, Big Country, on your dial, ya heardz me? And it's time to get this party crunked!"

I said to Shae in disbelief, "Your alarm is set to Big Country's morning show? There is definitely a problem."

Shae couldn't stop grinning. "Don't hate, it's not attractive. Besides, that my baby." Shae paused and cheesed so hard it's a wonder she didn't lose her teeth. "And I think it's sweet he gets to wake me and the rest of the campus up every morning."

"You up, Cornbread?" Big Country asked over the air.

"I'm up, baby." Shae stretched and smiled at the radio.

"Have my buttermilk-jelly biscuits and gravy ready for me about noon."

Buttermilk-jelly biscuits...and gravy?

"He is so fresh." Shae smiled a little too hard for me to even try and explain how nasty that whole creation sounded.

"You got me, baby?" Big Country said.

Shae spoke to the radio, as if she and Big Country were communicating telepathically. "You know I got you, daddy."

"That's what I love about you." Big Country's grin was loud and clear across the airwaves. Music started to play as he continued, "Now that my Cornbread is up, we gon' start this day off right. So, Stiles U, rise up out the bed, and as Sissy Nobby says, put an arch in yo back! Ya smell me!"

For some reason I think I did smell him.

Before I could tease Shae about Big Country being soooo country, my cell phone rang. I looked at the caller ID and all I could do was smile. It was my baby, Josiah.

"Hey, boo," I said, not caring about how loud and excited I was.

"Wassup, ma?" Josiah said as his voice melted like candy in my ears. "You up? You got a big day today."

"I know. I'm about to get up now. I need to get by the bookstore, I have about three more books to pick up." I was smiling so hard it's a wonder my dimples didn't meet inside my cheeks. "We were just listening to your boy, Big Country." I chuckled. "He's a mess."

Josiah laughed. "And you haven't heard nothing yet—wait until Wednesday when he has his morning bounce competition. People be lined up at the station like crazy. It's off the meter."

"I can imagine, and why are you so amped about it?" I teased my baby. "You're not planning on bouncing are you?"

"Funny, Seven. I got your bounce all right. I'ma bounce right on this court and kill this game."

"You gon' kill 'em, baby!" I said, a little too excited.

"I'ma knock 'em out."

"And I'ma be your cheerleader!"

"So you just stabbing me all in the back, huh, Seven?" Courtney spat as he beat against the wall.

Know what? I'ma ignore him.

"That's wassup," Josiah said. "But listen, baby, I have morning practice and then I have to get to class. I just called to tell you I love you and that I woke up thinking about you."

I swear my heart had melted from my chest into the phone. "I love you too," I whined.

"A'ight, then, give it to me."

I blushed, as I gave my baby a kiss through the phone.

"Gagging," Courtney said.

I slammed my fist into the wall, and while Courtney screamed I kissed my man through the phone again.

"I'll catch up with you later, ma," Josiah said as he hung up.

"Later." I held the phone to my chest and daydreamed about us one day being married.

"Awwl," Khya said, snapping me out of my trance. She flopped on the edge of my bed and laid back. "Love is such a beautiful thing."

"Yeah, it is." I smiled.

"Jamil used to call me on the phone, tell me he loved me and couldn't live without me."

"Really?" Shae said, walking over and lying beside Khya.

"Umm hmm," Khya said, sounding sad. "He used to do that all the time."

"So what happened?" I asked.

"Shaka-Locka came along and I had to bust out!" Khya said, extremely hyped as she sat up. "Dah'lin, did I tell y'all—"

"She looked like Precious," I said.

"Okay, well, did I tell y'all she had—"

"Four kids," Shae volunteered.

"They have heard it all, Khya. You tell them er'day. Not every day, but er'day." Courtney pounded against the wall. "And I don't want to hear it anymore. Okay? I've had enough, try sleeping with your broken heart and living with it. Just join the club with the rest of us and live with it...."

Khya hopped off the bed and picked up her nunchucks from her nightstand. "I'll be right back."

"Hurry up, Percy," Courtney said. "Lock the door, this heifer is crazy."

"I didn't think you wanted none of this," Khya snarled.

"But I do!" Percy's nasty mouth screamed. "You don't

even have to travel far; just meet me in the hallway. Matter of fact why don't we put on some cutthroat music and get married, just to say we did it?" He started to rap, "'Cause your accent turns me on and your pants are mighty fitted."

"Oh my..." Courtney said and I could swear I heard him slapping his hand over his mouth in shock. "I see right now I'ma need to call your mama and see if you've been prescribed medication."

"I'ma pimp," Lil Bootsy said as if he was beating his chest.

"What kind of pimp?" Courtney snapped. "Pimp of the fairies? Pimp of the short and won't grow-no-more-crew? I bet'not catch you on the playgrounds, trying to turn out the day care. You have one time for me to find out that that heifer you snuck in here the other night was really in kindergarten."

"I'm getting real sick of you..." Lil Bootsy carried on as he and Courtney continued with their morning ritual: an argument.

"You better go save your kin, Seven." Khya laughed, as she put her weapons down, and the three of us started to prepare for our day.

"Didn't I tell you he really wasn't related to me?" I said as I headed to the shower. "I could've sworn I made that perfectly clear."

9

I see you flirting
But his head you won't be turning...

—JORDIN PRUITT, "BOYFRIEND"

Seriously, I didn't know what was worse: standing in line for an hour while holding three heavy textbooks; or Courtney standing behind me and confessing his life story. Filling me in on how he was best friends with my cousin Zsa-Zsa—but had more credits than her and was able to finish high school a year early. How he really hated drama, but couldn't seem to shake it. How his thuggism was steadily tested and he wondered if it had anything to do with his rainbow assortment of boas, and how if I was a little more voluptuous—about a size eighteen–twenty— and didn't talk so much, he would think about making an honest woman out of me.

Can you say: throw up all up in my mouth?

I couldn't wait to break free of this place. The book-store was ridiculously packed and the crowd seemed more like one at a half-priced shoe sale instead of buying over-priced textbooks.

"I sure hope I don't sweat my finger waves out." Courtney faintly wiped his brow and tossed his boa from one side of his neck to the other. "'Cause a line this long don't make no sense!"

"Would you calm down?" I turned around to face him. "Actually, if you want me to pay for your book, I will." I looked at the seven-dollar paperback of Milton's *Paradise Lost* he held in his hand. "You don't even have to worry about paying me back. Just leave. Just go, please."

"Are you trying to get rid of me, Seven?"

I paused. "No, Courtney, what makes you think that?"

"I was just checking." He smirked. "Now, we need to be on a mission and find a hot hair salon in the neighborhood. I know you can't tell because I stay hooked up, but my roots are hit. They're so thick that when I run a comb through my hair I swear I can hear crickets."

T...M...I...can somebody smack me, please? I just wanna wake up somewhere else....

"Now, Seven, I want you to brace yourself," Courtney said somberly. "Because there's something I've been meaning to tell you. Now, it's going to catch you off guard and surprise you."

"Surprise me? Really? What is it?" I did my best not to get excited, but God only knew what Courtney had to say. I just hoped it had nothing to do with my boyfriend.

"And I hate to tell you this, but people can be so cruel. So, I figured it was better coming from me than someone else."

I took a deep breath. "What is it? Just tell me."

"Okay." He popped his lips and patted me on the back. "Well, I just want you to know this: there's a terrible rumor going on about me."

"What?" I said, clearly not expecting him to say that. "Rumor? About you?"

"Yeah, and like most rumors—except the ones I spread— it's not true."

"Okay."

"It's just people hating on me."

"Would you get to the point?"

"It's ugly," Courtney said, pouring on his usual the-atrics, "and I'm really hurt that people would spread this about me."

"Would you just tell me what it is?" I said, losing pa-tience.

"Okay, okay, brace yourself."

"I'm braced."

"The rumor is that I...that I...that I'ma talk-too-much drama king. With nothing else to do but mind other peo-ple's business."

I was stunned....Did he actually think that was a rumor? Judging by the glimmer of tears in his eyes, he did. This was crazy. "Wow, Courtney...I don't, umm, even know what to say."

"Horrible, I know. And Seven, you know me better than that."

No, I don't. Nosy and in everybody's B.I. is exactly who I know you to be.

"And your room is next door to mine."

And I wish like heck that it wasn't.

"And you know I mind my business," he carried on.

And you mind my business...and Khya's...and Shae's...Percy's...the girl down the hall's...the RA's... and when it comes to stalking folks online you have Khya beat....

"Why do you think people would say that about you, Courtney?" I asked.

"'Cause people love to spread hate. Well, I'm all about love."

"I know, Courtney, I know." *I know that you love to be all up in somebody else's Kool-Aid.*

"I feel like Michael Jackson," Courtney said, as I finally moved to the front of the line.

"Michael Jackson?" I placed my books on the counter.

"Yeah, all I want is to make the world a better place."

I turned my head from one side of the room to the next. Was somebody playing a joke on me? Really, was I on *Hell Date* and nobody told me? "Courtney, let's just, ummm, pay for our books so we can part ways."

I looked up at the cashier and my friendly smile quickly faded. I couldn't believe this. I blinked my eyes repeatedly, yet the vision didn't change. The cashier was the same chick who I'd seen in Josiah's face, one too many times.

This was the closest I'd been to her since Big Country's party. The chick was cute—I hated to admit it. But my mind wouldn't deny it, even though it was something that my mouth would never spit. She was about five seven, with caramel-colored skin, and her lips were twisted to the side as she rang up my books one by one. My eyes scanned her name tag: TORI. Don't ask me why, but suddenly I hated that name.

I looked back into her face and wondered if Josiah had ever looked at her and thought she was pretty. A moment after that thought invaded my mind I quickly snapped out of it and popped back into reality: I was wifey and she was simply some random broad who went to school here and worked in the bookstore. So whatever. I cocked my neck to the side and softly rolled my eyes.

"Your total is three hundred dollars and seventy-four cents." She sucked her teeth. "Cash or credit?"

"Oh no, she didn't!" Courtney said in complete shock. "Got manners anyone?" he spat. "'Mickey D's drive thru is the only one hiring with that attitude. But umm, you can take it down over here."

I handed her my debit card and said, "Courtney, we have class in a little while, so we're not even going to waste our time over here."

"Whatever," she said dismissively, and a few minutes later she said, "Well, you need to take some time and go to the bank, 'cause your card has been denied." She said it a little louder than she needed to. "Now, unless you have another form of payment you need to step to the side."

"What?" I said, completely surprised. "My card was what? Are you trying to be funny?"

"You see this line," she said dryly. "I don't have time to crack jokes with you. Now your card is denied!" she practically shouted.

I couldn't believe this. There were a million huffs, puffs, and sighs about how I needed to hurry up; and the longer I stood here the more aggressive the people behind me became.

"Oh hold up," Courtney turned to the girl complaining behind him. "You can calm your behind right on down, 'cause special-ed classes don't start until next week anyway!"

"Seven," he said, tight-lipped, "what's the deal? Now, I can only hold this mob off but for so long before we gon' have to jump Barney." He pointed to the girl standing behind him. "Now, wassup?"

I looked at Tori. "Can you just try my card one more time?"

She swiped my card and after a few seconds she said, "Still denied."

"It's cool," I said, trying to play off my embarrassment, but feeling as if I needed to find a sand pit to bury myself in. I tried not to turn around and look at the agitated line behind me, but I couldn't help it. There were a few understanding and compassionate eyes, but not enough for me to have her try my card for a third time. "I'll be back," I said and turned to Courtney. "Pay for your book and I'll catch up with you in a few."

"Nah." He placed his book on the counter. "I can get this book another time." He hunched his shoulders as we headed for the door. "Things happen."

But this wasn't supposed to happen. The only thing that wasn't covered by my scholarship were my books and my mother knew that. . . . So why wasn't there any money on my card? I looked at my phone and saw that I had another hour before my first class started. "Courtney, I'ma catch up with you later. I need to call my mom."

"Okay, Seven," he said. "I'll be in the caf if you need anything."

I watched him disappear from sight and then I walked out of the bookstore and found a secluded bench to sit on. I quickly dialed home and crossed my fingers that my mother would answer the phone. God knows this was not the time for Cousin Shake and his shenanigans.

Someone answered on the first ring. "Hello?"

It was my mother. "Hey, Ma," I said, relieved it was her.

"Hey, honey!" she said, extremely excited. "How are you? Are you eating? Are you getting enough sleep? You're not staying out too late, are you?" My mother had yet to take a breath. "I saw a story on *20/20* about college kids and drinking binges—"

"Ma—"

"And with us being in different states, I'm unable to keep an eye on you."

"Ma—"

"I know what you're going to ask me," she said, "and no, Percy going to school there was not my idea. But anyway back to the drinking. You're not twenty-one and you know better than to touch any alcohol. But if for some godforsaken reason you decide to act like you don't have any home training, mess around, and get drunk, just know that you do have a mama who will come down there and straight wreck shop. Okay? So don't and mama won't. Now what's going on with you?"

Finally I could speak. "Ma, I just left the bookstore to get the rest of the books I need for my classes and my debit card was denied."

The phone went completely silent, and then my mother said, "Oh my goodness! I completely forgot." I could hear her voice filling with tears. "All I had to pay for were your books, and I can't believe I didn't remember. Things have been so hectic here. Your stepfather was laid off again, your father's company folded. Toi needed me to · help her with Noah's day care. Your brother has outgrown everything—the boy is just about taller than me. And Cousin Shake is helping me as much as he can, but he's helping Miss Minnie with Percy's tuition too."

My eyes filled with tears, I didn't know what I was going to do. My funds were beyond low. All I had to my name was seventy bucks and I needed half of that to get my hair done. "Ma." I took a deep breath. "I think I should try to find a job—"

"Absolutely not! We've already discussed that college is your job and good grades are your pay. At least for this first year. Period. I can take care of you. Now I will have the money in your account by next week, Monday."

"Next week Monday! Ma, classes start today... this Monday."

"Seven, professors won't expect you to have your books the first week. It'll be okay, and by the time you wake up on Monday morning the money will be in your account. And I'll put in a little extra for your pocket, and everything will be fine. Okay?"

"All right, Ma." I may have said that, but there was no way I believed it.

"I love you, Seven, and I'm sorry, baby. I'll try my best to see if I can get the money to you sooner."

"Don't sweat it, Ma. I know you're trying."

"I have to go now, Seven." I could hear tears rattling her throat. "I love you." And she hung up.

Tears streamed down my face, and I fought with all I could to wipe them away. This wasn't the end of the world. I didn't think....

10

With you I fall so fast...
I hope it lasts...

—Ashlee Simpson, "Pieces Of Me"

Just when I thought I'd already strolled through hell, I walked into my creative writing class, ten minutes late.

The professor's name was Dr. Banks, and from the look she shot me I could tell that this woman didn't play. She handed me, and a few other students who crept in behind me, a class syllabus.

"Let me make this clear to you all," she said as she walked around the classroom. "This is not high school. This is Stiles University. And while you may be your parents' babies, you are young men and young ladies to me. I expect you to arrive to class on time." She pulled the rim of her glasses down the bridge of her nose and it seemed her eyes landed on me.

"After today if you are more than five minutes late, then I will not allow you in my class. If you miss your homework, I will not remind you that it is due; your falling grade will teach you. And you are to have your books"—

she looked at my bare desk—"the next time we see each other.

"Also, I will not accept any notes from your parents. Please keep all pets away from your homework, sleep at night"—she tapped on a dozing student's desk—"and not in my class. I am here to teach you, and together we will enjoy the love of creating literary art. Hopefully, when you leave my class you will have learned something that you'll carry with you for the rest of your lives." She looked around the class, and if I'm not mistaken I think she cracked a smile...well, at least a small grin.

"Now let's get started." She clapped her hands together. "The first expression of writing we will explore is writing fiction...."

O...M...G...why couldn't we start with poetry? I don't know anything about writing fiction.

"Does anyone know that there is more to fiction writing than first and third person?"

No, and I never really cared. I write poems—that's why I took this class...along with needing—what I thought would be—an easy elective.

The professor looked around the room, and seeing that no one chimed in, she continued on, "There's second person, third person total omniscient, third person limited omniscient, stream of consciousness...."

This was so not my day. I didn't mind learning about writing fiction; it's just that it would've been easier to start with poems. I swore nothing was going my way this day, and just when I thought things couldn't get worse the professor said, "If you will refer to your syllabus you will see that your first assignment will be a short story."

Jesus, please...

*   *   *

Three classes back to back, all the professors pretty much gave the same freshman speech about us not being babies but being high school graduates. They all had the same policy about lateness and at least one of them made sure that we understood that they already had what we wanted to get. Blah...blah...blah...

I hated that I wasn't as excited about my classes as I really wanted to be....I mean, it was no secret that I loved school. Heck, I worked hard to get here, but I was soooo embarrassed about not having my books that it kept me from enjoying my classes.

And it wasn't like I was lazy and simply needed to go to the bookstore. My mom didn't have the money for my books...and that was a hard pill to swallow.

The sagging economy seemed to affect everyone, even my middle-class family. We never had money woes and my mother worked two jobs to make sure we never felt a pinch. I always had a part-time job. But now I was broke, and totally dependent on somebody else. Thank goodness my meal plan was included in my scholarship or I would be on the corner with a sign that read HELP A SISTAH OUT, PLEASE.

I was so glad to be back in my dorm room. I tossed my backpack on my desk, kicked my heels off—which after my hustle from class to class around this humungous campus I would not be wearing anymore during the day...unless I was on a date. I pulled my hair back into a single shoulder-length ponytail and lay out like a snow angel across my bed.

I closed my eyes and the very moment I prayed for sleep there was a knock on my door.

Please...oh please...do not let this be Courtney....

I laid on my bed a few minutes longer contemplating if I really wanted to open the door, but before I could decide the knocks beat against the door in succession.

Despite the short distance I took my time walking to the door, and when I opened it, all I could do was smile, because suddenly my bad day had floated away.

Josiah leaned against the door frame, gave me a sexy smile, and said, "Yo, somebody told me that this hot and fly girl named Seven lived here, and that I needed to come check her because she had a big day today."

"Oh, really?" I blushed. "I'm Seven and I've had a horrible day."

"Really?" Josiah said, and pulled me by the belt loop to his chest. "What happened?"

I recounted for him what happened today, and then I said, "And my creative writing professor. OMG, yo, that lady was something else."

"Yeah, some professors are like that. But it's cool." He kissed me. "You're smart. You'll get through it, and when all else fails and this is all said and done, you're going to get further in life simply by being Josiah Whitaker's girl anyway."

"Excuse you." I chuckled in disbelief. "Feeling yourself, maybe?"

"Nah, just a little confidence." He kissed me passionately.

A few minutes in our kiss, "All right, all right," poured from behind us. "Enough of that." It was Shae and Big Country.

I wiped my lip gloss from Josiah's lips and said, "Don't hate."

Shae laughed as we all entered the room. Big Country and Josiah exchanged dap and we sat coupled up on me and Shae's respective beds.

"Yo, this is hot," Big Country said. "Ya smell me?"

"What, boo?" Shae asked him, while stroking his cheek.

I promise you this bearilla here looked more like Rick Ross than Rick Ross did himself. I was tempted to ask Big Country if he could rap, but I didn't want Shae to get offended; so instead I said, "What's hot, Melvin?"

"Us, being here like this," he said. "You know, like old times."

"Yeah." I chuckled. "This is sorta like old times."

"Uhmm hmm," Big Country agreed, "and now that we've gotten a little older and you not as sensitive, shawtie"—he looked at me—"I can tell you, man, you used to get on my nerves real bad."

What did he say? Who is he talking to? Me? "You better get your boyfriend, Shae. That's exactly why we used to beat y'all in every game we played and took all ya lil money."

"Hollah!" Shae slapped me a high five.

"Nah." Josiah smirked. "Ain't no hollah. You've never beaten me."

"Shawtie, stop lying," Big Country said.

"You, are crazy." I laughed. "Shae, would you tell 'em?"

"Yeah." She nodded. "We pretty much had y'all shook."

"And when was this?" Josiah asked.

"Arizona's," Shae said. "Ringing any bells? We whipped y'all—"

"Azzes!" I started hunching my shoulders and doing a dance.

"We let y'all win," Josiah said.

"Oh yeah?" I arched my brow. "Puhlease, you know you're making things up, me and Shae could beat you two in anything."

"Not in hoops." Josiah gave a sly smile.

"No, 'cause you're ten feet tall," I spat.

"Hmph," Shae said, hyped, as she stood up. "I believe I can take him."

"Shae," I said, tight-lipped, "didn't we already have this conversation about you not growing anymore?"

"True." She sat back down.

"Just give it up," Big Country said. "We're the kings. We can beat y'all in just about everything."

"Oh really?" Shae twisted her lips. "Well, name something besides ball and I betchu we'll take you."

"Bowling," Josiah said.

"Oh please!" Shae stood up and slapped me a high five. "We will bury y'all!"

Josiah and Big Country looked at us for a moment, and then they fell out laughing. "I'm not trying to hurt you, Seven." Josiah snickered.

"You can't hurt me," I said, "'cause I'ma get the last laugh in the end."

"Fa'sho'," Shae said.

"Well then, why don't we be about it," Big Country challenged.

"A'ight," Shae agreed. "Twenty bills."

"Pause." I looked at Shae like she was crazy. "I don't have no money, girl," I whispered.

"Me either, but this is called a short-term investment, a gamble on something that has a high probability to pay us and the only risk we take is time." She arched her brow. "I learned that today in Accounting 101."

I smiled and looked at Josiah. "Forty bills."

"That's my girl," Shae mumbled.

Josiah stood up and snickered. "Let's go knock them down real quick, Big Country, and take all their lil money."

"Let's," Big Country said as we walked out the door. "Seems they need to learn once more who's the boss."

"You know y'all cheated, right?" Big Country said, as we left the bowling alley and walked the few short blocks to campus. Shae and I were heartbeats away from missing the 2 A.M. freshman curfew we had during the week; but the fact that we each returned twenty dollars richer was pretty much worth the risk of the RA slapping us with a violation ticket.

Shae and I each waved the twenty-dollar bills the boys had lost in their faces.

"We didn't cheat," I said. "So don't even think you're getting your money back." I tucked it in my bra.

"If I wanted it back," Josiah said, as his phone—which had been ringing pretty much all night—now rang again, "I'd go in there and get it."

"Whatever." I gave a playful smirk. "And who keeps calling you, like they spotted you on the milk carton or something? Geez."

He walked up close to me and said, "Why? Are you jealous?" He slid his hands in the back pocket of my jeans.

"Do I have a reason to be jealous?" I hoped like heck my voice sounded as if I were telling a joke, although I was serious as cancer.

"Never." He kissed me softly on the lips. "You know you're number one."

"And who's higher than number one?"

"No one," he said as we started to kiss passionately. And just as the stars and the moons aligned and sweet darkness settled upon us, Big Country said, "Y'all wanna hook that up at the Super 8 or something?"

I gave Josiah one last peck on the lips, and he said, "Good night."

"Good night?" I whispered against his lips. "But you didn't answer my question."

"What question, Seven?"

"Who keeps calling you?"

"Seven." He pressed his forehead against mine. "You have to stop sweatin' me. I don't know who was calling me, since we've been together not once have I picked up my phone. And I haven't picked it up because when I'm chillin' with you I don't care. Which is what I want you to do: stop caring, focus on me. There're a million girls out here, but you're the only one that I know is for me. All these other chicks are on it because of basketball and what they know I'll have when I join the NBA. But I'm not thinking about that. I'm thinking about you, and me, and us. A'ight?" he said softly.

Maybe he has a point. "A'ight," I said as my heart skipped beats.

"Straight, now give it to me," he said and I slid my arms around his neck and kissed him again. "Now, good night," he said, giving me a few last pecks.

"Good night."

"All right, Big Country." Josiah stepped out of our embrace. "I'll catch up with you." He walked backwards out to the courtyard, blew me a kiss, and winked his eye at me. "I love you," he mouthed as he faded into the night.

I swear I couldn't move. All I could do was stand on the

bottom step of my dorm and bask in the beauty of love…
a feeling that I desperately wish I could explain, but I
couldn't. All I could do was feel it. …

"All right, shawtie, gon'-get now," Big Country snapped
at me, disrupting me from gettin' my glee on. "Cut me and
my Cornbread some space, smell me?"

"What?" I frowned.

"Let me put it like this—skip yo behind inside."

"Excuse you." I frowned. "And good night to you too."

"Good night, shawtie," he said as if I couldn't leave
soon enough.

The doors closed behind me and I heard him say to
Shae, "Now plant one on me and I want a real sloppy one
with extra gravy."

11

Every time I look up
He be sliding through in
the F-150 pickup...

—CIARA, "OOH BABY"

The crisp amber of the late Louisiana afternoon hovered over us as heavy sun showers blew drops of rain into our faces. We fought to stay dry beneath the glass awning, where we stood for the last hour waiting for the trolley. Our backs were against the cold storefront window while a neon pink sign blinked CLOSED above our heads.

We'd just left Trina's A Cut Above the Rest, which at first glance looked to be a hot-pink-painted hole in the wall. But it wasn't. It was the hair hot spot, where we spent our last few dollars—not to mention our entire day—getting my hair done in sexy coils of bouncing curls, Khya's bob laid, Shae's natural waves hooked up, and Courtney's finger waves redone.

I promise you, it was the pits trying to protect our freshly done dos from the elements. Let me say that again, *the pits.*

Josiah called this morning and told me he had a roman-

tic date planned for us and I needed to be at his apartment
by six o'clock so the dinner he cooked wouldn't be cold.

Follow me here, my baby cooked for me....

Well, now I had a problem because it was already 5 P.M.,
and not only did I have a twenty-minute ride back to campus, I still had to freshen up and get dressed. And where
was the trolley...? I don't know. And what made matters
worse is that on the weekend this thing ran like a turtle
and we had absolutely no money for a cab.

"Breaking news!" Khya yelled and snapped her fingers—
as rain sprinkled into our faces.

"What?" we all said simultaneously as the plastic bags
we held over our hair rattled in the wet wind.

Khya blew a bubble and popped it. "I met a cutie."

"Who, Jesus?" Courtney snapped. "'Cause you have ran
through every other cutie on campus."

"Seriously," I said, never thinking I'd ever agree with
Courtney.

"Who is it this time, Khya?" Shae asked.

Khya popped her gloss-covered lips. "Devin, Josiah's
roommate. We saw each other in the caf the other day and
ole boy insisted on having my number. I knew my natural
effect would work and I wouldn't have to sprinkle no gris-
gris on him." She snapped her fingers, did a Beyoncé
drop, popped back up, and gave a Miss America wave. "I'd
like to thank the academy of swagger...."

Courtney twisted his lips to the side. "Two snaps up
and a fruit loop—"

Two snaps and a what?

"With that one-track-mind cutie," Courtney continued,
"I'm sure it has less to do with your swagger and more to
do with your Serena Williams–like booty. 'Cause I'm sure
he's trying to make it his duty to get up on that."

Khya paused. "Oh, snap, Courtney, I didn't know you could rhyme. You should be a rapper, you would kill it."

WTF? "That didn't rhyme." I frowned.

"Shut up, Seven," Courtney barked. "It did rhyme and here you profess to write poetry." He turned to Khya, and said as if he was highly impressed, "You really think I could be a rapper?" He stared into space. "That would be so hot. I've always wanted to be MC Rainbow." He stood silently in his spot, and then suddenly he started doing the running man. "I'm MC Rainbow in the place to be and if you catch me on Thursdays my name is Court-ta-nee...."

What'da... I looked at Shae and we laughed so hard that we each held our stomachs, opened our mouths, and nothing came out. Tears slid from our eyes, and I thought for sure I was going to pass out.

"Oh, y'all thought that was funny?" Courtney said, his feelings obviously hurt. "Would you like it if I laughed at you?" He pointed to me and Shae. "You better be lucky my mother taught me not to attack Jerry's kids."

"Okay...okay..." Shae did her best to stop laughing. "Courtney," Shae stammered as she wiped her eyes, "we're sorry."

"Yeah," I sniffed as I collected myself together. "Yeah, we are. Now let's get back on track—" I wiped my eyes. "Back to Devin. Khya, it's just something about him. I don't know if he's the cutie for you. When we were on second line he was too busy staring at your hips and D cups."

"And if he's staring at your breasts longer than your face," Shae said, "then he's clearly saying to himself, 'I'm 'bout to hit that.'"

"Hmm, Shae." Khya rubbed her hand across her chin. "You went real deep with that one. Is that where you think I went wrong with Jamil?"

"Stop the recording right there." Courtney wagged his finger. "We are not going there. Follow me here: Jamil ran off and married Precious; we have to let that go."

"Nobody asked you, Courtney," Khya snapped. "And why would you say something like that to me, when I'm the only one who didn't laugh at you being some running-man played MC Rainbow? Did I tell you that your rhyme was like 1995, they don't spit bubble gum anymore? Noooooo, I was considerate. I let you have your moment, and what you do for me? Take out your gun and blow away my dreams. You wrong for that, Rainbow."

"Running man?" Courtney said in disbelief. "Played? And bubble gum? I don't believe you said that, Khya. And you know I'm sensitive—"

"Umm hmm, whatever, and for your information Jamil didn't marry Shaka-Locka." She paused. "But wait a minute—" She stared off into space. "I did see he'd changed his relationship status the other day to 'it's complicated.' What da hell does that mean? Oh hell nawl." She pulled out her cell phone. "Let me call this mofo right now—"

"Put that phone away!" Shae screamed. "It don't matter. Let it go, girl. Puhlease let it go."

"You're right." Khya took deep breaths and threw one-two jabs in the air. "It don' madder. I ain't fidda let Jamil bother me. Do I look bothered, yat?" She asked and answered her own question. "Not. Ya heardz me? I got this."

"Khya," Shae said, "what you need is a man like my baby. Big Country is a real gentleman." She blushed.

"Yeah, right." I twisted my lips. "A gentleman who whispers to you about how he wants to sop you up like gravy and suck you off the ends of his cornbread."

"Dead," Courtney spat. "That visual just killed Courtney."

Khya batted her lashes. "Ignore them, Shae, because that is *sooooo* romantic."

"Ill." I gagged. "Both of y'all are sick."

"Don't hate, Seven," Khya said. "And anyway, Devin is different from most guys."

I paused and thought back over the last few weeks. "You say that every time. Everyone you meet is different. The dude you met the first night on campus was different—"

"And he was," Khya said. "A different kind of jerk. Did I tell you he told me I reminded him of his third baby mama—? Third..." she said slowly, "...baby...mama!"

"Third?" Shae said in disbelief.

"Third," Khya confirmed. "Not first, not second, but third baby mama."

"Oh damn," Shae said. "But what about the one you met the first day of classes—you said he was different too."

"He was." Khya nodded. "A different kinda broke. Did I tell you I saw him the other night rocking the corner with a tore-up collection cup? He wasn't playing an instrument, he wasn't singing. Nothing. Just straight-up begging."

"What did you do?" I asked in disbelief.

"I gave him a job application and told him he needed to go and hook that up."

"Oh...kay." Courtney chimed in. "Well...ummm...what about the cutie you met last week on Thursday?"

"Say this with me: cra'ay'zee. Like Jay-Z, but cra'ay'zee."

"Oh that's a mess," I said as I spotted our long-lost trolley creeping up the block. We stepped out from under the awning as the trolley headed up the street toward us. I took my fare from my purse and said, "So, Khya, what makes Devin so different?"

"He has one out of three chances to be picked as a first-round draft pick if he were to enter this year; he just signed with an agent...Oh yeah, and umm, he's cute. Yeah," she said as if she were agreeing with herself. "And he's, umm, nice. He said good morning to me. And, ummm, yeah, I just like him."

"And for all the right reasons too—" I stopped midsentence, I had to. Really...I did...because suddenly and without warning the world came to an end. And we'd been drowned, from our freshly done dos to our manicured feet with a heavy wave of rainwater, courtesy of an onyx and kitted-up F-150 pickup that skirted around the trolley, splashed water from the street to the sidewalk, and rocked our world.

It was like...like...a hurricane breeze had come over us. Scratch that, how about a tornado—yeah, that was it, a tornado had just hog spit on us and now we were buried in the drippings.

WTF?!

Instantly every...last...one of my curls melted. My hair slicked over my forehead and stuck to the sides of my face like black glue. Khya's bob had gone flat, Shae's natural waves had transformed into an afro. And Courtney, well, his finger waves made a loud crunch sound, and as if his hair were breaking free it shot straight up in the air, causing him to fall to the ground and scream, "Dead! Courtney's dead!"

The plastic bags that had only moments ago protected our hair were blown into the street. My clothes were stuck to me and I felt like I'd just bumped—and yes, I mean bumped—into the ocean.

Oh hell to da no!

And just when I thought we'd made it through the worst of things the trolley we'd been waiting on for over an hour closed its doors and rode past us.

I only have one word to say: stunned.

The kitted-up culprit reversed its way down the street and made a screeching sound as it halted in front of us and splashed even more water onto the sidewalk. "Yo," the driver said as he got out of his truck and slammed the door, "my fault, Lovely."

The driver looked me over and his eyes smiled, at least until he peeped Khya and Shae, who were clearly in space, and Courtney who laid on the ground screaming about his roots. "I didn't have the money for a touch-up!" he cried.

"Damn, lil mas,"—he paused and looked at Courtney—"And you, I'm really sorry about this. I promise you I didn't mean for this to happen."

I placed my hands on my soaking wet hips, crooked my neck to the left, and just when I was prepared to spaz, he boldly swept my hair from my forehead. "Seriously, beautiful"—he gazed into my eyes—"my fault. I shouldn't have cut in front of the bus like that."

For-real, for-real, I had every intention on being a pissed, raving lunatic, but instead I found myself spent... all because he was well...fine—hmm, let's make that beautiful—nah, that's not doing him justice either.

Let's try pretty—but then again...I wasn't sure what label to place on whoever he was; and though I tried to keep my eyes still, so that I could focus on being swollen,

I couldn't and my eyes roamed all over lil daddy like an oil spill.

His looks were so sweet that he put Reggie Bush to sleep. He was a grown-man-type fine. NFL player, Terrell Owens, but younger and with smoother almond-butter skin, deeper plunging dimples, a sexier cleft chin, marble brown eyes, and a smile that demanded your attention. Yeah, trust me, it was like that.

He wore a fitted and white V-neck tee that clung to his defined muscles and showcased a few of his tattoos; dirty-wash True Religion jeans; a G-Shock wristwatch; and a pair of Louis Vuitton sneakers on his feet.

And honey, his sexy New Orleans accent made me feel privileged to be south of the Mason-Dixon line. *Hollah!*

"Yo, Love, for real," he said, "I didn't realize how fast I was going."

"Oh, it's okay, lil tender," Khya said, snapping out of one daze and into another. "I happen to like the wet and slick-down look."

"Well, I don't!" I spat as my wet hair slung water all over the place. "Do you understand what I had to go through to get my hair done? And did you see my clothes?"

"My roots!" Courtney yelled before I could go on. "My roots!"

"I'll pay for your hair to get redone. All of you." The cutie pulled out his wallet as his sexy voice radiated with apologies.

But at this moment I could care less. I was so heated there was no way I could process anything he had to say. "No, what you need to pay for are driving lessons! 'Cause what you just did to our hair is straight out of control. If I was Tiger Woods's wife, trust me, it would be on!"

"I sooo sorry, ma. I got you." He gave me a sexy half-a grin. "Forgive me."

"Forgive you? I have a date tonight and you have ruined it!"

"Skip it then—we can go chill somewhere else."

I blinked. "You think this is a game? You out here using your car like a weapon—"

"It's okay," Khya said. "I like a lil violence."

"My roots!" Courtney screamed. "My roots!"

"I really don't believe this." I shook my head.

"Look," cutie said, "I've said I was sorry like a thousand times. And I am. Let me at least offer y'all a ride back to Stiles U. I don't mind. It's the least I could do."

"Ride back to Stiles U? I don't know you!"

"There's only one way to get to know somebody, Seven," Khya said, tight-lipped.

"Be quiet." I looked at ole boy suspiciously and said, "And how did you know where we were going?"

"I saw you in the bookstore the other day," he said.

I stood, shocked. "What? So you running all over town stalking me and when you couldn't get my attention you douse us with water? Is that your pick-up line?"

"All you had to do was ask me for my number," Khya said. "I'm not that hard to please. You didn't have to mess up my hair."

He chuckled. "It wasn't like that."

"I don't care what it was," I snapped. "I still don't know you."

"Zaire." He smiled and I was pissed off even more that his smile made him even cuter.

"Look," Shae said, "bump all that. Yeah you cute and all, but I got a man, so impress me with my forty-five dollars."

She held her hand out. "Twenty-five for the style and fifteen for the inconvenience."

Zaire pulled the money from his wallet and handed it to Shae. He looked at Khya. "What do I owe you?"

"Dinner, Red Fish Grill—"

"I wish you would go to a Red Fish Grill with him." I squinted. "You know what?" I said as another trolley pulled up and I held my hand out for it to stop. "You can skip yo lil bootleg behind on, driving like you're drunk or something. Don't think you being sexy compensates for you ruining my hair. Oh hell no. And you can keep your money, your phone number, and whatever else is behind that smile, 'cause Seven McKnight is not beat!"

"All that you saying"—Zaire leaned against his car as the rain washed over his body—"you don't even believe."

"Whatever." I looked at my girls and said, "Let's go!" That's when I realized that Courtney was still stretched on the ground. I turned around while standing in the trolley's aisle and yelled out the window, "MC Rainbow, get yo behind up and come on!"

A few minutes later Courtney stumbled on board.

Once we took our seats, I looked out the window and Zaire hit me with a soft wink. I leaned back, closed my eyes, and did all I could to erase his face from my thoughts.

12

Picture us married...

—Nas, "K-I-S-S-I-N-G"

True story, this is how I was supposed to be: teenage *Sex and the City*. Super-duper fly, in my black and fitted Bebe mini dress, equipped with all the right trimmings: four-inch pencil heels and sexy curls. Deliciously sick. But I wasn't.

The reflection that stared back at me from the bathroom's full-length mirror was ummm...ummm...yeah, you got it—one hot...mess! Let me say that again: hot... mess.

To say I was pissed would be an understatement.

I'd been standing here for the last hour trying to fix my hair and style it in every way imaginable. One side was braided because I thought a Mohawk, with natural curls flowing down the center, would've been hot. Not. It looked stoop'pid. The other side was gelled down—and quickly faded to a flaky wreck a few seconds after I slapped a handful of Ampro on it.

I couldn't wash my hair because I had no shampoo and the dryer that I had, had been had, and no longer worked.

Honey, let me put it to you like this, I was a wretched mess and the only thing that worked for me was this sexy black dress that I'd slipped into. That's when it clicked. I wasn't going...period. There was no way I could let Josiah see me looking busted. And yeah, I know he was supposed to love me flaws and all...yada-yada-yada. Whatever. There was no way I was about to step in Josiah's crib looking like queen of the misfits.

I took my cell phone and dialed Josiah's number. "Yeah," he said sarcastically while answering the phone, "you're only an hour late."

"I'm not coming," I said, getting directly to the point. There was no way I could sugarcoat it.

"What?" he said, shocked. "What do you mean you're not coming?"

"My hair is a mess." I recounted for him the story of how my curls went from sugar to well, you know....The only thing I left out was how the perpetrator made my heart beat a little too fast.

"Seven, we've been together for how long?" he said in disbelief.

"And you've never seen me like this."

"Remember that time you broke up with me and I came to see you—and your brother said you'd been lying in the bed crying for six months—"

"What about it? And it wasn't six months—it had only been two days."

"It was a week, but still—you were hit. Hair a mess, cold in your eyes."

"Whatever." I laughed. "And you didn't look too hot yourself, but anywho, I still didn't look as bad as I do now."

Josiah continued, "Remember last summer you were sick for a week and I came over to take care of you?"

"Yeah," I whined, remembering how sweet that was.

"Well, I hate to break this to you, but you looked so bad that a few times I had to remember how much I loved you."

Why was I smiling? This was not supposed to be a funny moment. "Whatever, let's not forget how I was practically your servant when you hurt your foot playing ball, and when you had the flu I made chicken noodle soup for you. Oh, what about when you had a stomach virus—? Should I go on."

My baby laughed. "So then you get my point," he said.

"I guess...but..."

"But what? You think your hair being messed up is going to turn me off or something?"

"It might." I looked in the mirror at my callaloo of hairdos.

"Seven, don't you get it by now? I'm seriously crushing on you. I don't care about your hair. I just want you over here. I have something special planned; Devin's gone out for the night—"

"Speaking of Devin, since when did he start liking Khya? He better treat her right."

"Time out. You know I don't believe in being in any of my boys' business. If Devin's kicking it to your girl, that's between them, and dinner over here is between us. Now come on."

"All right." I paused, looked myself over in the mirror once more, and said, "And you better not…"

"You told me you weren't going to laugh." I pouted as I stood at Josiah's apartment door, dressed in my sexy black number with my hair a complete mishmash. I was seconds away from going home. "I'm leaving." I placed the baseball cap I'd walked over here wearing back on my head and turned toward the hallway.

"No," he said as he tried to calm his snickering down. He turned me back toward him, removed my cap, and said, "Nah, chill." He kissed me on my forehead. "It's cool, you look kind of…ummm…kind of cute." He played in my hair a little and shot me a half grin. "Yeah, I almost see the vision. Almost and it's kinda hot."

I tooted my lips, yet a few seconds later they pushed into a smile. Which I hated. Because I wanted to be mad… but being here with Josiah I couldn't. He always had a way of seducing me into happiness. "Whatever," I said, clearly not knowing what else to say.

"Now, can we bring the party inside?" He grabbed my hand and led me into his apartment.

Immediately the butterflies in my stomach woke up. And not the ones that came alive every day when I saw my baby. The special ones that only fluttered when I stumbled upon an extra special memory, I was reminded of how much I loved him when he did something special like this.

Soft jazz played and there was a trail of rose petals from the front door to the dining-room table. Candles were everywhere, and they created a seductive hue that made me feel like everything I'd been through today was all worth it.

"Oh, Josiah." I held back tears of joy, as he stood behind me and wrapped his arms around my waist. "This is sooo beautiful. I can't believe you did all of this for me."

"Believe it." He smiled and kissed me behind my ear. "And when I get signed, I'ma fulfill your wildest dreams. I'ma buy you everything you've ever wanted. We are going to get married."

"Picture us married." I laid my head back against his chest. "Mr. and Mrs. Whitaker."

"Nah, Josiah 'The Dream' Whitaker and his wife. Now that's wassup. They gone span to you at the games, and the commentators are going to say, 'Is that...is that Mrs. Josiah?'"

"Feeling yourself, anyone?" I chuckled. "I have a name and it's not Mrs. Josiah."

"Oh really?" he said, sliding something unexpected around my neck. "So I may as well return this."

I looked down and Josiah had slid a white-gold necklace with a miniature diamond engagement ring hanging from it. I was in awe. This necklace was the most beautiful thing I'd ever seen.

"I figured it was a way," Josiah said, "to say that I want you forever. And one day I'ma get you a ring just like this one"—he lifted the necklace—"and place it on your finger."

Never in a million years did I expect this. This was... beyond a dream—because it was reality, but it didn't feel real. Does that make sense? Like, I was on a natural high and everything that I'd ever felt bad about—everytime I'd questioned if my relationship was meant to last forever, every speech my mother had ever given me about living my life, and all of her warnings about settling down too soon—had suddenly disintegrated and no longer meant anything.

"I'ma love you forever."

"I know you are." He kissed me. "Now, let's eat, 'cause I'm starving."

I looked at the dining-room table, which was dressed with a white linen tablecloth, silver cutlery, a gleaming silver dinner dome, and a bouquet of red roses laid in the center. Josiah held my chair out. "For the lady," he said.

"Thank you." I playfully curtsied and then took my seat.

Josiah sat directly across the table from me, and I blushed while asking him, "What's for dinner?"

"Filet fish, with a special sauce, lettuce, cheese, a side of fried potatoes, and for dessert apple pie."

"You cooked all of that? Wow. I'm scared of you."

Josiah lifted the dome and I almost fell out of my chair. "Burger King?" I couldn't believe this. "All this beautiful hype for Burger King?" I did my best not to laugh, but I couldn't help it. "You told me you cooked. And it's Burger King with the special sauce, lettuce, and cheese. Oh my…" I laughed. "All this for a number six?"

"Since when you become so funny?"

If I didn't know any better I'd think I hurt his feelings. I rose from my chair, walked over to him, and sat on his lap. "Don't be mad."

"I tried to cook," he said.

"What happened?"

"I burned it. Everything. The chicken, the vegetable, and the rice; I couldn't get it to come out the pan so I just threw the whole thing away."

"Awwl…"

"I started to get you a chicken tenders meal, but a few of my teammates were there and I couldn't see myself, a grown man, ordering chicken tenders. That's a little suspect."

"Oh please, Courtney orders chicken tenders every day."

"Exactly my point."

"That's ridiculous." I laughed until I cried and a few moments later Josiah joined me. He laughed until tears filled his eyes. This was the perfect scene...perfect. This was what being young, fabulous, and in love was all about.

We ate dinner, laughed, told jokes, recounted memories, and dreamed. Dreamed about Josiah being all that he'd ever wanted to be, a star player in the NBA. "Promise me something, Josiah," I said.

"What's that?"

"That things will always be like this."

"Always," he said as we kissed passionately. He lifted me from the chair and carried me into the mystic darkness of his bedroom where we capped off this beautiful night with the sweetness of sinful memories....

I was on cloud nine and felt like I'd just eased down the yellow brick road by the time I arrived back at my dorm. I held my stilettos in my hand, and tipped into the room, doing my best not to make any noise as I unlocked the door and pushed it open. But of course the door creaked.

"No need to sneak round. Ya mama ain't here," Khya said as she sat up in bed and Shae flicked the light on.

"Where you been, yat?" Shae added. "And don't say catching da wall, 'cause we know that ain't so."

"I was with Josiah." I lifted my necklace and showed it to them.

"That's beautiful!" Shae and Khya said, excited.

"What does that ring hanging from it mean?" Shae asked. "It's a promise ring, right? 'Cause you know we have a lot of years left in school."

"Shae, don't dry up the dream." I twisted my lips. "I'm not dropping out of school. I got this. And yes, it's a promise ring."

"Jamil gave me a promise ring once—" Khya said.

Before she could finish Courtney pounded on the wall. "Not tonight, Khya. Not tonight."

"Shut up, Rainbow!" Khya yelled. "Anywho, Seven, somebody dropped you off a package this evening. It was sitting outside the door when me and Shae came back from the dinner at the caf."

"A package?" I said, surprised, as I turned toward my desk and spotted a medium-sized cardboard box. I tried to shake it, but the box was heavy. "Who is this from?"

"I don't know," Khya said, "but I tell you what, they mixed some crazy glue in with that tape, 'cause it wouldn't pop open for nothing."

"You tried to open my box?" I said, surprised.

"No, girl, you know I respect your privacy."

I shook my head. *Leave it to Khya.* "Now open it," Shae said. " 'Cause I wanna know too."

I took a pair of scissors and popped open the top of the box. After sorting through mounds of white tissue paper, there were three textbooks. It took a moment before I realized that these were the very books that I needed. "What the hell?" I said in disbelief. The books were wrapped in red ribbon and topped off by a large bow and a note that read: *Since you wouldn't let me take you home I hope you'll accept this as my apology. Zaire.*

"What is it?" Khya pressed.

"Books," I said, completely flabbergasted.

"Books?" Shae frowned. "From who?"

"Zaire."

13

You changed the game
I like your thug style...

—CIARA, "THUG STYLE"

Two weeks later...

I sat in my creative writing class on pins and needles, as Dr. Banks handed back the short stories we'd all written last week. I prayed that I had an A; otherwise my mother would flip her lid—wait a minute. *Screeeeeeech!*

A smile loomed on my face. *How would my mother know if I don't get an A? She's not in my dorm room.* Don't ask me why, but I could feel the arch in back going from slump to straight. *There aren't any teacher–parent conferences here.* Now my neck was cocked to the right a little more. *My mother can't raid my book bag or keep up with my assignments the way she used to when I was in high school.* I twisted my lips. *Hmph, I got this. I'm grown.*

"Miss McKnight," Dr. Banks said to me, as she handed another student the last paper she held in her hand. "I need to see you a few minutes after class."

Excuse me?

I sat stunned. And don't even ask me what happened to my newfound posture because I was now round-shouldered and practically buried beneath my desk. Oh, and puhlease, don't even think I knew what the heck went on for the remainder of class because I didn't.

All I knew was that this lady was about to have my mother's foot on my neck. I needed this chick to understand that not only did I need this paper, I needed a decent grade....Otherwise it's "bye-bye, Seven." Because bad grades equaled scholarship being taken away. And the way my mother bragged to the church, the pastor said a prayer, and the church surprisingly gave me money, I knew that if I didn't do well I was gon' need Jesus on the main line.

And yeah, umm hmm, whatever, I know I just said I was grown, and I am grown. Well...like...a lil bit grown. Grown enough to be away at college.

Ugg! Who am I fooling? 'Cause I know that Grier McKnight-Eley, b.k.a. my mother, doesn't care. She will come down here and Louisiana will never be the same.

Why did I take this class? I looked at my cell phone for today's date and wondered if I still had time to withdraw.

"Miss McKnight," Dr. Banks called for my attention, "are you okay?"

I blinked. "Yes, ma'am, yes," I stuttered. "Ummm, yeah, I'm fine."

"Okay, well class has been over for about a minute and I've been calling your name to get your attention, and you seemed as if you were somewhere else for a second there."

I was. I was in hell. "Oh no, m'am, I just didn't hear you." I forced myself to grin, and I'm sure it was the stupidest smile she'd ever seen. "You wanted to see me?"

"Yes." She walked over and handed me my paper. I held my breath and thought to myself, *Hopefully a lot of people will come to my funeral.*

I didn't even look at the grade, I just started to explain. "Dr. Banks, I'm just so stressed out. I'm only a freshman, the economy is crazy—"

Dr. Banks looked perplexed. "What's wrong, Seven? You earned an A."

"What?" I looked down at my grade, and just like she said, it was an A and she had written *Excellent* by the grade. *WTF?*

"I don't understand," I said. "Why did you hold my paper until the end?"

"Because I wanted to know if you realized you had a special gift. Your story is wonderful!" she said with excitement. "I could really see and feel your main character. Your character development was awesome."

I'm sure, especially since the story really was about my grandmother when she started to date after my grandfather died and my uncle harassed her boyfriend everyday. I mean, I changed the names and added my own flavor, but still... "Oh, thank you so much. I tried hard to make it feel real."

"Well, you did a wonderful job and I could tell that a lot of time and effort went into it."

Chile please, I waited until the day before it was due to start it. "Thank you, I really tried."

"So I hope that you're an English major—"

Is she trippin'? Everybody knows that when you come to college you have to plan to earn a degree in making moola? And I don't remember English being on the list of degrees to have. Just sayin'.

"I know, I know." She smiled and said as if she could read my mind, "It may not seem as lucrative as some of the other disciplines, but it can be. You just have to work a little harder at it. But, I promise you it is as rewarding and with the talent that you have here, you could be an author, a professor, a journalist. The possibilities really are endless."

Umm hmm, yeah, okay. I did all I could not to raise my brow. "I'll have to keep that in mind, Dr. Banks, but right now my major is occupational therapy."

"Okay." She nodded. "But don't close the door on English too. You have a very special gift and I think you should share it."

With who?

"I teach other classes on writing fiction specifically. I hope to see you take them over the course of your college career. But until then I wish you the best. And if you ever need any advice on writing, come see me. It would be my pleasure."

"Thank you," I said, not knowing if I should be ecstatic or feel weird.

"Two snaps up and a fruit loop!" Courtney said as he dragged onto the courtyard, where we sat among tons of students who chilled and did their own thing. Some of the Greeks stepped, a few of the band members played a routine, some amateur athletes shot hoops, and everybody else sat on the cement park benches or the grass and chilled with their cliques.

Courtney dropped his backpack on the ground next to the set of benches where we sat. "Anybody seen Jesus?" He held his hand over his eyes like a sun visor and looked around.

"You too, huh?" Shae said as she shook her head.

Courtney flopped down on the bench next to Shae and directly across from me and Khya. He flung the ends of his powder-blue boa to the back of his shoulders and smacked his lips. "This trig class is kicking my—" He stopped short. "You get the picture."

"And my biology class." Shae wiped invisible sweat from her brow. "A mess."

"Hmph, well, rounds," Khya said, shaking her head, "I think I got y'all beat, 'cause my professor recommended that I drop his class."

"Say word?" Shae's eyes bugged.

"Word." Khya tooted her lips for emphasis.

"So what happened?" I asked.

Khya smacked her lips. "Well, I took this Greek mythology class because I needed electives and the class started at noon on Mondays. Which meant I could party late on Sunday night and sleep late the next morning. But, hmph, I had no idea this class would be talking about different gods and carrying on."

"You didn't?" Shae said, perplexed.

"Heck nawl!" Khya ranted. "I'ma Christian, ya heardz me? And when they started talking about all these different gods, I was like oh hell to the no, the devil is a liar, only one God, bey-be! And I guess that pissed the professor off so he looked at me and said, 'Do you have any idea who Alphadite is?'"

"And what did you say?" Courtney asked, clearly flabbergasted.

"I said 'That's Alphadite, short for Alphadite-Rakeesha Shanae Johnson-Smith. She was my friend Leroy's lil cousin's god-sistah's brother's second baby-mama. She lives in the Third Ward, and will rob you blind.' After that the professor pulled me to the side and said, 'You need to get out while you're ahead.' Now ain't that a mess?"

"A complete mess." Shae shook her head. "Khya, Aphrodite is the Greek god of beauty."

"Looka here, Shae, you got your downfalls," Khya said, "and I got mine."

"I know how you feel," I said, "because my English class is—"

"English?" Khya cut me off and sucked her teeth. "Are you trying to be funny? Who fails English? You speak English. Did you go in there and start speaking Creole, Seven, trying to be fancy? You gon' mess around and they gone put you in ESL."

"First of all," I said defensively, "I can't speak Creole and I'm not failing. I'm just having a little trouble with—"

"With what?" Shae spat. "English is super easy."

"Excuse you," I said. "English is not always that easy, and don't hate because the classes you all are complaining about I'm handling with ease. And anyway it's my creative writing class—"

Courtney looked at me and smirked. "It gets worse?" He shook his head. "Now you're having trouble with a class where you get to make things up? Somebody lied and told you you were smart, didn't they? No wonder Zsa-Zsa never talked about you. But see, I was put in your life to get you to see the light and understand the truth of your slowdation." He stood up, puffed out his chest, and started to sound like a Baptist preacher. "I come before ya today, chu'ch—"

"Well…" Khya and Shae said, sounding like church mothers.

"To help our dear sistah, Seven, out, now hmmmm..."
He hummed and then continued his tirade. "She need to
know, Lawd, that she slow, y'all, and she need our help—
Jesus!" he screamed. "Please shine Your light!"

"Would you shut up?" I looked around at the few eyes
that were staring our way.

He placed his hand on my forehead. "Help her, saints!"
Can you say embarrassed?

"Help her to know," Courtney continued his sermon,
"that if she doesn't shut up complaining about English
while we're over here dying in the other classes, and poor
Khya has even been asked to leave, then we gon' have to
come for her throat, Lawd! Hallelujah, Amen!"

"That was good, Courtney," Khya said. "You should be
like a, ummm...a preacher."

I whipped my head around toward her. "Would you
stop assigning MC Rainbow careers?"

"You think so, Khya?" Courtney said, ignoring me and
popping his collar.

"Yeah," she said, "but you know what you'll be even
flyer at?"

"What's that?" Courtney said as if he was in awe and
waiting for Khya to hire him.

"A choir director. Something about the boas you wear
and those finger waves in your hair tells me you would put
it to sleep, fa'sho'."

"Yeah, and I can play a mean tambourine too," Courtney bragged and started waving his arms in the air as if he
were directing a symphony that only he could hear.

"I'm 'bout to update my status"—Khya blew a pink bubble and popped it—"and tell er'body about you being a future choir director and see how many people click the like
button for my comment." Khya picked up her phone,

snapped a picture of Courtney, updated her status, and the next thing I knew she went from zero to sixty and started going off.

"That's the heifer who keeps sending cyber martinis to Jamil!" Khya stood up on the bench and yelled over to a clique of girls. "Let me tell you something Nastyazzdot-com, I ain't the one! Now send Jamil another drink, please do it and I'm bust yo—" Khya came to a complete halt, jumped off the bench, and said, "Stop the press." She looked at me and pointed. "Seven is that—"

"Zaire," I said, more to myself than I did to her. Don't ask me why, but my heart thundered like crazy and instantly I wondered if every strand of my hair was in place, especially since I had styled it in natural waves that hung to my shoulders.

I quickly glanced down at my clothing:

Fitted jeans—check.

Pink fitted tee with AM I MAKING YOU SWEAT? written across it—check.

Okay, okay, I'm buggin'. I don't even know this dude. Besides, I got a man. So, I'ma just walk over there and say thank you for the books. Yeah, that's what I'll do, say thank you and be out.... I sucked my stomach in—and though I was pear shaped and most of my sexy weight went to my size-fourteen hips, at this moment I was so self-conscious that my belly felt like I had a nine-month-old fetus in it.

Be calm and play it cool, Seven. You got this.

I boldly walked away from my crew and over to Zaire, who exuded an aura of straight-up confidence. Like that Jay-Z, grown-man-type swagger. It was like he knew... that everybody knew... that he was dope.

He wore a black Yankees cap, a pair of black jeans, a black sweatshirt, an iced-out chain, and a pair of Marc Jacobs sneakers on his feet. His smile lit up the sky as he sat at one of the courtyard's gaming tables, slammed dominos down, and laughed with another cat—who put me in the mind of Drake but with a fly buzz cut, three parts on the side, a goatee, and, from what I could see, a crazy nice body.

Never noticing me standing to the side of the table, Zaire raised up from his seat, slammed his hand down on the table, and hollered, "Dominos!" He grabbed a bundle of money that sat on the side of the table, smiled at his friend, and playfully said, "All I do is win-win-win..."

"So does that mean," I interjected, "that you're going to pay me the money you still owe me for my hair?" *Why did I say that? That is not what I was supposed to say. The hair thing is so played now. Dang. Should I leave now or wait for him to bust out laughing?*

Zaire turned around and stared at me. His eyes clearly ran over my body and his gaze dropped compliments every step of the way.

"Nice view," he said with all the cocky confidence in the world. "But you know what's funny?" He stroked his goatee. "I distinctly remember trying to give you the money for your hair and my number for a date and you turned them both down. You remember that?" He sat back down in his seat, and somehow I eased up close enough to him that I was practically standing between his legs.

"I remember being pissed." I batted my lashes and struggled to keep my lips from forming a smile.

"And now?" he asked.

"Now—" I paused. I couldn't fight it anymore and my

lips were full-fledged cheesing. "I'm not mad anymore. Especially since you were nice enough to buy me those books I needed. Thanks. I appreciated that."

"It was the least I could do. I owed you that."

He stared at me intensely, locking eyes with me for a moment too long and causing me to feel frozen in my spot. An awkward silence lingered between us, and then I said, "So...ummm...I didn't know you went to school here."

"I'ma sophomore, bey-be." He gave me a half grin and looked me over again.

"What's your major?" I asked.

"Pre-med. All day."

"That's what I'm talking about." I knew I sounded stupid, or silly, or both. "A degree in moola." *I needed to shut up.*

"Nah." He gave me a sexy grin. "It's not about the money. It's about the love of wanting to make a difference."

Before I could decide what to do he asked me, "What are you majoring in?"

"Occupational therapy."

"Really?"

"Yeah, I mean...I have a passion for English, but like that is sooo not a moneymaker."

"That's interesting," he said. "I didn't take you as the type of girl who was caught up in dollars."

Shut down. Maybe I should just pick my face up off the floor and simply walk away now.

As I went to say something that was probably just as ridiculous as my previous statements, "Hey, Cuz—" interrupted me.

I turned around only to see Percy, standing there in a three-piece sky-blue tuxedo equipped with the smedium vest and ruffle shirt. And just when I thought it couldn't get worse I noticed the burgundy velvet cape hanging around his neck. "'Sup?" He gave me one of his dumb smiles. "It's my birthday. I'm the big one-eight."

"Happy Birthday, now run away," I said, tight-lipped.

"You don't be talking to me like that!" Percy snapped, and I wanted to choke him. "I'm the older cousin!"

"You are not my cousin," I said, agitated.

"Oh really, well, we just gon' see what my stepdaddy Shake has to say about that!" and he stormed away.

By the time I turned around toward Zaire he was falling out in laughter. "Yo, beautiful, you shouldn't play your lil big cousin like that."

"Whatever." I laughed. "Long story."

Zaire walked up to me and, getting bold, took my hand. "You're cute. I like that."

I knew I need to back up... but ummm... I was too scared that if I moved my nervous knees just might give way. So all I could do was stand there for a moment and say, "So ummm, you're from New Orleans originally?"

"Yeah," he said, slightly put off.

"That's wassup," I said, sounding the queen of dumb. "So umm, you live on campus?"

"Nah, I have my own spot, not too far from here though. Maybe you'll let me show you around one day."

"What day?" rained from over my shoulder. I didn't even have to turn around to know that was Khya. "Wednesday's free and the weekend of course." Before Zaire could get a word in, Khya turned to Zaire's friend, who was still seated. She stood before him and said,

"Pause. Hold up—who is this lil Drake and Eminem combo? I need introductions please."

The guy laughed and said in a deep and sexy voice, "I'm Chaz."

"Oh wait." Khya held her chest. "I thought I was about to pass out 'cause you sound..."

"Sound what?" Chaz said, curious.

"So..." Khya said slowly, "damyum...cute." She snapped her fingers. "Let's just skip the formalities and get to the boo-lovin'. I'm Khya, I'm single, and if you play your cards right a few years from now we can lock down November fourth as our date to have the same last name."

This chick was straight-up trippin'!

Chaz smiled and his eyes gave Khya the up-down. "You know what, ma. I might have to look into that. November fourth a few years from now? Well, depending on how soon you give me your number and let me take you out, then I just might be able to free up that date."

Finally, I was able to collect my knees and take a step toward Khya. "Seven," she said, "this is the future Mr. Khya, Chaz."

He laughed. " 'Sup, ma."

"You got it," I said. "And where are you from?" I looked at Chaz and recognized his accent. "New York?"

"Brooklyn, son." He smiled. "Or Brooklyn, bey-be, as my boy would say." He pointed to Zaire. "I'm glad he ran into you again."

"Really?" I said, taken aback.

Chaz smiled and looked at Khya. "What time on Wednesday?"

Khya blinked, "Umm, we can make that happen at about seven. I just need to cancel a date with this lil cutie named Devin who is working my nerves, and then me and you are a sho'nuff plan. Ya heardz me!"

"You wanna join them?" Zaire asked me. "Or we gon' do our own thing?"

I really needed to tell this dude that I have a boo, but for some reason this has yet to fall from my lips.

Before I could answer, "Hey, Zaire," cut across me. It was Tori, Josiah's groupie. I rolled my eyes to the sky because, I promise you, I hated the sight of this chick.

Zaire nodded at Tori and said, "Wassup?"

"I haven't seen you around here in a minute," she said.

"I been around."

"All right, well take care." She waved and shot a sick smile at me.

Zaire quickly returned his attention back to me and I fought with everything I could to play off my feelings of uncertainty. But I had to get away, I had a boyfriend and feeling like this made no sense.

"I'm good." I smiled at him, gave Chaz a tiny wave, and walked away.

Now don't ask me why—especially since my friends were all in the courtyard—but I didn't stop walking until I was back at my dorm and sitting on the edge of my bed. All I could do was fall back on my pillow and wonder why I had butterflies in my stomach for someone other than my man....

14

Everything was beautiful between me and him
And here comes you and your big mouth...

—JILL SCOTT, "GETTIN' IN THE WAY"

Monica's "Everything" danced through my sleep and in and out of my dreams at least a million times before I realized it was my cell phone ringing. I didn't know that I'd fallen asleep until I was waking up. I stretched across my yellow sheets and curled my knees into my chest. I didn't want to move. All I wanted to do was finish my nap...but I couldn't, because my cell was going off again and that's when it clicked: Monica's singing was the special ring tone I'd attached to Josiah's calls.

Instantly my heart thundered in my chest. I quickly prayed that everything was okay. I mentally scanned through my week's schedule, but I couldn't remember us having any plans that I'd missed. That's when I remembered that we didn't...because Josiah had been away at a game in Atlanta and he was due to come back tonight.

A smile gleamed on my face. I bet he was already here and anxious to see me. I flipped through my zillion missed calls—all from him—and all ten of his text messages read, "You need to call me. Where are you?"

I dialed Josiah's number and the phone barely rang before he answered, "Yo."

I was smiling so hard I knew he could hear it in my voice. "Hey, Budda!" I said, calling him by the special nickname I'd given him.

"Yo, for real," he said sternly and seriously agitated. "Where you been all day?"

I was a little taken aback by his tone, and then I thought, *He's jealous. How cute.* "After class I came back to my room and fell asleep. That's how I missed your calls. So how was your game?"

"I lost!" he snapped.

"Oh, Budda, I'm sorry."

"What are you sorry for? I woulda won, if I didn't find out that you were up in the courtyard in some dude's face a few hours before I was due to play my game. If I didn't hear that I woulda been straight!"

"Whoa!" I snapped. And for a moment I had to talk myself out of going off. "What is your problem?" I growled at him. "And who are you talking to like that? You don't be cussing at me!"

"Man, whatever! Here I am, away at a game, doing everything not to mess up, and the first time I'm outta state you in some cat's face. Are you kidding me, Seven?"

"What are you talking about?!" I found myself screaming at the top of my lungs as my heart raced in my chest. I sat straight up and felt like...like I was in a complete daze. Was this really happening? "What man?!"

"Don't lie to me, Seven."

"You are really outta pocket!"

"I'm outta pocket? And you're running around here all up in ole boy's face. And then I hear that this is the same cat who bought all your books for you! Is that your dude now, Seven? You playing me?"

"What are you talking about? I'm not playing you, I love you."

"Yeah, a'ight, but if I was in the courtyard in some chick's face, I would've been every kinda dirty, no good nothing. And then you lied to me!" he said in disbelief. "You told me your mother sent money for your books!"

"She did! But it was a problem with her card at first—"

"Liar!"

"Don't call me a liar!"

"How about this? I don't call you at all. And since you wanna act like some lil greasy ghetto bird, then handle that. 'Cause I'm not!"

"Josiah!"

Silence.

I called his name again and when he didn't answer I realized that he'd hung up on me.

Can somebody please tell me what...the...heck...just happened here...?

I sat in silence on my bed and tears bubbled in my eyes. I did all I could not to cry, and suddenly I had an epiphany.... *That trick, Tori!* She worked in the bookstore and she was in the courtyard today! Oh, hell no! I picked up the phone and called Josiah a zillion times back to back before he finally picked up. "What?" he snapped.

"Who told you I was in the courtyard? And who told you about the books?"

"Don't worry about it—somebody who cares that I know the truth!"

"Oh really." I chuckled in a pissed disbelief. "Since you calling me accusing me, based on what I know that beyotch Tori told you, then you need to make sure that you deliver this message. Tell that trick that when I catch her I'ma slaughter her!"

"Whatever, Seven."

"Oh, it's whatever?" My feelings were hurt and they sank lower into the pit of my stomach with each passing moment. "I can't believe that this chick called you to tell on me. Why does she care so much? Huh, Josiah?"

"'Cause that's my friend and anyway it ain't about her, it's about you!"

"About me? No, this is about you and how you just spat another lie—hmph, or maybe that one's the truth. First you said, you didn't know this trick! Then you say, she was somebody you knew in passing, and now this ho is your friend? What's next? She's your girl?"

"Don't be trying to twist this around on me. Girls come at me all day every day, but I'm up here trying to upgrade you."

"Upgrade me? I know you don't think I'm on it like that?! I knew you when you had braces and a head full of naps. Don't play with me."

"I'm not the one playing. You're the one who was practically sitting in this dude's lap—"

"I wasn't sitting in anybody's lap!"

"Yeah, right, you all holding hands and practically kissing him! I can't believe this!"

"It wasn't even like that!"

"It doesn't matter what it's like, 'cause I'm done."

"Oh, you're done?" I couldn't believe he'd said that. "So we're through? You're breaking up with me based on something some lil hood bugger, hollah-back trick told you? Then cool. What, you think you're irreplaceable? Hmph, you must not know 'bout me!" I felt tears about to break free from my eyes and cause my throat to spring into a scream, but I fought back my emotions with everything inside of me. "I don't give a damn. Do you? And if you think I was kickin' it with somebody else and playing you, then step to the left! And you and your lil broke-down skeezer can have each other. 'Cause guess what Seven's doing? That's right, you got it! Leaving yo stank azz alone!" I tossed my cell phone across the room; and the next thing I knew my eyes were running with a river of tears and all I could see were my dreams of being with Josiah forever fade to black. . . .

15

It won't last forever
But now it hurts like hell...

—CHERISH, "LOVE SICK"

O nce the day faded to night and I found myself sitting in the shadow of the moonlight, I wondered what I was supposed to do now. I mean, like...was I supposed to feel happy, because I stood my ground? Or sad, because I lost my man? Or indifferent because I didn't understand what had really just happened. All I knew is that I felt like I was in space and as bad as I wanted to call Josiah and make up with him...my pride wouldn't let me.

So instead of giving in to my heart, I let it turn to liquid and stroll its way down my cheeks.

I'm finished though and I may cry and hurt, but he will never know how being without him kills me.

I fell backwards onto my bed, placed my pillow over my face, and cried myself into oblivion. I cried so much that it took me a minute to realize that my phone was ringing. Instantly, I prayed that it was Josiah, but once I picked it up off of the floor and looked at the caller ID I saw it was my mother; and I went from being in mourning to having an attitude.

I started not to answer the phone. But then…if I didn't…she would only worry, especially since I hadn't called home in over a week.

Forget it. "Hello?"

"Seven McKnight," she said without missing a beat, "did you forget that you had a mama?"

"No, Ma, I didn't forget." I was doing all I could to swallow my tears.

She carried on, "Actions speak louder than words. And what is this mess with you telling people that Lil Bootsy isn't related to you?"

"He's not."

"He's Miss Minnie's son and they're family."

Oh God, I really can't do this.…Really, I can't.… I rolled my eyes to the ceiling. The last thing I cared about was Lil Bootsy a.k.a. Percy. "Okay, Ma, if you say so."

"Now, how are your classes going?"

"They're cool. I got an A today on one of the stories I wrote."

"Fantastic, look at my lil scholarship-having baby!"

"Yeah," I said, unimpressed.

"And how are your roommates, Shae and Khya?"

"They're cool."

"Uhmm hmm. Okay, well, you want me to keep up the twenty questions or do you want to tell me what's wrong?"

How does she know something's wrong? "I'm fine, Ma. It's nothing." I tried my best to sound sincere.

"Seven, I know you better than you know yourself."

I swear I hated that line.

"And besides," she continued, "I'm more than just your mother. I'm a woman who has been seventeen and in love. And I'm also a pretty good listener."

I know she didn't think I was about to confide in her. Puhlease, she is playing too much.

"And no matter what you tell me," she said, "I'ma love you anyway."

I paused.... I mean, I really did need to talk and I wasn't so sure if I was ready to talk about this to my friends, so maybe...I'll try my mother's listening skills. "Ma, you have to promise to listen and no passing judgment in the middle of my sentence."

"Seven, I'm offended. I never do that."

All I could hear running through my mind was my sister's voice saying, *Oh, yes, you do.* "Well, me and Josiah... it's been like—"

"A struggle."

Did she just finish my sentence? "Ma, you said you would listen."

"I'm sorry, you're right. I'm listening."

"And at first when I got to school it was sort've hard, because we had some misunderstandings, but then we fell back into place. But tonight, we had a really bad argument, and we broke up." I could feel tears pounding on my tonsils. "And I don't know what to do."

"Oh my baby," she said. If I was sitting next to her she would've kissed me on the forehead and fixed me a glass of warm milk. "Listen, Seven, I knew when I dropped you off at school that something was bothering you, but I didn't say anything because I figured I needed to give you some space to handle it. And when you were ready you would talk to me."

"Ma, I don't even know what to do."

"I know you love Josiah. And I know you have been with him since high school. But when people grow up and move on to college, things change, life changes, and situations don't always stay the same."

"What are you saying?"

"I'm saying that you're young, Josiah's young, enjoy your life. Maybe a break from the relationship isn't a bad thing."

"So I should just give away my boyfriend—"

"Give him away to who?"

I paused. "I'm just saying, I don't really need to hear the 'too young for love' speech."

"First of all, watch your tone, and second of all, I never said you were too young for love, but I will say you are too young to be stressing over some man. If Josiah's acting funny, or the relationship doesn't feel right, then leave him alone. You are not giving him away. He's not an object. And let's not lose sight here—he may be an NBA hopeful but you are the prize."

"You're just saying that because you're my mother."

"No, I'm saying that because I know what you have to offer and if Josiah or any other lil boy can't appreciate you or they're causing you grief, then leave them alone."

Does she really think it's that easy?

"Enjoy your life," she carried on. "You never know what can happen for you. Heck, you may even meet someone else. But until then you dry your eyes and remember that you have a choice in what you will and will not accept."

I could kick myself for opening up my mouth. "Okay, Ma," I said, hoping it shut her up. But it didn't.

"Now when we get off the phone," she continued, "you

will do what you want to. But just remember this, becoming a woman is knowing your limits, knowing when you've cried enough, and knowing that when love starts to hurt it's not love anymore."

"All right, Ma, I need to call you later."

"I'm sure you do. Love you, my Fat Mama."

"I love you too, Ma," I said with a drag.

Once the call ended I sat on my bed, held the phone in my hand, and replayed everything my mother had just said to me and hated that it made sense.

I heard Shae and Khya's voices from behind the door and I tried to dry my face quickly. But it seemed I was too late though. They stood there in the dark and Khya asked me, "What, you tryna set a mood? Let me know before I flick the light on. 'Cause I ain't tryna see no jimmies, but then again—"

"Khya!" Shae snapped.

"You can turn it on!" Courtney yelled as he knocked on the wall. "I been trying to listen for the past ten minutes and in between her whispering on the phone—trying to fake out me and my glass to the wall—I don't think nothing much is going on!"

Normally, I would've cussed him out, but I knew if I opened my mouth tears would've trembled my words.

Shae flicked the lights on and then turned back to face me. "Seven," she said in shock, "you been crying? What's wrong? What happened?"

"Yeah, yat," Khya said, surprised. "Why are your eyes all red and swollen?"

My friends were obviously concerned and there were two ways I could play this. I could fold into my heart and release all my secrets. Tell them what went down tonight and how for the last few weeks I'd been walking around with a certain level of insecurity about my relationship. I could cry on their shoulders, have them feel sorry for me, but risk never hearing the end of this. Or I could wipe my face, claim the redness and puffiness of my eyes are due to allergies and act as if all is well with the world.

I'll take the latter.

"Please, girl." I waved my hand. "It's nothing wrong. You know my allergies act crazy sometimes. But I'm cool." I looked at Khya. "So you kicked it to Chaz for a minute?"

"Yeah," Khya said, excited. I could see Shae staring at me, as if she could tell that I just spat out the biggest lie of my life.

"So how did he seem by the time you left the court-yard." I hoped I was playing my feelings off well. "'Cause you know you will dump a cutie in a minute."

"Fa'sho'." Khya grinned and shot me a high five. "But he was cool. I mean I've never dated outside of my race before, but hmph, he was a lil cutie, for real."

I couldn't take Shae's staring, especially since I felt like I knew what she was thinking. "What's wrong, Shae?" I asked.

"Nothing." She twisted her lips. "Not a thing." She sat down on the edge of her bed. "Just thinking about acting skills."

I fought hard not to roll my eyes to the ceiling. This was the downside to having a best friend who knew me way too well.

"So looka here," Khya continued, "the Q's are having a hot party tonight."

"Word?" I forced myself to smile. "Where?"

"It's off campus, but not too far, only down the street."

Khya smacked her lips in glee. "We have to be there." She sorted through her side of the closet.

"Two snaps up and a fruit loop, honey, Prince Courtney will be in the hiz'zouse!" Courtney shouted as he banged on the wall. "And don't try and leave me either! I'm 'bout to be a beast tonight!"

16

Be clear: I may have felt like the world had ended, and like all I wanted to do was crawl under my covers and cry until the end of time, but make no mistake I placed my tears on pause and repped well for all the fly girls. There was no way I could stay in the dorm and drown in my sorrows.

Inside of me was a war, but I did all I could to hide bombs dropping from my heart to my stomach...especially since I knew if I confessed to my friends I would be a bumbling mess by the time it was all over with. And I wasn't ready for that.

So, instead I fought against everything in me to act carefree during our pre-party ritual. Cherish's throwback "Do It To It" played on the radio while—in between doing spontaneous dances—we huddled shoulder to shoulder in the sole wall mirror and put our Cover Girl faces on.

"Look at you, Seven!" Khya said as she stood back and admired me. I was dressed in a passion purple, spaghetti strap, and fitted dress. The dress fell midway down my thigh and was simply too fabulous for words. My makeup was tight and my hair was straight. I slid on four-inch pencil heels and was ret'ta go.

"Flyness will do it for you every time." I hunched my right shoulder forward and started to get my Naomi Campbell on.

Shae and Khya laughed. After I was done strutting back and forth across the room I looked them over and said, "Divalicious as usual." Khya wore a fitted miniskirt with a rhinestone-trimmed halter, wedge heels, and a fake tattoo of a blooming rose on her thigh. Shae wore a pair of black leggings with a strapless top that rode her body like red paint and three-inch stilettos.

We were so fly that calling us cute would've been an insult.

My stomach felt queasy but I kept a smile on my face. "Let's roll!" I said, excited.

"Yeah, bey-be," Khya spat. " 'Cause I got a wall to catch."

"Shh," Shae whispered. "Maybe if we ease out we'll be able to leave Courtney. 'Cause I am so not in the mood for him tonight."

"You know what, Shae?" I said. "That's a good idea."

"Then we need to slip our shoes off so he doesn't hear us creeping out," Khya suggested.

We each took our heels off and held them in our hands as we slowly crept into the hallway, softly closed and locked our room door. Thank God Courtney was nowhere in sight.

"I think we're safe," I said, looking around.

We eased onto the elevator and once the doors closed we cracked up laughing. We laughed so hard that we cried at the vision of Courtney running around looking for us. "Okay, okay," Shae said, "we have to calm down or we're going to mess up our makeup."

"You're right," I said, wiping the corners of my eyes. We each looked at ourselves in the elevator's mirrored walls and dusted whatever wrinkles the laughing caused. Once the elevator stopped we took one last glance at ourselves before stepping off and running into what felt like a screaming brick wall. "Oh hell to da first *and* second snap, y'all tryna leave me?"

It was Courtney and he was pissed. "I put my glass to the wall and what do I hear? Nothing. And then I head into the hallway and what do I see? Elevator doors closing with y'all up on it and crying in laughter. So leaving me is funny to you three now? What you think, Courtney is a joke?" When we didn't answer he spat, "You best not say nothin'! Now, look me over and tell me I'm cute so we can go bust in the door."

Courtney got his top model on before us and that's when I realized that I wasn't the only one stunned, we all were. Why did this dude have on a leopard bodysuit with leopard booty shorts, a matching boa, and leopard-print high-top Converses on his feet?

"Don't hate now, divas." Courtney continued to model. "Peep it." He placed his hands on his hips. "Love it. Feel it. 'Cause with Court-ta-ney it's all about the coordination."

I'm speechless. Completely...and utterly...speechless.

"How do I look?" Courtney asked.

I blinked and said, "You look...just like your name should be MC Rainbow."

"And you know it!" Courtney snapped his fingers and continued his rant as we walked out the building. "They ain't gon' be ready for da Prince, honey! 'Cause da Prince 'bout to kill it." He broke into doing the running-man dance. "I promise you when I step in the room that party will never be the same."

O...M...G...

After a few moments of Courtney's never-ending antics, our hypeness returned and I did all I could to keep up with my friends and their feelings of excitement as we headed to what was sure to be crunked.

My heart lagged behind me, but I was determined that I had to get it together, because there was no way I could feel like this for the rest of the night.

So bump it, I swallowed whatever residue my tears left behind and pushed back the overwhelming urge to spill my guts. I did all I could to genuinely join my crew's saunter as we glided down the street. And I almost made it...almost... at least until we spotted Josiah leaning against the hood of his car and saying, "So this is it?"

For the second time in one night I was frozen.

I tried to play it off and continue walking, but then he said it again, "So this is it?"

Shae and Khya turned to me, while Courtney obliviously continued dancing down the street.

"Is that Josiah?" Khya asked.

"Yeah, that's him," Shae said and turned to me. "Is he talking to you?"

"Seven," Josiah called my name.

"Yep." Khya nodded. "I do believe you are the only one around here named Seven. But why is he on a dark street looking for you? My stalker radar is going off and I'm concerned."

"I don't know what his problem is," I snapped.

"Well, is he your problem?" Shae asked. " 'Cause I don't care what you say, but you seemed upset earlier."

I promise you everything in me said *Keep it moving and walk away.* That I didn't owe him any explanation or a conversation. If anything I owed myself not to be aggravated with the bull. But seeing him, standing there and leaning against the hood of his car, with the street light splashing over him, made my heart want to be soothed by his voice. Like maybe he had the magic words to make me feel better and put an end to my internal torture.

"Yo, for real," Khya said, tight-lipped to me, "if something happened between y'all and you need to kick it with him for a minute, then you need to handle it."

"Yeah," Shae chimed in, "just keep count of how many times you've been handling things."

See, comments like that are part of the reason I keep my business to myself.

"All right." I glanced over at Josiah. "I'ma umm, catch up with y'all later."

"Okay," Shae and Khya said as they continued toward the party. "Deuces." I stood in the center of the sidewalk for a minute before I took in a deep breath and turned to Josiah. I walked over and stood in front of him. There was a moment of loud silence, and then Josiah said, "So is this how you droppin' it?"

"Droppin' what?" I did everything I could not to become emotional. Ever since I saw my mother cry like a wounded baby and my daddy still left her, I vowed no man would ever see me like that.

"Droppin' this, droppin' us, dropping everything we ever had together. So this is what it comes down to, nothing?"

"You dropped it to nothing! And anyway, didn't you call me a lil easy ghetto bird? So what you sweatin' this bird for?" That was the only thing I could say that would keep the tears at bay. "I'm doing me."

"Yeah, it seems." He looked me over. "We break up and you're headed to a party."

"What? You thought I was gon' sit at home and cry over you? Psst, please. I didn't even cry when my father left my mother so I'm certainly not about to cry over this. If you wanna believe some slimy rat over me, then it's whatever. I through wit' it."

"Why must you be so hard all the time?"

" 'Cause that's who I am? What you want? Me to be all over you like all these other chicks—"

"I don't want these other chicks. You're the only one I know that's for real."

My heart thundered when he said that, but still I felt like ice. "Yeah, well, I don't know if you're for real."

"Me? You're questioning me?" he said, flabbergasted. "When you were the one in some cat's face?"

I rolled my eyes to the sky. "All that you saying is so played. For your information and had you asked me, I would've told you that I went over there to tell him thank you for my books."

"So you admit it?"

I ignored his last statement and continued, "My mother forgot to place money in my account and when I went to use the card it was declined. The night that we had your lil Burger King surprise and my hair was accidentally splashed, the dude today in the courtyard, was the one who did it. Him buying me books was his apology."

"How did he know you needed books?"

"Because," I said, exhausted, "he was there when I was played like garbage by your lil girlfriend. Okay? It was nothing more than that! So don't come at me crazy!"

"And you couldn't tell me that!"

"Obviously not," I snapped.

"So are you seeing this dude?"

"Oh my God!" I screamed. "I don't even know that dude. He dropped a box of books at my door like he was Robin Hood or something. I can't help that. That's not my fault. I'm not the one with some lil chicken stalking me— hmph, or maybe I am, since she's all telling on me. For real, when I see that chick, it's gone be all over with. And then you believe this girl over me? Nah, I'm done."

"So we're finished?"

After a long and hurt-filled silence Josiah said, "Seven, this is out of control, and maybe I should've asked you, instead of accused you—"

And when did that lightbulb go off? "Yeah, you should've."

"But I was so mad that I couldn't even think straight." He grabbed my hands. "Seven, I love you. And when I think of you with somebody else, I lose it. At first I felt like Tori was trippin' when she called me. And for real, I cussed her out and told her don't ever call with that mess again—"

Why did him saying he cussed her out make my resistance start to melt?

He continued, "But then when I called you and you didn't answer my calls—I freaked and I lost it. But I lost it because I'm in love with you. You my lil shortie, you know that."

He paused as if he expected me to respond, but I couldn't.

"So if I hurt you—which I'm sure I did—then I'm sorry. But you have to understand that I was hurting too. And if you decide that you never wanna be my girl again just know that I truly loved you and I'm sorry."

"You really hurt me," I said, leaning nervously from one foot to the next. "I can't take anything and I just feel like something isn't right between you and that girl—"

"It's nothing going on. I told her to stop talking to me."

"But Josiah, I feel like if it is something then you just need to come clean now. Like, just let me bounce while I can keep it together and keep it movin'. I just can't—" I paused. "I don't want to be hurt."

"I would never hurt you. I love you. Now what I need to know is if you love me too."

A million thoughts and a million reasons why I needed to turn away and leave him standing here floated through my mind.

For one, I loved him too much; and when I saw my mother fall apart after she and my dad divorced I promised myself I would never love anyone that hard....

But I failed.

And here I was in the middle of the night, with Josiah, understanding for a brief moment my mother's tears. This kinda love was too deep to be shaky and too shaky to be deep.

I didn't like being so connected to Josiah. Connected like...if I let him go, then I became anxious that another girl would quickly take my place. Or like...if I let him go then I'd be scared of what happened next, especially since I had no dreams without him at least being in the background. But was that connected or was that settling?

My mind told me that we needed space. As a matter of

fact it screamed it, but my heart wanted him close. I couldn't let him go, but I couldn't let him play me either. "You can't talk to that chick anymore," I said, giving in.

"Already done," he said.

"You can't ever question me based on some mess somebody else brought to you about me."

"Never."

"And you have to always be honest with me."

"I would never lie to you, Seven. So wassup?" He gave me a cute one-sided grin. "You gon' leave me broken hearted or you gon' be my girl again? What, you want me on one knee?" He laughed, and grabbed me by my waist. "What, you want me to sing?"

"Oh no." I chuckled. "Puhlease, don't sing!"

"So what are you saying?" He tickled me a little and I ended up squirming and folding into a ball of laughter pressed against his chest. "I'm sorry." He kissed me on my forehead.

I thought about my actions for a brief moment and truthfully I was a lil extra when I was in Zaire's face . . . and yeah, maybe I should've told him about the book situation. "I'm sorry too. I guess I should've told you."

"It's cool, but what you do need to tell me is that you love me." He pressed his lips against mine.

"I love you."

"You better," he said as we started to kiss passionately and the full moon eased its shadow onto our backs.

17

I can't tell you what it really is...
I can only tell you what it feels like...

—EMINEM, "LOVE THE WAY YOU LIE"

I'd sat in the library for over an hour and nervously tapped my pencil against my lips. My MAC lip glass stuck to the eraser every time the pencil hit it, but it was the only thing I could do that distracted me from wondering why Josiah was just coming through the door.

I hated that my heart and mind both aligned with the worst every time I thought about, how lately Josiah was never on time and was always unapologetic whenever he arrived.

I was slippin' and I knew it; and I was being tripped and tipped off of my game and I knew that too. But I was the culprit. Because I knew better, but I couldn't stop the train that my heart told me was bleeding its way through.

So I went along with the program, casted myself as the happy and nag-free girlfriend, and hoped that our life stumbled upon a script that let me play satisfied all the time.

Josiah walked over to the table and sat down in the seat

next to me, "Hey, baby." He leaned over and pecked me on the lips.

"Hey," I said, a little drier than I should've. "What took you so long?" I asked him.

"Practice," he said a little too quickly. "My fault." He looked at his watch. "So wassup, did you find anything on Priscilla—Patricia—?"

"Phyllis Wheatley," I corrected him and chuckled. "How are you going to write a term paper on someone whose name you can't even remember?"

Josiah shook his head and laughed at himself. "I'm trippin'. In a minute I was 'bout to call her Margaret."

"It's official." I cracked up. "Something's off with you."

"Maybe instead of writing a term paper I'll just write a rhyme and spit." He started banging out a beat on the table with his hands. "Number one on the scene tryin' to live a dream, but my professor's tripp'in', 'cause he's say'ing I need to be rippin' on a poetic chicken, but I ain't trippin', 'cause I'ma 'bout to be rippin' the court. The NBA court. Now"—he looked at me—"hit me with an old-school human beat box."

Don't ask me why I fell into the trap of being silly, but I did. I cupped my hands around my lips and took it so far back with my beat boxin' that er'body in here probably thought that Slick Rick and Doug E. Fresh had made a come back.

"Wicka-wicka word!" Josiah tossed his arms across his chest in true 1985 fashion and we both fell out laughing. I laughed so hard I cried.

Now I knew why I held on to loving him: he lit up the room. "Courtney rhymes better than that," I teased him.

"Courtney?" he said in humorous surprise. "Oh, you went to the bottom of the sea with that one."

"Excuse me!" The librarian stormed over and said in a forceful and stern whisper, "You must quiet down or you will have to leave." She pointed to the door. "This is a library. Not a night club!"

"I'm sorry," I said as I struggled to stop myself from laughing.

"My fault," Josiah said. "It's cool. No problem."

The librarian walked away, and Josiah whispered, "I got it, we ditch the research and ask the librarian's old behind about Phyllis Wheatley. I'm sure they knew each other."

I snickered and as the librarian whipped back around toward us we quickly acted as if we were reading. She walked slowly back to her desk and shot us the evil eye every few seconds. "You better not get me thrown out of the library," I whispered to Josiah.

"Come on." Josiah smiled. "Let's get thrown out."

"Are you crazy?" I chuckled. "Heck no."

"You play it too safe, Seven. You need to change it up a little bit."

"Change it up to what?"

"I don't know." He looked me over in my tight jeans and pink fitted tee that had a rhinestone tiara on it and script that read, ANTI-DRAMA QUEEN, and he said, "Like wear another color besides pink all the time. Try blue." He laughed. "Don't be so resistant to change; everybody needs to try something new."

I didn't think that was funny. "Seriously," I said, holding back the urge to ask *what exactly did that whole spiel mean?* "The only newness you need to try is studying and writing this paper. Unless you want to try a new position off the court called benched—especially if you mess up in your classes."

He paused. "Funny, Seven."

I knew that pissed him off—but whatever, I didn't like the slickness of his last comment.

When I saw how quiet Josiah became I thought... maybe... I was being a little extra and too sensitive.

But so what? Where was he that he showed up here an hour late?

He said practice.

I don't buy that.

Why am I doing this?

'Cause you're crazy.

"Josiah." I pointed to a stack of books on the table that I'd gathered when I first arrived. "I pulled out several books for you. After we see which one is the best source of information, I think we should check a few things out online, and then head to the caf for dinner, 'cause I'm starving."

Josiah looked at his watch. "Let's sort through the books first and then we'll see," he said as his cell phone started to ring, "what time looks like."

He's conscious of time now... okay.

Josiah quickly looked at the number on his phone, sent the call to voice mail, and slid the phone back in his pocket. He picked up the first book on the pile and thumbed through it.

I wanted to ask him who was calling him, but I was scared that question would lead to an argument... which is why I guess it caught me off guard when he volunteered the information. "That was Big Country. We're supposed to hook up. He's probably wondering where I am, because I was supposed to be there already. But I wanted to come and kick it with you." He kissed me on the lips. "A'ight, now let's get back to the books."

"Kick it with me?" I said, taken aback. "This is not about me; this is about you needing to do your term paper for your American Literature class or risk riding the bench."

"Would you stop saying that?" he snapped. "I got this."

"Okay," I said nonchalantly.

"So which book do you think I should use?" he asked.

"Well..." I said, shifting the pile of books and pulling out one from the bottom. "This one seemed to be pretty good. It gives a wonderful breakdown of Wheatley's poetry."

"Really?" he said as his phone rang and he acted as if he didn't hear it.

"Are you going to answer that?" I just had to ask him.

"Nah. Country can wait a minute."

"Why don't you just call him and tell him that you have to finish gathering information for this paper?"

"Seven," Josiah said as if he needed me to calm down, "it's cool, I got this. Now finish what you were saying."

I fought off the urge to sigh and instead said, "This book gives a good breakdown of Wheatley's poetry and explains that most of her work speaks of being saved from Africa and being grateful to be enslaved in America."

Josiah looked at me as if I'd lost my mind. "Really?"

"Yeah," I said, excited, "look at this." I turned to one of Wheatley's poems and said, "What do you think she meant by 'Twas mercy that brought me from a pagan land?' She was speaking of the slave catchers saving Africans from Africa and bringing us to America."

Josiah frowned. "I don't want to support that type of thinking in my paper. Nah, we need to find someone else."

"No, we don't." I paused. "No, *you* don't, I mean. You'll write about the interpretation of Wheatley's poetry and

then you'll explain in the body of your paper that although Wheatley had a philosophy that we know was
never true, she was representing the thought process of
her time. And you'll also write about how she defied and
challenged the systematic brainwashing of the ruling soci-
ety, by even being able to read and write, and having the
talent to formulate such poetry that has stood the test of
time and will always stand the test of time."

"Damn." Josiah blinked. "You got a thing for this kinda
stuff, huh?"

"I love poetry. I write poetry."

"Really?"

"Yes!" I smiled and my heart skipped beats at his interest. "My favorite poet is Gwendolyn Brooks."

"Yeah, that's wassup. She used to be with some old
brothahs or something." He snapped his fingers and when
a lightbulb seemed to go off he stopped. "The pips. Gwendolyn Brooks and the Pips."

"That was Gladys Knight; and they were a music group,
not poets."

Josiah laughed. "I'm just messing with you, Seven. I
knew that."

No, you didn't. Which is why I didn't crack a smile. I
simply said, "Okay." And returned my attention back to the
books on the table.

"So, wait." Josiah placed his hand over mine, as I went
to turn a page. "What kind of poetry do you write?"

"What?" I blinked in disbelief. Was he really interested
or was he playing with me? "I write about different things.
Mostly about love."

Josiah's face lit up. "So you over there curled up in your
dorm room, writing poems about me?" He smiled.

I paused. *What did he just say?*

"So hit me with it." He carried on.

"Hit you with what?"

"One of the poems you wrote for me. I'm listening." He folded his arms across his chest.

For a split second I thought about losing it and cussing him out for having turned into an arrogant creep, but something inside of me quickly said, *Chill.* So instead of flipping the script, I looked in his eyes and said, "Well, recently I wrote a poem...and umm...right now it's titled 'Incomplete,' because I haven't finished it yet, but this is what I have so far:

> We once shared a pulse
> the same air...easy...free
> And then you started
> to see me...as one with you
> but not you with me...
> And I tried to fight
> for a defining space in your life
> But it was the universe's plight
> for yesterday to be our sweetest
> and today be our weakness..."

Josiah stared at me for a moment and I wondered if he understood what I'd just said to him. "That was deep, Seven," he said. "You need to put a beat to that, send it to Nicki Minaj or Trina and they would probably rip it."

"Excuse you?" I blinked in disbelief and frowned.

"Oh, God, here you go," he said, exhausted. "I was simply saying your poem was hot. And you're about to throttle me. Now look, if you wanna play with some words, handle that, I'll support you all the way. But what's gon' put us on the map is me. And I got us covered. All I need for you to do is stay fly and by my side."

I put on a fake and extremely exaggerated southern accent. "Yas, sah, boss. Do you needs me to throw meh shoes way too? 'Cause I'ma sho' you want me barefoot and belly big." I rolled my eyes so hard I'm surprised they didn't fall on the floor. "You have lost your mind."

"So what, you don't believe in me?"

"I believe in you. But I believe in myself too...and ummm FYI...I'm not getting a degree in bare feet and babies."

"I never said that." He shook his head.

"Let's just get back to your paper."

"Yeah, let's."

We each picked up a book and after a few minutes of scanning through them, Josiah said, "I need a favor."

I wanted to say, *You need to ask whoever you been hanging with*, but I didn't. "What's that?" was the alternate.

"I need you to help me out—well, in the long run it'll be helping us out—and hook this paper up for me."

"Hook it up?"

"Write it."

"Your brain must be sucking on lollipops, 'cause that idea was utterly crazy."

"Seven, you already know that being on the team I have to keep my GPA up."

"Then you need to study or get another dream."

"Listen, Seven, you're good at this type of stuff—" He pointed to the books. "Me, not so much. Especially since, when I read poetry all I see are a bunch of words on a page that make my head hurt. Now math, I'm straight, even science, but that English literature nonsense, nah, not for me."

"Well, it needs to be."

"So what are you saying, you can't help me out?"

"I'm helping you, right now. I could be partying, but I'm in the library. I'm hungry, I could be eating, but I'm in the library. I could be working on my own paper, but I'm in the library with you. It's a thousand *other* things I could be doing. But since you're my boyfriend I'm here to help you."

"I need more help than this. I need you to write it. Please. I've been so busy, all these games and now this paper is due and I can't mess up my GPA. Because then I'm messing with my basketball scholarship."

"There's a simple answer to all of that, Josiah."

"What's that?"

"Do your work."

"So after we've been together for three years, you can't help me out this one time? That's what you're saying?"

"I don't believe you're asking me something like that."

"Seven, listen, I got a million things to do."

"Me too!"

"But you're not an athlete. You don't have the pressure that I have. And for real all these coaches care about is being at practice and working the court."

"Then ask your coach to write your paper. Your emergency is not my problem. I'm not writing your paper for you. I'll help you, but writing it? No way."

"Okay, so forget me, right? All of a sudden you can't be there for me?"

"You are really going to the left."

"I need you."

"And I need you!" I said a little louder than I should've. "I need you to be my boyfriend. The old one. The one I had in high school who loved me! Not this new NBA, riding-his-own-jimmy one!"

"Is that what you think of me?"

"I don't know what to think of you," I said as his phone started to ring again. "Oh my God!" I spat out of frustration.

"Look," he answered the phone, "I said I'll hit you later. I'm doing something." And he hung up. Then he turned back to me. "You know I love you, Seven. And what I'm trying to do, I'm trying to do it for us—"

"Us? I don't even know us anymore."

"Really?" He paused and became extremely silent and so did I....

A few moments later he said, "Maybe I need to join Country earlier than I planned."

"Maybe you should." I really wanted him to feel the sting of my words, but I didn't want him to leave. Why didn't I just control my mouth?

My mind told me I was being extra. My heart told me to ride it out. But what was I riding out? This was not the script I'd mentally rehearsed when I stood in the mirror and put my cute and happy face on. The plan was to act like the beautiful, wonderful, and understanding girlfriend. Not the nag, the witch, the ungrateful chick who had a man and couldn't appreciate him.

But the problem was I didn't feel appreciated.

And I needed that. I wanted that.... But instead I had this... whatever this was....

"I'm buggin'," I said, not knowing what else to say. "And I'm sorry."

"Seven," Josiah said, looking me in the eyes. "I know it's frustrating and yeah, our relationship is different. But going through this will only make us stronger."

Maybe he was right. "Yeah."

"So, I just need you to swing with me. I got you. Now can you please, help me out just this once?"

"What do you want me to do, Josiah?" I said, more like I was giving up than giving in.

"I want you to write my paper for me, please."

"All right." I folded. "But this can't become a habit."

"It won't. I promise."

"Okay," I said, defeated.

Josiah rose from his seat and said, "My ride or die." He winked at me.

"You're leaving?" I said, surprised.

"Yeah, baby, I need to go and check Country. He's been going through some things lately."

"Really?"

"Yeah, and don't mention it to Shae, because I probably shouldn't have said that to you."

"What are you talking about? Is he cheating on her, because if he is I *will be* telling her and we will be coming through, you can believe that. It'll be just the excuse I need to molly-whop lil Biggie's behind!"

"Would you chill? He would never cheat on Shae. It's some man-to-man things we need to discuss. Now I'm out." And by the time I realized he'd thrown me a deuces sign instead of giving me a kiss, he was gone.

I sat in my seat and stared at all the books on the table. I couldn't remember how this study session turned into being for me... but it had....

A million thoughts of what had gone wrong in my relationship rushed through my mind; and just when I promised myself that I would control the things I said from now on and that maybe...just maybe...that would make things better between us, I felt someone standing behind me.

"I get it now," poured from over my shoulder. Instantly a smile emerged on my face and I was ridiculously cheesin' from ear to ear. As soon as I realized what I was doing I capped it and watched Zaire appear from behind me. He leaned against the edge of the table and his seductive cologne made love to my nose.

I couldn't stand that he was so cute, and so thugged out, and had a swagger that made him the king of irresistible. He most def could rock the cover of *GQ*. "You get what?" I tried to fight off my blush...but couldn't.

"I get why you tossed me to the left and left me in the shade."

"And what did you come up with?"

"That you have a boyfriend."

"By golly"—I stood up and stacked the books—"you've got it."

"So where did he go?"

"And why are you so concerned?"

"I'm not." He stroked my hair behind my ear. "But he needs to be concerned."

I batted my lashes in awe of Zaire's boldness. "And why is that?"

"Because, leaving you here with me, isn't in his best interest."

"Really?"

"Nah, even you know that."

"Oh no," I said sarcastically, "another one on his own sack."

Zaire chuckled and said, "Don't even play me like that. It's just that I know and you know that this moment, might be the moment, that leads to another moment, that leads to the right moment, and the right moment will be the very moment that you stop running from me and give me at least five minutes of your time."

"Just five minutes?"

"Yeah, that's all I'ma need."

"And why is that?"

"Because after five minutes with me, I have no doubt that you and ole boy will be a wrap."

18

You can be my superman
Save me here I am…

—CIARA, "PROMISE"

Somewhere between me realizing that Zaire had nick-named me "Love" and his funny imitation of the ice grill I gave him the night he ruined my hair I relaxed my wall of defense enough to smile and laugh….And at the very moment when I caught myself and peeped what I was doing, it was too late to put the wall back up, because I was all in. "You are too funny," I said.

"Yo." He gave me a one-sided grin. "I thought you were about to cut me that night."

"I wouldn't do that."

"Yeah a'ight," he said, and his southern accent teased the butterflies in my stomach. I swear he was just too sexy. "I've heard that before."

"No, I'm serious." I nodded for emphasis. "I'm from Jersey, baby, and we don't bring knives to gun fights."

"Word?" He chuckled. "It's like that?"

"Fa'sho'." I popped my collar and dusted my shoulders off. "Ya heardz me?"

"Oh, you think you're tough, huh? What camp you reppin' for?"

I carried my silliness on. "I'm reppin' for the pretty
brown girls." I threw up fake gang signs and Zaire cracked
up, which caused me to roar in laughter too.

Before I could calm myself the librarian's Easy Spirit
heels clicked and she stormed over to the table. "There
are no more chances left after this one!"

Don't ask me why, but that caused me to crack up even
more. "I'm sorry," I said in between snickers. "You're
right." I did all I could to calm myself down. "It won't happen again."

Once she left, Zaire looked at me and without hesita-
tion I locked into his gaze. "Let me take you out," he said.

That's when I knew I needed to fall back. I'd been too
silly and too serious—all at the same time—and this whole
deal had gone on for a few minutes too long.

"I can't do that." I shook my head.

"Why?"

"I have a boyfriend."

"A'ight." He paused. "So let's be friends then."

"Yeah, right." I twisted my lips.

"Seriously. I won't push up on you anymore. I'll let you
take the lead; and when you're ready to be more than
friends, you let me know."

"And what if I'm never ready?"

"Love"—he leaned off the table and stood up straight—
"I'm not even worried about that. Now grab your purse,
let me get the books for you, and we bounce."

I couldn't help but wonder how I'd gotten here—
where butterflies jumped in my stomach and my heart
thundered uncontrollably for someone other than Josiah.
This was crazy.

"Just friends." I grabbed my Coach bag, slid it on my shoulder, and handed Zaire the books I needed to take. "We homies, right?"

"Just kickin' it." Zaire gave me a pound as we checked the books out and walked outside to where his black F-150 pickup was parked.

"Good," I said, as I slid onto his black leather seats, "because as long as we're friends I can keep it real with you: a sistah is hungry."

"Your treat?" Zaire started the ignition. "'Cause I'm hungry too." He backed out of the parking space.

"What?" I said, taken aback. "Don't kill the dream, Zaire, you cannot be broke."

"Me? Broke? Never." He smiled and looked at me, and our gazes locked longer than they should've. "But I don't go around treatin' my homies." He turned back toward the street.

"Oh you buggin'. Then scratch the boy deal, I could be more like your, umm, sister."

He pressed on the brake, came to a complete stop, looked at me, and said, "You could never be like my sister. I've already imagined too many things we could do together."

"Are you being fresh?"

"Nah, we pot'nah's, right? So I'm just keeping it real." He started to drive again.

"You keepin' it real all right," I said. "Real fresh."

He laughed. "So where you wanna eat?"

"I don't know." I shrugged. "All I know is that it better be slammin'."

"We're in New Orleans, Love," he said and made a left onto a major street. "Er'where we go the food is tight."

"Aren't you confident in your city? All I know is that if the food—that you're treating me to—isn't good, then it will be a situation. Just sayin'."

"What are you, a mafia mami or something? You're way too beautiful to be so 'bout-it, 'bout-it, every time I see you."

"Would you have me any other way?"

"Wow, that wasn't even five minutes and already I can have you?"

Silence. Complete and utter silence. I didn't know what to say to that, especially since I practically slipped out "yes."

"Why do you do that?" he asked, interrupting my troubling monotony.

"Do what?"

"Why do you freeze up with certain things or at certain times? Why don't you just say what's on your mind?"

"I don't freeze up," I insisted. "And trust me, I have no problem saying whatever."

He chuckled. "Nah, what you don't have a problem with is bringing it, Ms. Brick City, but I'm talking about just expressing yourself without all the homegirl ra-ra—"

"Homegirl ra-ra? That's what you think of me?" I didn't know whether to chuckle or be pissed.

We stopped at a red light and Zaire turned toward me and said, "You really wanna know what I think? I think you're beautiful, smart, sexy as hell. And I also think that you are a lil extra at times because you're scared."

"Scared?" I couldn't believe he said that. "Scared of what?"

"Let me ask you this," he said as we started to drive again. "You and ole boy, how long y'all been together?"

"Since high school. About three years now."

"That's what I thought."

"Okay," I said, "you're thinking a lot of things, but when I ask you what your thoughts mean, you're not telling me."

"A'ight, this is what I think. I think that you and ole boy are going through some things and you're scared of what or who comes after him, because he was your first boyfriend. You're scared of being hurt, so you're holding on to him, hoping and praying that you can press pause or rewind back to a time where you could see yourself being with him forever."

"And, what? You don't think I see myself being with him forever anymore?"

"Nah."

Is it that obvious? "I've been with Josiah for a long time. It's not that simple to cut him off."

"I didn't ask you to cut him off."

I paused. "I know...but I'm just saying that I'm obligated."

"Really?" Zaire said, taken aback. "Well, you don't seem the type that would nix an obligation and you sho' don't seem the type to be sitting here with me if I wasn't making your heart skip extra beats."

I hated that he was right. I really need to get off of this serious kick. "Ummm yeah." I tossed a chuckle into the air. "My heart skipped extra beats out of fear, 'cause first you stalked me and then you practically kidnapped me. So yeah, it's skipping extra beats 'cause I'm a lil scared." I chuckled.

"Yeah, right." He looked at me out the corner of his eye.

"You're scared of me a'ight, but we both know it's not because I stalked or kidnapped you. It's skipping beats because you're feeling me and fighting it like hell."

I paused and a few sarcastic things I could say entered
my mind, but none of them felt like the right thing to say.
So, for once, I gave a simple answer. "Maybe you're right.
Maybe I am scared for a few different reasons."

For a few still minutes silence hung in the air, and then
Zaire stretched his arm over the seat and his hand draped
over my shoulder. I wanted so bad to press my head
against his chest.

"Awwl, isn't this special," I said, hoping to get some silliness to change up the seriousness in the air. "You wanna
be my superman? Take me, here I am."

"You want me to be your superman?" he said without
flinching, or laughing, or dismissing what I'd just said as
Seven's mouth being out of control. "If so, just keep it one
hundred with me."

True story: I didn't know how to keep it one hundred
with him. I didn't know what to say, or how to act. Zaire
was different from Josiah. They were the same age, but
Zaire was grown, had an aura that clearly said he handled
his business and handled it well. Seriously, Zaire had a
swagger that would knock the most experienced woman
off of her feet, so you can image what it did for me.

And I knew that Zaire was too serious for me to be
overkill with the silliness. That wasn't going to impress
him, and my sarcasm didn't amuse him...at least not for
long. He seemed like...like he wanted me to be me...but
I was scared to be. I'd been that with Josiah and look...

"I'm not into being all emotional" was the closest I
could get to expressing how I felt.

"All you have to do is keep it real."

"I do keep it real, but I have to keep it safe too."

"Being safe and being scared are two different things."

"And we're going this deep…because…of…what, a few burgers off the dollar menu?"

Zaire chuckled. "I don't eat fast food. And I guess you're looking for an escape route out of this conversation. But it's cool, Love, I got you."

"I know you do." I shouldn't have said that, but I couldn't help it. I hoped he took it as me being sarcastic, and not as a Freudian slip.

Not knowing what else to do or say, I turned the music up and said, "Stop the press! This throwback is my jam!"

Cherish's "Do It To It" filled the air and I started to sing, "Bounce wit' it/drop wit' it/lean wit' it…"

"I thought you wanted to listen to the song."

I stopped singing for a moment and said, "I am listening to it."

"Nah, you live and in concert." He looked at me quickly and gave me a soft wink.

"You don't like my singing?" I slid over—just a little—not too much, but enough. I knew we were sitting a little too close to have placed one another in the friend zone… but I guess…it was what it was.…

"Your singing's a'ight." He laughed. "But you probably shouldn't drop out of school to pursue a career in it. But then again, you're cute though, so if Rihanna can get a record deal maybe somebody could hook you up."

"You are such a hater." I laughed.

Before he could respond his cell phone rang. He slid his hand in his pocket, took his phone out, pressed the talk button, and placed the call on speaker. Which completely took me aback, especially since Josiah spent most of his time pretending his phone wasn't ringing.

"Hello?" he said.

"Don't hello me, Grandson," an older woman with a heavy Louisiana drawl snapped. "Where have you been? Sunday was yesterday and I didn't see you!"

Zaire turned to me and mouthed, "It's my grandmother."

"What you got some lil girl you lookin' at?" his grandmother continued. "Huh, you better tell me something, 'cause I need to know why me and Ling didn't see you yesterday!"

"Well, I—" Zaire attempted to say, but his grandmother's words ran over his.

"I said to Ling that it must be, because you smelling some lil girl—"

"Yo, chill," Zaire said, and then he quickly added, "I didn't mean to say that, m'am."

"I was getting ready to say I know you're not talking to me like some street vixen."

I was doing all I could not to laugh, but I just couldn't stop imagining a heavyset black woman with a wooden spoon in her hand, prepared to beat Zaire with it.

"Big-Maw," he said affectionately, and for some reason I could imagine him once being five and saying that. "I explained to you that I have to work sometimes on Sundays."

"Yeah," his grandmother said and her voice drifted toward disappointment, "but you know it's only me, you, and Ling. And I need to see my baby at least a few times a week."

"Big-Maw," he said as if they had held this conversation a thousand times, "I'm nineteen, I'm not a baby anymore."

"No," she said, giving in. "You're a man, you've always been a man, even when I was changing your diapers, you had the eyes of a man. But when I don't see you, I miss you. Which is why I like to cook your favorite on Sundays: gumbo with crawfish, shrimp, and sausage, fried catfish, cornbread, mustard greens, dirty rice, stuffed tomatoes, and beignets with praline and caramel sauce? But it's okay, me and Ling will have another lonely night, with all this food, and no grandson in sight."

Zaire ran his hands over his face. I could tell he was torn.

But I wasn't. I whispered to him, "Can you put her on hold for a minute?"

He nodded. "Hold on for a moment, Big-Maw." He placed the call on mute and said, "Wassup?"

"Look, I don't mean to be all up in your business with Big-Maw, but her spot sounds like the place to be. Now we can kill two birds, she gets to see you and I get to eat."

Zaire gave me half a grin. "Are you sure? 'Cause she is going to talk you to death. I don't think you're ready for a bayou grandmamma."

"Grandson," I teased him, "me and Big-Maw gon' be cool."

19

Here's what I wanted to see: Zaire's grandmother standing on her gallery and smiling at us.

Here's what I never expected to see: how devastated the Lower Ninth Ward still was—years later after Katrina.

Half of the block Zaire's grandmother lived on reminded me of what I'd seen on TV five years ago—when my mother and Cousin Shake scrambled for the phone to make donations to the Red Cross. We watched people cry, scream, look for relatives, and hold on to dead bodies as if they were crown jewels. But when the cameras left town and the news stopped showing the clips, I thought that maybe...somehow it had all been put back together again. Especially since in the French Quarter, where campus was, it was pristine.

But ummm...this place was like a ghost town...well, not quite...because somehow in the air there was life. Like the people who hung on their porches and waved at Zaire as we passed by, seemed happy. There was also a lingering of blues music, and the sound of saxophones danced in the breeze, children ran around, and neighbors chatted their hearts out.

So the neighborhood was alive, I just didn't understand how—especially since there were abandoned houses scattered about with windows broken and jagged edges of glass gleaming all over the grass like morning dew. There were houses with black *X*'s spray-painted across the front door, marked with the number of bodies found inside.

There were plots of land that may have once held a home but now only held sticks, boards, broken windowpanes, and strangely enough thriving palm trees.

A community of housing projects were at the end of the block, and amazingly they stood perfectly sound, which is why I couldn't understand why the windows were boarded up and a seven-foot barb-wired fence created a fortress around it.

Yet, despite all of this there was life in the air; and for the first time since I'd arrived in New Orleans, I felt like a tourist.

"What's wrong, love?" Zaire said as he opened the truck's door for me and helped me to get out.

"I just didn't expect that things were still like this. . . . I thought—"

"They were all cleaned up?"

"Well, yeah. Do you know how much money, my mother, my cousin, and I mean, well—millions of people donated?"

Zaire shook his head. "A lot of people donated money and a lot of things were fixed, some businesses were re-opened, the French Quarter was maintained, Stiles U was able to remodel a few things on campus, FEMA bought us some poisonous trailers, threw us some food. A lot of things happened, they just didn't all happen back here."

"I see that, yet everybody seems so…" My voice drifted as I looked around, "So happy. Despite the obvious devastation."

"What devastation?" Zaire said as he took my hand and turned me around toward him. He pulled me close to his chest, rested his hands on my hips, and said, "I want you to close your eyes and imagine something for me."

I quickly complied, especially since standing here like this felt like heaven. "Closed," I said.

"Imagine that it's the day after an angry river has stampeded its way through your city. Trees are everywhere, your neighbors' vehicles are in your yard, or stuck in the remaining trees and hanging there like Christmas ornaments. Your neighbor that you've known all your life is floating dead down the street, your dog, your neighbor's dog, zillions of dogs, cats, dead animals everywhere and the animals that survived are in the trees, holding on for dear life, but every few minutes you hear splashes hit the water.

"And then you remember—that before your grandmother made you go to bed the night before—your uncle, his girlfriend, and their baby were on the first floor watching the news and wondering if they should've left and went to the Superdome with everybody else.

"And now—the next day—you're standing on the roof with your grandmother and you can't find your uncle's family anywhere. You can't go down to the first floor because it's a toxic sea from the floor to the ceiling. Besides, you're only thirteen and you're scared as hell, because not only is your uncle's family unaccounted for, you don't know where your mother, your father, your little brother, your aunts, cousins, friends, you don't know where anyone is. All you know is that you are standing in the belly of the beast, trying to figure out why you hadn't died but were clearly in hell.

"Now"—he took a deep breath—"once you have a grip on that image, open your eyes and look at me. Do I look like a six-foot-three-inch-tall piece of devastation?"

I opened my eyes and tears slid down my cheeks. "No," I said quietly.

"Now let me show you something else," Zaire whispered against my cheek. "Turn around and look." I wiped my face and turned toward the street. "You see that family?" He pointed. "They all survived Hurricane Katrina, no one from their family died." He pointed to another house. "You see the little girl jumping rope in the yard?"

"Yeah," I said, as I wiped more tears from my cheeks.

"She was floating down the street, in a baby carrier, with her dead mother floating beside her. Now you see that man sitting on the porch watching that same little girl?"

"Yeah."

"He saved her. He and his wife adopted her, and guess what?"

"What?"

"Before they adopted her, his wife couldn't get pregnant, and now they have three children. You see that couple?" He pointed to a lavender shotgun house, with deep purple shutters and a small gallery.

I wiped my eyes and laughed a little at the odd, but cute couple. The older woman had smooth chestnut skin, large breasts, wide hips, and stood about five three. Her hair was dyed the wrong shade of auburn for her complexion, but nevertheless she rocked a short and cropped cut. She wore a pair of black jeans and a floral shirt. The man standing next to her with his arm around her shoulders was a balding Asian man whose eyes were so slanted they sunk into his cheeks and for a moment his face looked as if it only wore a smile.

"What about them?" I asked.

"The day after the hurricane, he came down the street with his boat. He didn't know anyone; he was just looking to help and he did. He saved a woman and her grandson, and shortly after that, they fell in love, and he asked her to be his wife. And before him, she'd been a lonely widow for twenty years, who swore she would never remarry or date again."

"That is the sweetest love story I've ever heard."

"So what devastation? There's life here, love here. We love our city, our homes. Some of us don't know any place but New Orleans, and we want to be here. So, yeah, things could be cleaned up and more houses could be put back together, but there is no devastation. There's only God's perfection, and now"—he pointed to the ramshackle houses and littered plots of land—"all we're waiting on is for man to do his part."

I turned back to Zaire and I wanted to kiss him and melt into his embrace, especially since I felt like at this moment, everything that I'd ever done and had been going through was supposed to lead me here.

Zaire looked into my eyes and as his lips moved toward mine, the scream of "Grandson!" halted us.

I turned around and the couple from the lavender shotgun house waved us over. "Would you come on down here before this food gets cold? I can't stand no cold and old food!"

"Big-Maw's calling," Zaire said, as he grabbed my hand and we walked toward the gallery where his grandparents stood.

"Well…well…well, looka here." Zaire's grandmother stood with her hands on her hips and smiled at us. "Ling"—she turned to her husband—"Grandson has brought home some company. And she just as cute as she wanna be. Got some meat on her bones too. I like that. Lawd knows I can't stand no chile too skinny. Now, Grandson, introduce us so we can go on in the house."

Zaire shook his head and smiled. "This is Seven, and Seven this is my grandmother, Mrs. St. James-Wong—"

"You can call me, Big-Maw," she said, taking over the introductions, "And this is my husband, Ling. And you can call him Ling. He likes that."

Ling looked at me and smiled. "Welcome."

"Thank you."

"Now, is your name really Seven?" Big-Maw smiled. "Like God's perfect number?"

"Yes, m'am," I said, excited that she knew the meaning of my name.

"I love that name." She looked at Ling, and said, "Remind me to play seven hundred, and zero-zero-seven, in the lottery. Now come on in here. The table is already dressed. I just have to fix your plates. Now, listen—" She carried on as we walked in behind her, "My show, *The Real Housewives*, is on." She turned to me. "You watch *The Real Housewives*?" Before I could answer, she said, "Well, I do. So I'ma have to join you and Grandson for dessert, because I need to watch my show first."

"I understand." I smiled. "My mother loves that show."

"And me too." She chuckled as she led us into her country-style kitchen.

"You can sit here, Seven." Zaire pulled out a chair for me to sit in and he sat across from me.

"Now, Seven, are you in school?" Big-Maw asked me, as she fixed our plates.

"Yes, m'am. I'm a freshman at Stiles U."

"Okay." She sat my plate in front of me, picked up a pen, and walked over to the refrigerator. "In college. Check." She pointed to a handwritten list on the freezer. "Now what kind of folks do you have? Where's your daddy? Your mama? You got any babies—?"

"Whoa, time out," Zaire said in complete shock. "Big-Maw"—He walked over to her and placed his arm around her shoulders. Their backs were turned to me. "What are you doing?" he said, tight-lipped, and I did all I could not to fall out laughing.

"I'm checking my list and checking it twice. I'm like Santa around here, and you're my prize, so before I can give you away I need to make sure she's not a rag picker. So like I said"—she turned back to me—"you got any babies?"

"No, m'am." I smiled.

"Look at those dimples, she just as cute. Okay, Grandson, I think we may have a match here."

"Big-Maw, would you chill? It's cool. We're just friends."

He walked back to the table and arched his brow as if to say, *Told you.*

"You're friends?" Big-Maw squinted. "Nawl, what y'all doing is playing. 'Cause if I hadn't called you when I did, you'd be out in the street in a lip-lock right now. And the next thing I know I'da been cussin' out my neighbor, Lu-cille."

"Y'all still at it, Big-Maw?" Zaire questioned. "Seven, the only time they ever got along was the day after the hurri-cane."

Big-Maw sucked her teeth as she sat Zaire's plate in front of him. "Let me tell ya somethin', gul, hard times will make a monkey eat pepper, okay? So, I have tried with this woman. But she loves to run her mouth, honey. The other day, a funeral came through here, so me and Ling joined second line and who was there but Lucille. And do you know what she did?"

"What she do, Big-Maw?" I said.

"Dah'lin, she was dropping sexy eyes over at my Ling."

I snapped my fingers. "Oh no, she didn't."

"Oh yes, she did." Big-Maw snapped her fingers in re-sponse to mine.

"And what did you tell her?"

"I told her, it don' have'ta be beans and cornbread time, but it can be."

For the first time since I met Khya, I was stunned speechless. Beans and cornbread? "What does that mean?"

"It means I will brang it. I told her I 'taint da one. I will work a gris-gris on you, have you all confused. Now play wit' me, ya hear? Or ya heardz me, as the young people say."

"A'ight, Big-Maw," Zaire said, "you can't be busting out voodoo queen at somebody's funeral."

"Hmph, Grandson, Lucille better ask about me. Any-way, baby"—she turned to me—"you two go ahead and eat and when my show goes off, I'll be in here to have dessert with you." She smiled at me and then turned to

Zaire. "Don't you miss another Sunday." And she walked out the room.

"She is too cute," I said to Zaire while studying the amount of food that Big-Maw had piled on my plate. There was shrimp gumbo over rice, fried corn, fried okra, collards, a piece of fried catfish, chicken, and cornbread. I must've blinked a thousand times, trying to figure out where to even start. I mean, like, ummm, I was a big girl, had wide hips, and wore double digits when I bought clothes, but ummm...dang. I looked up at Zaire and he cracked up.

"What, Love?" he said. "Didn't you say you were hungry?"

"Yeah, but I can't eat all of this."

"Now you know you didn't get all those sexy hips from eating salad," he teased. "You know you're used to eating like this."

Did he just call me fat?

Zaire seemed to read the look on my face and quickly said, "I didn't mean anything by that. I was just messing with you."

My face remained twisted.

"Now see, Love, you're too cute to be mad with me. She fixes everybody's plate like that. Look at mine."

I glanced down at his, and he had more food than I did.

"A'ight." He rose from his seat and walked over to me. "Stand up."

Reluctantly I did as he asked and stood. He sat down in my seat and pulled me onto his lap. He reached for his fork, and said, "We gon' knock this out together." He began eating from my plate and just like the perfect scene from the perfect movie, Zaire and I laughed and joked and before we knew anything, we'd cleaned my plate.

"Just friends, huh?" Big-Maw walked into the kitchen. "Young people." She shook her head. "Y'all come on in here with me and Ling so we can have some beignets and tea."

We sat down in the living room and Big-Maw served us. We talked about everything under the sun. Ling told us how he loved Big-Maw from the moment he saw her. Big-Maw talked about how her family went from being a large unit to it only being three of them, with the exception of a few cousins that were sent to Texas after the hurricane and never came back.

Big-Maw showed me photo albums, Zaire told me stories about his mother, and Ling told us how he'd come to New Orleans for a fishing vacation, found the love of his life, and never returned to China.

The night was perfect. Simply beautiful and by the time I returned to campus I was even more confused than when I left. I was feeling Zaire like crazy, but I had a boyfriend, one I'd been with since high school.

I looked out the window of Zaire's truck and then turned to him and said, "Thank you."

"For what?"

"For tonight. I had one of the best times of my life."

"Maybe we can do it again?"

"I can't."

"Why?"

"Because it wouldn't be right. And I mean like"—I took a deep breath and released it out the side of my mouth—"I want to stay in this moment, I do....But we both know

I have a boyfriend...and if I do to him what I'm praying like hell he's not doing to me, then I'm just as guilty and I don't want that."

Zaire smiled at me and kissed me on my forehead. "Don't stress, Love. We homies, right?"

I hesitated. "Yeah."

Zaire gave me a pound and said, "You need me, you call me. You wanna hang out, I'm here, a'ight?"

"All right," I said and placed my hand on the door's lever. I didn't get out though, and don't ask me what came over me, because I don't know. All I know is that I felt an urge to kiss Zaire. And for once, I didn't want to feel obligated to anyone and anything. I didn't want to give a care about partying, designer labels, stilettos, bling, grades, what my mama would say, or any other BS that my mind was trippin' on.

I turned to Zaire, wrapped my arms around his thick neck, and kissed him. I knew he was surprised, but he kissed me back and our tongues spoke a language all their own...French...Spanish...Haitian patois. This was beyond beautiful. I felt like...like...I was traveling all over the world: France, Spain, Italy...and just as I felt myself giving in to this out-of-body experience...my telepathic travel stopped at Josiah's doorstep.

"Wait," I said as Zaire's kisses moved down the center of my neck. "Zaire," I said softly, thinking for a moment that I shouldn't stop him and that's when I realized that my phone was ringing. I knew by my ring tone that it was Josiah. "Zaire, stop." I lifted his chin with one hand and placed the other on his shoulder.

"What, what? What's wrong?" he said as if he'd been in a daze.

Before I could answer my phone stopped ringing. "I can't."

Zaire stared at me long and hard.

"Zaire, I just..."

"It's cool, Love," he said as my phone started ringing again. "Your obligation is calling."

And he was right, I was obligated to Josiah. "Good night." I held my phone in my hand and got out of the truck.

Once I stepped into my dorm Josiah was calling me again.

"Hello?" I answered.

"Yo, Seven."

Don't ask me why but my heart was thundering. "Yeah?"

"Where are you?"

"Why, what?" I stuttered. "I'm in the dorm."

"Oh, okay."

"Why?" I said nervously. "What's wrong?"

"I just wanted to tell you that the paper you'll be writing for me has to be at least five pages long, a'ight? So give yourself enough time to start and finish on time."

I blinked. "That's it?"

"Yeah. I'll check you later though."

"Okay."

"One." He hung up and I stood there wondering if it was possible to win a war against the inevitable.

20

If it's not like the movies
That's how it should be...

—Katy Perry, "Not Like the Movies"

It was 6 A.M. and just as I was able to stop my mind from wrestling between thoughts of Josiah and Zaire, this is what filled the air: "Wasuuuuuup! Big Easy, yeah, baby, it's Big Country on da scene, coming to you all the way from your Stiles U AM dial, bringing your airwaves coffee to ya, baby! Ya heardz me! Now rise and shine, 'cause it ain't beans-and-cornbread time, it's what?"

"Time to wake up!" Shae completed Big Country's sentence.

"You got it, time to wake da hell up!" Big Country carried on, and the sound of his voice rose from Shae's radio and completely wrecked my nerves.

"Could you turn that down?" I tossed the covers from over my head and turned to Shae, who looked at the radio and smiled. "I can't believe you're gawking over the sound of his country twang."

"Are you hatin' on my baby, Seven?"

"Y'all know what?!" Khya wrestled with her sheets until

she unwrapped herself and sat up. "You two got a bad habit of talkin' while I'm tryna to finish my sleep."

"Tell 'em, Khya," Courtney banged on the wall and complained. "'Cause Lawd knows I need my sleep too. I didn't get back from the 'Boys Who Like Zebra Print' party until one this morning. And between Seven's funky lil cousin and Seven sliding out of that black F-150 pickup at one-thirty A.M., looking like a bowl of mustard greens and guilt, I've been up all night."

"F-150 pickup?" Khya looked at me and squinted her eyes.

"Would that happen to be the same pickup that splashed water in our hair?" Shae asked.

"Pause." Courtney banged on the wall. "Two snaps up and a fruit loop, Seven, was that baby-daddy last night? I'll be right over there for details."

Before I could flip and put all of them in their places, Courtney banged on the door. "Open up!"

"I'ma fight him," Khya said, as Shae opened the door for Courtney.

"And you gon' die too." Courtney walked in the room, and growled at Khya. "You don't be grittin' on me as soon as I walk up in here."

O...M...G...

I blinked my eyes at Courtney in disbelief. "Are you serious coming in here like that?" I looked at Shae and Khya and they were in just as much shock as I was. Why did this fool have green sponge rollers in his hair, a zebra-print leotard, zebra-print slippers, and a matching boa?

"Why would you come over here looking like that?" I spat.

"What?" Courtney flung the ends of his boa to the back

of his shoulders. "I sleep in this every night. I know, it's sexy, right?" He winked his eye. "Make y'all look at me and imagine thangs. But guess what?" He flopped down on my bed. "Ain't none of y'all my type. Mouths too big and ya too nosey. But you my girls though. Now, Seven, wassup with you? You on the creep-creep?"

"First of all, Zaire and I only grabbed a bite to eat," I said and purposely left out the details. "And second of all"—I gawked at Courtney and twisted my neck—"I don't remember inviting you into my business."

"Well, I ain't going anywhere." Courtney blinked. "So you may as well let me in."

"How did we get stuck with you?"

"Stuck?" Courtney frowned as he took my spare pillow and tucked it under his head.

"You can have that." I rolled my eyes.

"You a feisty lil thing early in the morning." Courtney smiled at me. "Keep it up and you just might turn me on. I like a lil aggression. Now tell me, wassup with you and Black Love and don't leave out any details. Start from the moment he walked up to you and said, 'You, woman, you come to me, man, and we get together and get our freak on.'"

"Is that your pick-up line, round?" Khya frowned. "If so that's why you're lonely and skipping around here in leotards and carrying on. You got issues."

"And what you got, Khya? 'Cause you're lonely too! At least I'm not talking about an imaginary boy named Jamil every few minutes!"

"First of all me and Jamil got a love thang; and it's real. And furthermore, I'm far from being lonely, boo," Khya snapped. "'Cause I been kicking it to Chaz, honey. Didn't you read my status update?"

"Oh my." Courtney smiled. "You and lil Eminem got a vanilla and chocolate groove going on?" Courtney jumped up off of my bed and started doing the pop, lock, and drop it. "Getcha swirl on, getcha-getcha swirl on!"

I wanted to be mad, but all I could do was look at Courtney and laugh. "You are crazy."

"And you're fresh." Courtney stopped his dance and returned to the bed. "Now right after Khya fills us in on her lil homeboy, we gon' move on to you. We're listening, Khya."

Khya smiled. "Okay, he's really cute and sweet."

"Okay." Courtney batted his eyes. "Tell us more."

"And he plays football."

"Touchdown!" Courtney jumped up in glee. "She scores! Khya found us an MVP!"

"Another athlete, Khya?" I looked at her perplexed. "Girl you got more groupie'ism than me, 'cause I can't handle it."

"And why is that?" Shae asked, and I knew she was serious, because of the look on her face. And besides that, out of everyone in the room Shae was the only one who knew me and Josiah when. . . .

"Is there something going on with you and Josiah?" Shae asked.

"Not really, it's just that half of the time I feel like he's somewhere else," I confessed.

"And the other half?" Shae asked.

"I feel like he's with someone else."

"You think he's cheating on you?"

"Oh no!" Courtney sniffed. "I can't take being dogged. Not again, Lawd, not again!"

"Would you cut it out?!" I looked at him as if he'd lost his mind. "For once I'm trying to be serious and you're carrying on."

"I am being serious. I don't joke this early in the morning," Courtney snapped. "And as a matter of fact, I don't have to take this! It's obvious you don't want me in on your lil funky secrets anyway." His voice trembled.

Is he about to cry?

Courtney carried on, "And here I love you three like sisters and this is how you treat Courtney?"

"It's not like that, Courtney," I said, feeling guilty.

"Then apologize to me." He slapped my hand with the end of his boa.

"My fault, Courtney."

"Okay, now tell us what's going down." His attitude quickly snapped back in place.

"I don't know." I hunched my shoulders in defeat. "A big part of me loves Josiah and wants to be with him no matter what, but another part of me is tired."

"You're young, Seven, you need to live," Courtney said, and for once he sounded serious. "You have plenty of time to settle down."

Shae spat, "First of all, she's been with him since tenth grade and before this moment she wanted to keep him forever, so forgive me, but I seemed to have missed something here."

"Just because she's been with him for a while doesn't mean she should be unhappy," Khya added.

"I'm not saying that. Of course she shouldn't be unhappy," Shae snapped, "but no relationship is perfect."

"At seventeen," Khya said, "if your relationship is not like something out of a movie then dump him. Move on to the next athletic scholarship. You know, Seven, there are a few golf players here and the brothahs are tearing up the greens."

I waved my hand as if I were trying to get attention. "Whenever you all want to know my thoughts let me know."

"I want to know your thoughts," Shae said.

"I feel confused." I fought tears back. "Like, I want to love Josiah so bad and I want things to be the way they used to be, but he's not who I fell in love with. He's arrogant. And the only time I hear from Josiah is when he needs me to do something for him or he wants some becky."

"Then maybe they're right," Shae said. "Maybe you should walk away."

"And let some other chick win. Hell no."

"Win what?" Courtney blinked. "He has some money or something? 'Cause all the college students I know are broke."

"She doesn't want him to break up with her," Khya said, "and then he ends up in the arms of Shaka-Locka. And the next thing you know they are happily ever after. I feel you on that."

"Dead!" Courtney screamed. "Courtney's dead at the hundred millionth mention of Shaka-Locka!"

"Shut up." Khya shot Courtney the evil eye.

"I say stay on the creep. Josiah doesn't have to know," Courtney said.

"Are you crazy!" Shae snapped. "You don't encourage her to do anything like that. 'Cause as soon as we find out he's creeping on her we would be all over him. Seven"— she looked directly at me—"you know you're my girl, and you know I will miss us all hangin' tight, but if you feel like you two need a break then you need to be honest with Josiah and step."

"I'm not giving him away!" I looked at Shae as if she'd lost her mind.

"It's not giving him away! And you just said that you were tired."

"I didn't mean tired as in done. I meant tired as in I want things to go back to the way he used to be."

"What if they don't go back? What if they *can't* go back?"

"They will!"

"How do you know that?" Shae pressed me.

"Because, if they don't then I won't know what to do." Tears ran down my cheeks. "Once Josiah and I got together I never imagined being without him." My words were steadily getting caught in my throat. "What am I supposed to do?"

Shae and Khya walked over and joined me and Courtney on my bed. We were all huddled together on a twin-sized bed, like a pathetic pack of teenagers and I was the ring leader.

"Why didn't you tell me this is how you felt?" Shae asked. "Why did you hold this inside?"

"I didn't know what to do and I still don't."

"If it's making you feel like this, Seven," Courtney said, "then you have to let it go."

"He's not the worst guy in the world," I said, hating that I confessed anything to them. "That's not what I'm saying."

"Then what are you saying?" Khya asked.

"I'm saying that I love Josiah. It's just not the way it used to be."

"Well, you're a big girl now," Shae said, "and we're not in high school, screaming ballin', we're in college and if you are not happy then you need to move on."

"I'm not leaving him."

Shae stared at me long and hard and said, "Well, if you want to stay with Josiah you need to tell him how you feel. Then you need to make it a point to stay out of F-150 pickups and leave all the other boys alone. Cheating is not a good look."

I hated that she was right. "You're right." I wiped my eyes and twisted my lips.

We all sat in silence and I hated, hated, hated that I'd confessed anything other than that things were perfect to them. The last thing I wanted was for this to be thrown back in my face at a later date. "I'm good though." I glanced over at the clock. "So listen, it's time to get ready for class."

"Are you sure you're okay?" Khya asked.

"Yeah, I'm straight, girl," I said with a little too much enthusiasm.

"Okay, 'cause if you want, I can get some of Josiah's hair, make a voodoo doll, and the next thing you know he'll bust out looking like Midget Mac. Ain't nothing but a word."

"Somebody need to call the police on you!"

"You know what, Courtney..." Khya said as she and Courtney quickly became engulfed in an argument. I left them standing there because I had other things to deal with, like how I just spilled my guts when I should've kept my mouth shut.

I walked into the bathroom and as Khya and Courtney's exchange of insults lingered behind me, I heard Shae say,

"Seven." She squeezed into the bathroom with me and the space was so tight, that all we could do was face each other's reflection in the mirror.

"Shae, I'm okay," I said, hoping to stop her before she got started.

"Look, I didn't come to lecture you, I didn't. But I know you and I know that you hold a lot of things inside."

"I said I'm all right."

"By you saying that to me, it says that you're not."

"Shae, look, I'ma big girl and I told Josiah that if he wanted to do other things—see other girls—then I was out."

"Why does it have to be on his terms? If you want to be out, check out. Now we're girls so I'ma keep it real with you. I don't want to see you become that chick we swore we would never become."

"And who is that?"

"The one that accepts anything. If Josiah is not treating you right, then step."

"You really think it's that simple?"

"After you realize that your happiness is what matters, then yeah, I think it's that simple." And she left me standing there, staring at nothing but my reflection.

21

I'm doin' me...
And this is what I'ma do 'til it's over...

—Drake, "Over"

I'd been at war with my thoughts for a week. It was a struggle not to think about the grenades that exploded in my stomach everyday; but I played it off to the best of my ability. I swear, I was tense all the time; and all I really wanted, more than anything, was to get back to being me... and doing me.

But I couldn't.

I was this other chick—some fragile and super-sensitive girl who walked on eggshells around her boyfriend, prayed that she said the right things to him, and hoped that the phony smile she shot everybody was believable.

That was me: out of my mind.

I looked over at Shae and Khya and was thankful that the glow of my laptop didn't wake them; after all I'd been up since three this morning working on Josiah's paper.

I really didn't need to give it to him until tomorrow, but given that I was doing everything I could not to face my problems I found myself with more than enough time to knock this out.

My aim was to be done and out the door before either Shae or Khya got up, which is exactly why I'd dressed for the day hours ago.

Oh, wait, let me back up, 'cause another new thing the reinvented me had been doing, since the confessional with my friends, was avoiding them whenever possible. Especially Shae. I couldn't take that her looks said more than her mouth did. And I know she thought I was stupid... and maybe I was... but this was my life and it wasn't a crime to want to keep my man... or was it?

I typed the closing sentence on Josiah's paper and saved it on my portable disk drive. Instead of printing it out here, I decided I'd go to the library and do it.

I closed my computer and just as my feet softly hit the floor this is what rocked the air: "Wasuuuuuup! Big Easy, yeah, baby, it's Big Country on da scene, coming to you all the way from your Stiles U AM dial, bringing your airwaves coffee to ya, baby! Ya heardz me! Now rise and shine, 'cause it ain't beans-and-cornbread time—"

"It's time to wake up," Shae said as she peeled the covers off of her face and stretched.

All I could do was roll my eyes to the ceiling. So much for my evacuation plan.

"Hey, Seven." Shae peeked over at me. "You're dressed already?" She looked at the clock and then back to me. "It's seven A.M. Girl, I feel like I haven't seen you in days."

"I know," I said, purposely keeping it short and curt. I walked over to my desk and packed my backpack.

"I saw you were up late last night," she continued.

"I was." Another short and curt answer.

"So what time did you get up and get dressed?"

"A while ago." I slipped on my Coach sneakers.

"Oh...kay." Shae cleared her throat. "Why were you up so late?"

"Why are you sweatin' me with all of these questions?"

"Sweatin' you?" Shae said, taken aback. "I didn't realize that's what I was doing."

"Well, you are," I said as bitterness settled on my tongue. "So back up."

"What did I tell y'all about waking me up like this?!" Khya snapped as she took her pillow and slammed it over her face.

Shae and I both ignored her. I placed my backpack on my shoulder while Shae sat up on the edge of the bed and said, "So what's really good with you? Why are you acting like this? Is it about Josiah?"

"Look, not today, okay?" I said, pissed off. "Now tomorrow might be a better look, but as for right now, I'm not feeling your comments."

"You need to check yourself, 'cause I didn't do anything to you, and all that bass in your throat you need to give it to your disrespectful boyfriend!"

"Whew, that sounded a lil harsh," Khya said, snatching the pillow from over her face. "Y'all need to chill, we don't need to be trippin' early this morning."

I ignored Khya, looked at Shae, and said, "Pause." I gave Shae the warning eye. "Back up, for real, though. 'Cause, yes, I love my man, but if he was disrespectful to me, which he is not, then I would leave him alone. Puh-lease, believe I am not on it like that, okay? So shut it down. And for your information, not that I owe you an explanation, but me and Josiah are fine, so you can return to your lane."

"And you need to return to being yourself, forget Josiah, and remember he is not the only boy in the world. Trust." Shae sucked her teeth. "That's exactly why, when I saw him the other day, I read him."

"Boo'yowl!" Khya said. "Shae was all up in his grill!"

I stood stunned and not because Shae had cussed him out, but because nobody told me that all of this had gone on around me. The real me was really MIA, fa'sho'.

"He's a straight creep," Shae spat.

"I don't need you to fight my battles," I snapped.

"Well, you're not fighting them."

"I've heard that one before," Khya said, " 'cause that's the same thing my friend Sharri said to me when I was about to take Jamil back."

"Fail." Shae frowned. "We are not going there again, Khya. It's not about you and Jamil."

"And it's not about me and Josiah either." I rolled my eyes.

"Oh, I believe it is," Shae insisted, " 'cause you know he's doing his thing."

For a moment I could've sworn that someone had just sliced my throat. "You need to fall back," I said, tight-lipped. "And what *thing* are you talking about? Josiah would never cheat on me."

"Would you just face facts? You know he's capable of cheating, 'cause he was with Deeyah when he was pushing up on you."

"And you say that to say what—?"

"Well, how you get 'im is how you—."

"That's a low blow, Shae," Khya said.

My chest felt like a hot and sharp knife had just sliced through it. I hated that I had to serve her. But there was nothing else left to do, other than to run off and cry because what she said was the truth, and I surely wasn't about to do that. So I had to black.

"Why are you all up in my neck wit' it, though? Especially since you will never know what it's like to walk in my stilettos, okay, so let's not forget that you were sorting through my leftovers when you chose Big Country."

"Oh, you wrong for that, Seven!" Courtney screamed as he pounded on the wall. "You owe her an apology."

"Whatever." I sucked my teeth. "All I'm saying is that your rah-rah about Josiah, Shae, means nothing to me, 'cause from where I'm standing you're not in my league." I flicked my right hand as if I were performing a magic trick. "Now step off."

Shae frowned. "Are you serious? The only reason I'm not gon' put you on a platter and feed you to the wolves is because I know that you're going through something with Mr. Nothing. But understand this: you aren't the only one who can straight black. Believe dat. I'ma let you live, but the next time it's gon' be a problem.

"And by the way, maybe when you had the chance you should've chosen Melvin, instead of throwing such a treasure away. Then you'd know what it's like to have a real man and not a real disrespectful jerk. But you didn't do that, and yes, Big County is *now* my boyfriend. And he may not be what you want him to be, but he is everything I want and need. So you don't have to be feelin' him, 'cause I am."

I clapped my hands sarcastically. "Do you, Shae." And I

walked out the door with tears bursting at the seams of my eyes, dying to slide down my cheeks.

I did all I could to outrun my thoughts as I raced to the library. Shae and I had never had a fight like that...and I knew I needed my bestie, I just didn't know how to turn off the defense mode, even with someone who I knew loved me unconditionally.

I was officially losing it.

No seriously.

I am.

I mean...who was I?

Who am I?

Have I really turned into that chick...the dumb chick?

Was Shae right?

Or was she buggin' and just didn't understand what it was to be in love with a man like Josiah?

But am I really in love or holding on to what used to be love?

I'm nuts.

Tears streamed down my face as I looked around the library, and knew I needed to get out of here. I walked out to the courtyard and found me a secluded corner.

I needed to talk to somebody. I really did....The problem was I'd just thrown my best friend away. I looked at my cell phone and thought about calling my sister Toi. After all when all else failed there was always family to fall back on, so I took my chances.

"Hello?"

"Toi?" I said, confused, and then I realized it was my mother. I rolled my eyes to the ceiling. I was soooo not in the mood for her probing.

"Seven?" my mother said. "Is that you?"

I sighed. "Hey, Ma."

"Is everything okay?" she yawned.

"Yeah, it's okay," I said with no conviction. I pulled my knees to my chest and wiped the silent tears that slid down my cheeks.

"Oh, okay, are you sure?"

"Yeah. I just, ummm, wanted to ask Toi's opinion on something."

"Well, she left for school already and she forgot her phone at home. I saw your number so I answered. She should be home about three."

"Oh...kay."

"You sound like something's wrong. You know you can talk to me, I'll put being your mama aside for about five minutes."

I chuckled. "Ma, I've heard that a million times and it never works for you."

"Okay." She laughed. "Maybe it doesn't, but I'm willing to try. And since I'm not there to kiss your boo-boos when you fall down, I can at least listen and see if that will make you feel better."

I needed someone to talk to, but my mom...? I sighed; here I was again, walking into the trap of spilling my guts to my mother. I felt like I could hear my sister screaming, *DON'T DO IT!* But I couldn't hold this in for another minute. "Me and Shae just had a big argument."

"Oh you guys will get through it. When you were little"—my mother laughed—"you fought all the time and the next day you two were back to being best friends."

"I'm not so sure, this time. Like this time was different."

"Okay, so what'd you two fight about?"

I swallowed. "Josiah."

"Really?" my mother said and I could imagine her brow rising in the air. Knowing my mom, she'd sat up in bed and clicked her reading lamp on. "What about Josiah?"

"I don't really know how to explain it."

"Just say it."

"Well, you know things are different with me and Josiah. And I'm just so confused."

"Are they worse than the first time we talked about this?"

I swallowed. "Yes. He doesn't answer his phone when I'm around. And when I'm not around I can barely get him on the phone. There's this girl that keeps lurking everywhere. Josiah's not interested in anything that I have to do, unless he wants some—" I paused—I'd completely forgot who I was talking to.

"Are you sleeping with him?" my mother said, shocked. "Let me tell you something, little girl, you're playing a grown woman's game, but you can't take care of no baby and I'm not! And you better be using protection because AIDS is a roaming bullet with no name!"

"I'm not having any babies! I'm not getting AIDS! And you said you would listen to me!"

I could hear my mother as she swallowed extremely hard. "You're right. I said I would listen. But I have to ask you this, why are you holding on to him?"

"Because I love him!" I snapped. "I'm just confused about it."

Surprisingly my mother didn't address my tone; she simply said, "Love isn't confusing, it's quite clear."

"Being confused is not illegal."

"Are you confused or in denial?"

"I'm not in denial. Josiah and I love each other."

"So then, what's the problem? Live your life and love your boyfriend."

"Ma, you don't mean that."

"No, I don't, but that's what you want to hear, and honestly, I'm ready to turn off the listening ear and get to the mama mode. You know what; skip all that, I'ma just get to it. You're down there in Louisiana playing grown and doing grown-woman things with Josiah, so you need to be able to hold your own. And if you can't then that's a clear indication that you don't need to be sleeping with him."

"Ma—"

"I'm not done! Now I may not have always been perfect and I know that me and your father's divorce had more of an effect on you than it did your sister or brother, but one thing that I hope and pray you learned from me divorcing him is that you are your own woman, who doesn't settle for bullcrap! And no matter how much I want to coddle you, and kiss your boo-boos I have to give it to you straight with no chaser."

"Ma—"

"I know you wanted me to listen, and I tried, and what I'm saying to you may not be the most politically correct thing, but it's the truth. Now, you mean to tell me that as beautiful as you are, as talented, and as much as you have going for yourself, that you're settling for a relationship that is offering you nothing?"

"I'm not settling. I love him."

"No, you're in competition with whoever this other little girl is."

"No, I'm not!"

"Yes, you are and I know it, and you know it! Every woman has been there and the next thing you know you start imagining things; and becoming consumed with stuff that doesn't even exist and meanwhile he's off living his life."

"But I already told Josiah that if he wanted to do his thing then he could step."

"Seven, baby, he's only nineteen and most nineteen-year-old boys do not announce to their girlfriends that they are ready to move on, they just do it, and it's up to you to catch on. What you have to do is take back your power and control."

"He doesn't have control over me!"

"Then let him go, Seven. I told you before that you needed to think about taking a break and now I'm straight-out telling you, you need to step away from this relationship. Do you think that Josiah has missed a meal? Do you think he's losing sleep? Losing any games? No. You don't need his permission to leave him. Just do it."

"It's not that easy to leave. I love him."

"And that's all you keep saying, so I'm clear that you love him, but what I'm not clear on is if he loves you. And I'm not saying that Josiah is the worst boy in the world, but I am saying that he is young, and that although he may care about you, it's obvious that he wants to experience some things without you. Let him. Do you and do you till it's over. Trust me, it will be okay. Someone else will come along and you will live."

My chest felt like it was caving in. I had to get off this phone. I looked at my watch—I didn't even have time to drop Josiah's paper off now. I needed to get to class, and from the way this conversation was going, I couldn't get there quick enough. "Ma, I don't mean to be rude, but I have to get to class."

"No problem. I love you, Seven, and I hope you understand where I was coming from."

"It's cool, Ma, I got you, and I know you love me. I'll talk to you later." I couldn't hang up fast enough.

22

I was physically in class, but mentally I was in Josiah's apartment, trying to convince him why we needed to get our relationship back on track.

This was sick and I knew it, but I couldn't help it. And I wished there was a way I could rewind time and erase the pivotal moment when things changed between us.

"Okay, everyone," Dr. Banks said as she stood in front of the class. "Your papers on the history of African American fiction are due today. So please pass them forward."

Rewind…what did she say? Did she say paper? What paper…? Oh…my…God! I sorted through my backpack, grabbed my class syllabus and it read, *History of African American fiction due…twenty percent of your grade.*

Dead. Completely dead, buried, and in hell.

For the rest of the class I avoided eye contact with Dr. Banks; instead I mentally rehearsed how I could convince her to allow me to hand in my paper late. A million excuses floated through my mind, ranging from a sick grand-mother to a dead cat.

When class ended, I lagged behind the rest of the students and once the professor and I were the only two left in the room I approached her. "Dr. Banks, can I speak to you for a moment?"

"Yes, of course." She smiled at me.

"I, ummm." I bit the corner of my bottom lip. "I wasn't able to hand my paper in today."

"Really?" She arched her brow. "And why is that?"

'Cause I've been doing my boyfriend's homework. Not to mention that I've been going through so much drama it will cause your head to spin.

"I got mixed up with the date and thought that it was due next week."

"Umm hmm."

"So I was hoping you would let me hand it in late."

Dr. Banks paused. "I don't accept late work."

"Dr. Banks, I really intended to be on time. I've just had so much going on that I got confused with the date. Please, let me give it to you next week. I really can't afford to lose twenty percent off of my grade. I have to keep a certain grade point average to maintain my scholarship."

"Miz McKnight," Dr. Banks said with a slight southern drawl, "you've said the operative phrase, 'you have to maintain.' Now I don't mean to be cruel, but I simply can't allow you to give me a late paper."

"No one has to know."

"You are an excellent student, very talented, and quite gifted, but if I give you an opportunity to hand in a late paper then I have to offer it to everyone."

Tears filled my eyes.

"I know this may seem harsh, but college is the place where you will learn how important it is to stay focused, stay on track, and hand your papers in on time."

"Okay," I said somberly.

"Have a good day." Dr. Banks grabbed her briefcase and walked toward the door; once she reached the threshold she said, "Miz McKnight."

God hates me....

As I walked out of the classroom my heart felt like it was beating in my throat, and by the time I got to Josiah's apartment I felt like I'd been in a war.

I stood outside of his door and rapped softly at first, but after a few minutes and no one answered, I rapped harder, and a few minutes after that I rapped harder and laid on the bell.

The door snatched open and Josiah's roommate, Devin, stood there wiping his eyes. "Yo, what's up with you? It's early as hell." Devin looked me over. "But you sexy as usual." He pulled the end of one of my curls.

Ugg, he was so grimy. I smacked his hand. "I am not trying to wash my hair today, so keep your hands off of me, okay? And besides, don't you have a class you need to be getting to?" I said.

"Nah, only freshmen get stuck with early-morning Monday classes."

"Whatever," I said sarcastically, as I pushed my way inside. My eyes scanned the mess of empty pizza boxes, open soda cans, and CD cases all over the living room, and then I looked back at Devin. "Where is Josiah?" I started walking toward Josiah's room.

"Yo, wait," Devin said, catching my attention. "Yo, he umm"—he smirked—"a lil busy."

"First of all I know my name is different from most but it's not 'Yo.' And second of all, I'm not in the mood to be playing with you."

"Listen, *Seven*, Josiah is in class, a'ight?"

"He doesn't have classes on Monday, so save it." I placed my hand on Josiah's doorknob.

"Trust me, Seven." He looked me over. "I'm not the one playing with you. If I had you, I wouldn't have you on rotation; you would always be with me."

"What the hell are you talking about?" I whipped around toward him. "You know what, just go somewhere and kill yourself."

"Damn." He chuckled in disbelief. "That was cold."

"Yeah." I frowned. "Exactly, I'm cold on you." My heart thundered as I opened Josiah's door slowly. I could hear Donell Jones's "Where I Wanna Be" playing lightly in the background and I could smell perfume in the air as I pushed the door open.

I stood silent and still for a moment, and then my eyes focused on absolutely nothing. There was nothing to see, other than a few LeBron James posters, an unmade bed, a wall of sneakers stacked neatly in their boxes, and a basketball.

"I told you he wasn't here," Devin said. "You didn't want to listen."

"You told me he was busy." I sucked my teeth.

"He is busy. I'm sure wherever he is, he's doing something."

I rolled my eyes. "You are such a hater. I'm not going to

even let you get under my skin. Just tell him I'll be back later after my classes are done."

"I'm not his secretary. I don't deliver messages." Devin smirked. "Now, unless you're joining me in the shower, you need to bounce."

I flicked my hand in the air. "Whatever." I walked out the door and slammed it behind me.

For the rest of the day I couldn't concentrate. I'd been to all of my classes, and if you asked me what happened in them, all I could have come up with would be a blank stare.

I must've texted Josiah at least a thousand times and in between my schedule I called him a thousand more.

This was the slowest day on Earth and by the time my classes were over and I returned back to my room it was six in the evening. Shae and Khya were sitting on their beds, watching TV. As soon as I walked in Shae slipped her shoes on and left; shortly after, Khya came and sat Indian style on the foot of my bed. "You know you were wrong," she said, "and you really hurt Shae's feelings."

"Khya, tell me something I didn't know. It seems that lately I'm always wrong."

"I bet you didn't know her period is late and she thinks she may be pregnant."

"Shae?" I said, completely taken aback. "Are you serious?"

"Let me tell ya somethin', yat. I play a lot of games, but a late period ain't one of 'em."

"Pregnant? Shae? She can't be pregnant," I said in disbelief. "Why didn't she tell me?"

Khya chuckled. "You're kidding me right? Seriously, Seven, you have not been yourself. You don't laugh like you used to, we don't chill like we did when school first started. It's like a tornado came through here and stole our clique. Like, we used to catch da wall tough and now, if you're not snapping our heads off, it's all about Josiah."

"Khya—"

"Let me finish. Before Hurricane Katrina put me and my family out of the projects and then the city of New Orleans put us out of New Orleans—courtesy of them closing the housing projects—and we ended up in Texas, I never felt close to anybody. I always felt like it was a matter of time before something crazy happened and they would be gone from my life; so I kept my guard up. But when I came here and met you two and we clicked the way we did, I let my guard down, and now it's like we're Xscape, you're sleeping with Jermaine Dupre and our lil group is a mess."

What kinda analogy… "Wow, Khya, I didn't know you felt like that."

"Yeah, we all feel like that," Khya said. "So, anywho, round, I'm not the one to lecture you. I'm just putting it out there to you that you're not acting like the Seven I know. You have definitely turned into number eight."

"You mean negative eight." Courtney pounded on the wall. " 'Cause you have been around here cussin' er'body out."

"Why are you in our conversation, Courtney?!" Khya screamed. "I'ma press peeping Tom charges on you."

"Do it," he growled.

"Whatever," Khya said, and turned back to me. "As soon as you and Shae make up we can hit this party."

"Party!" Courtney screamed. "I'll be right over for the details."

Before Khya or I could think to lock the door Courtney was standing in our doorway. "Who's having a party?" he said. "So I'll know what to wear."

"The Deltas are having a party," Khya said. "And if you go, Courtney, you better be on your best behavior, especially since I'm thinking about pledging."

"Oh, isn't that cute." Courtney batted his lashes. "But you shouldn't be a Delta, you should pledge G Phi G."

"G Phi G?" Khya and I said simultaneously.

"Do they have a line on campus?" Khya asked. "I've never heard of them. What does it stand for?"

"Ghetto-Phi-Ghetto." Courtney placed his hands on his hips. "Matter of fact, y'all could start a chapter right here on campus. And your catcall could be, 'I'm 'bout to catch da wall, bey-be!'"

"Looka here, lil whoady," Khya spat, "you have crossed the line...!"

And the next thing I knew they were in a full-fledged argument. They were going at it so hard that I almost didn't hear my phone ringing. I looked at the caller ID and it was Josiah.

I breathed a sigh of relief and walked into the bathroom to get away from Laila Ali and Sugar Ray Leonard. "Hello?"

"Seven," Josiah said, "I'm sorry I missed your calls. I've been chilling with my boys in the Third Ward."

"What time did you leave? Because I was at your apartment early this morning."

"Oh my fault, I should've called you and told where I was."

Really? I blinked. *He's never said that before.*

"Well, baby," he continued, "I won't be home until tomorrow. It's Gerard's birthday so we'll be out for most of the night."

Gerard? "Who is Gerard?"

"One of my teammates."

"Teammate? I don't remember seeing a Gerard on the roster."

"Seven, could you please stop with the questions? I was just calling you to tell you I love you and I was thinking about you. All right?"

"All right," I said reluctantly.

"Did you finish my paper?"

"Yeah, but—"

"Thanks—look, I'ma hit you tomorrow, a'ight? They're calling me. I'm coming!" he yelled into the background.

"Josiah—hello...hello..." I said as I realized that he'd hung up and when I called him right back he didn't answer. I held my phone in my hand and wondered what the heck that conversation was really about.

23

You used to love me...

—FAITH EVANS, "YOU USED TO LOVE ME"

Clearly, I was trippin'. I was in the middle of a jam-packed party, Souljah Slim's throwback "Love Me or Love Me Not" rocked the spot and what was I doing?

You got it—thinking about Josiah. But check this: surprisingly I wasn't really entrenched in thoughts of how to make my relationship better. What had a hold on me was the feeling that Josiah had blatantly sold me some bull.

This is when I needed Shae. I mean Khya was my girl, but Shae was like my sister. Khya had texted Shae to come hang with us; she refused. And when I texted her that I was sorry and we needed to talk, she didn't respond.

I didn't know what hurt worse: losing my best friend or losing me.

Khya was seriously dropping a slow bounce mixed with a West Indian whine on some dude who was too busy looking at her booty to genuinely get his dance on. Court-ney danced in the corner, by himself and threw his arms in the air as if he was about to bust into karaoke at any moment.

After the DJ dropped a few more tunes, I turned to Khya and said, "I'm getting ready to go."

"Go where?" She stopped dancing and wiped sweat from her brow.

"Home."

Khya rolled her eyes to the ceiling. "You told me we were going to try and hang tight tonight."

"I know, Khya, and I'm sorry, but I just don't feel right. Like I need to go and lie down or something. My stomach is sour."

"Uhmm hmm." She twisted her lips. "You owe me big time."

"You can stay if you want to," I said.

"Nawl, I'd rather go back to the dorm, curl in the corner, and whisper to my boo."

"What boo?" I said as we walked out the door, leaving Courtney behind.

"Chaz, girl," she said as we walked up the street toward campus. "I am so feeling him."

I hesitated. "When you two are hanging out...do you ever see Zaire?"

"Why?" Khya gave me a one-sided smile. "Do you like him, Seven?"

"He's okay."

She rolled her eyes to the sky, "Come on, we're girls. You can tell me."

"You better not say a word." I pointed my index finger at her.

"Who I'ma tell?"

"Well"—I hesitated—"Yeah, I have a tiny crush on him. But I told him we could only be friends. Just kickin' it."

"Why did you do that?" She frowned. "Girl, you 'bout crazy as Tiny and T.I."

"Tiny and T.I.?"

"You know—loco. Don't make no sense that they have nothing to do but get arrested time and time again. Like I told Jamil, 'Why you keep getting in trouble for the same thing—?'"

"Khya—"

"And you know I said it," she said, not coming up for air. "*And* I told him while you over there with your palms sweatin' on bars I'ma be catchin' the wall. Feel me? That's why, when Jamil got in trouble last summer and he called me, I was like, 'Oh, no, you better call Shaka-Locka—'"

Nope, not going down that road. "Khya!" I called for her attention. "This is supposed to be about me, not Shaka-Shake-whatever her name is."

"Shaka-Locka, and you're right. This is about you and you being real extra with Zaire."

"I have a boyfriend."

"Girl, please, you have said that to er'body. And er'body is tired of hearing it. Seriously, you're my girl, so I have to tell you the truth, you're starting to sound like a scratched CD."

"Oh no, you didn't!"

"Yeah, I did. But you know I love you, girl." She pinched my cheek.

"Whatever." I chuckled.

Once we arrived on campus; my stomach flipped into knots. I thought about going by Josiah's apartment, just to see if he was really there or not; but a hundred reasons why checking up on him was a bad idea popped like flashes of light in my mind. Yet, a hundred more reasons why I needed to push those feelings to the side and show up at his door anyway, took precedence over anything else. "Khya, I'ma catch you later," I said. "I'ma run by Josiah's for a minute."

"Girl, I'm not letting you roam all over campus by your-self in the dark."

"Khya, the building is right here. What are you talking about?"

"Oh, no, we're in this together."

I looked at Khya and laughed. "You're not slick."

"What?" She blushed.

"You just said you were crushin' on Chaz and now you're trying to go with me, hoping to see nasty-behind Devin."

"Don't hate, Seven. Mr. Nasty is cute."

"But he's a yuk muk."

"Hmph, Mr. Yuk Muk is being courted by a few scouts, honey. Never close off your options. Never."

I shook my head as Khya and I headed into the lobby. Once we approached Josiah's apartment door, I heard people laughing and music playing, from behind.

"Oh, they're having a party and didn't invite us?" Khya said. "Oh hell, nawl, if Groupie4life is in here, it's gon' be a situation."

Before I could ring the bell, Khya pounded on the door, and a few seconds later it opened.

"Hey baby, the pizza guy..." Tori's voice faded as she looked into my face. "...is here."

I stood completely still because I felt like if I moved my body would break. Tori stood at Josiah's door wearing nothing but Josiah's basketball jersey and her panties. Tears beat against the back of my eyes like a tin pan left in the rain, but there was no way I could break down and cry. At least not right now . . . and most-def not right here.

I looked over at Josiah and he stood bare chested in his basketball shorts, holding two glasses of grape Kool-Aid in his hands.

I swallowed and looked at Khya. I knew she could see the hurt in my eyes and maybe that's why she took the lead and said, "Oule, Seven, come on in here, girl, let's make sure we get the full view of what exactly is going on here." She boldly walked inside and I walked in behind her.

Our heels clicked like top models as I did all I could to keep my knees from buckling.

"Seven—" Josiah called my name. He placed the glasses on the table and said, "It's not what it looks like."

"Oh really?" I turned to Khya. "Shall we go over the list for 'he's standing here guilty and he's still denying that he's cheating'?"

"Yeah," Khya said, "let's go over the list. Hit it."

"Okay." I looked Josiah over. "I believe number one on the jerk-off list is another chick answering the door and he's standing here practically naked, with two glasses of Kool-Aid in his hands."

"Side bar," Khya said. "Seven, fa'real dough, dawg, I'm trippin' off this fool drinking Kool-Aid. Don't nobody drink Kool-Aid anymore." Khya shook her head. "I swear nothing's worse than a cheap jerk." She looked at me and said, "We gon' give him two checks for that."

"Seven—" Josiah called my name. "Let me hollah at you for a minute."

I continued, "On to the next item on the list: A trick standing in his apartment with his jersey and her panties on...says to me they were gettin' it in—"

"Clearly, they were gettin' it in; and from the looks of things after they ate they were gon' get it in some more," Khya insisted. "Know what? I'ma put a check by the item that says, 'How to know if your man needs his behind bust.' "

"You two are going a little too far," Tori said, pissed. She looked at Josiah. "They need to leave."

"Make me leave!" I snapped. "I dare you!"

"Chill," Josiah said to Tori, and she immediately sucked her teeth and said, "I don't believe this."

"Believe it." Khya twisted her neck. "Happens to the best of skeezers every day."

"I'm not a skeezer!" Tori snapped.

"Oh you're right, tramp. You're not. What would you prefer, ho? Prostitute? Strip-er?"

"Josiah!" Tori screamed. "You better—"

"Didn't I just tell you to chill?" Josiah said. "Seven, let me hollah at you for a minute." He reached for my arm and I snatched it away. "Please, I need you to understand!" he said.

"I hate you!" ripped from my mouth without me thinking twice. "Now understand that!" I tried to hold my composure, I really, really did, but I couldn't do it any longer.

"Seven, I'm not going to keep saying this, I need to speak to you. You at least owe me that!"

"I don't owe you a thing!" I promise you, I wanted to spit in his face.

"Seven—"

"No!"

"Josiah," Tori snapped, "what are you doing, and why are you explaining yourself to her?"

"Stay out of it!" He cut his eyes at Tori and then looked back to me. "I didn't mean for it to go down like this."

"I don't believe this, Josiah!" Tori screamed. "I'm out of here!"

"You ain't going nowhere," Khya said as she looked Tori over. "Who you think you're fooling and if you do leave you'll only be back in the morning, so you may as well fall back. This is what happens when you in second place, scallywag!"

"I'ma about to—" Tori attempted to say before Khya cut her off.

"About to what? Don't tell me, just do it, because when I get ready to steal on you, you gone be on the ground and that's all to it. No forewarning. Just bam, all up in ya grill! Now what—wassup?" Khya took a boxer's stance.

"Seven—" Josiah reached for me again.

"Don't." Tears snatched my voice from my throat and halted my words. I fought through everything in me that wanted to fold and break down. I looked at Khya and said, "Let's go."

"Let's go?" she said, surprised.

"Let's . . . go . . ."

"Seven," she said, tight-lipped, "I know you're upset, but we at least need to pimp smack this chick." She looked Josiah over and continued, "Hmph, he might be twenty feet tall, but it's two of us, we can take him. And I'm not even worried about homegirl." She pointed to Tori. "'Cause she bet'not get in it!"

"Khya," I said sternly, "they're not worth it."

"Seven," she practically begged, "just slug him one time.

Please. I got a mini pair of nunchucks in my purse and I
promise you, when I get through with this fool, his mama
gon' feel his pain."

"No!" I looked at her and the tears I tried to hold back
were making diamonds in my eyes. "Let's go!"

Khya stared at me, and then she said to Josiah and Tori,
"You better hope I don't see you again, 'cause I will be
packin'!" She took her nunchucks out her purse and
swung them around her arms. "Trust! I'm looking for a
reason to unleash the season of beatin'."

We turned toward the door and stormed past the pizza
guy, who no one knew had been standing there, and by
the look on his face he'd watched this entire episode un-
fold.

My adrenaline pumped on overload and my head was
spent. I did all I could to steady myself as we walked back
to our dorm. I knew Khya didn't know what to say and
neither did I.

All I knew is that I felt like I needed an asthma pump,
but I didn't have asthma. I needed to be somewhere quiet
where I could lie down and pretend that none of this existed.

Once we were at our building Khya said, "Seven, hold
up. Wait, something just came over the newsfeed." She
looked down at her phone and then back to me.

"What?" I said with my throat feeling heavy.

"Ummm, hmmm, you know what? Never mind."

I hate when people do that. "What? What is it?"

"Nah, it's okay."

Oh God. "Would you just tell me?"

"Okay." She looked at her phone, peeped at her watch,
and then looked back at me.

"Khya, what...is...it?"

She swallowed. "You know I'm sensitive and I'ma always be there for you. And I know we're supposed to be
going upstairs to handle your heartache, but you know all
we gon' do is go up there, cuss him out to each other, and
maybe cut up some of his pictures. You'll scream about
how you should've known better...yada-yada-yada. Oh
and you may break down and cry and I'll tell you it'll be
okay...but, at the end of the day none of this would have
changed the fact that you caught him standing butt naked
in the middle of his living room with homegirl."

"He was not butt naked."

"You know what I mean."

"And what does that have to do with anything?"

"Okay." She took a deep breath. "I just read over the
newsfeed, that the football team is having a midnight
cookout and ummm yeah"—she snapped her fingers—
"we need to be there."

"A cookout?" *Did she just say a cookout?* "I'm not up to
a cookout, Khya."

"Yes, you are, Seven." She placed her arm in mine. "And
look at it this way, if nothing else we could go there and
you could eat. You know you haven't eaten in about two
days, especially since you've been so stressed out over
Josiah. So like, you can eat and I can mingle."

"Khya—"

"Seven, please." She folded her hands in a prayer position. "And I promise you when we come back I'll stay up
with you and we'll cry together all night. Deal?"

24

I'm on some new 'ish
I'm chuckin' my deuces…

—CHRIS BROWN, "DEUCES"

Ican't believe I let Khya talk me into this. I really
should've been in my dorm licking my wounds, but instead, I was in the middle of a crowded cookout…at midnight…on a Monday.…

Can you say hot mess? Know what, I'll say it for you…
hot…barnyard…mess.…

"Seven," Khya whispered, "there goes Groupie2damax,
and she's all over Jaquil."

"Who's Jaquil?"

"He used to be number forty-six on the football team,
but now his number is dismissed because his drug test
came back positive for steroids. So, word is that he's trans-
ferring to Trinity U, which is not a Division One school."
Khya laughed. "So why she's all over him, I have no idea. I
swear, this chick's groupie skills are a wreck."

"Khya, maybe she likes him; and maybe him being in a
Division One school doesn't matter."

Khya blinked. "Shhh, you can't ever say that again." She

looked from side to side. "People will think there's something wrong with you. And the next thing you know, somebody has said something crazy and I have to bust out Brucilla Lee on 'em and start swinging my Kung Fu weapons. Now, follow me here, this is how we roll: once we find out that a college athlete's future is secure and there's a possibility of being on one of those rich-women reality shows, then we consider falling in love with him."

"What kind of philosophy is that?" I couldn't help but chuckle. "What happened to love coming first?"

"Didn't you just learn your lesson about love being first in your life?"

"That wasn't love—that was the result of Josiah feeling himself."

"True. And I mean, don't get me wrong, girl. I'm all for love, it's a beautiful thing. But business is always number one. And until then we explore our options. Hey'yay!" She started doing an end zone dance.

All I could do was look at Khya and crack up laughing. "You are a mess!" I laughed until it became infectious, and the next thing I know Khya stopped dancing and had cracked up too.

"On the real though, Seven," Khya said, "right now we just need to live and have fun. Why be tied down anyway? I mean, my motto is 'If you're single, don't stress—be fresh.' " She struck a pose.

"True...but it's just that I was with him for so long. He was my high school sweetheart."

"Well, Seven...I mean...you are entitled to be hurt. And who knows"—she waved at a passing cutie—"maybe you can move on to some new 'ish."

"Puhlease," I twisted my lips, "some new 'ish is the least of my problems."

"Really?" interjected its way into my conversation. "And what's the worst of your problems? Your phone not working?" I didn't have to turn around to know that was Zaire.

I fought hard not to smile, but it killed me.

Chaz walked over to Khya and instantly she melted like butter. "Hey boo-boo." She gave him a soft peck on the lips.

Once I composed my face and was able to hold my smile and blush at bay, I looked up and into Zaire's face. I promise you, this dude put the F.A.H. in fine as hell.

"You have a bad habit of sneaking up on people" was all I could think to say. Saying anything more than that would've had me cheesin' too hard.

"And you have a bad habit of not checking in with your homies," he said.

"Homies?" I frowned, forgetting for a moment and then quickly remembering that I was the one who came up with that label for us.

"Oh," Zaire said, taken aback. "We're not homies anymore?"

"Y'all homies now?" Khya looked at me and then to Zaire. "When y'all become homies?"

"A minute ago, Khya," I said dismissively, hoping she would let it go. Then I said to Zaire, "I could say the same thing about you too, homie. You could've called me."

"Nah." Zaire walked up so close to me that not even a slither of air could get between us. "The last time we were together, after we left my grandmother's house, the ball was in your court."

"Grandmother?!" Khya said in disbelief. "Seven, you've been all in his Maw-Maw's house, and you didn't tell us? Did she serve food?" Khya looked at Zaire.

"A full-course meal," he answered.

"You have eaten a home-cooked meal since you've been here and you didn't say anything? You wait until we get back to the room," Khya said in disbelief. She turned back to Zaire. "And what did she serve?"

"Some of everything," Zaire said.

"Gumbo?" Khya pressed.

"Yep."

"Mustard greens?" she carried on.

"You know it."

"Pork chops?" Her eyes popped open.

"Fried."

"O...M...G....Baked tomatoes?"

"Stuffed, baked tomatoes."

"Beignets?"

"With praline and caramel sauce."

"Oh hell to da nawl! Seven, do you understand that you have been inducted into this family? No wonder you didn't throw any punches tonight or trip too hard, 'cause you over here cupcakin' with lil Bayou daddy at his Maw-Maw's house. Wait until I tell Shae that you been skippin' out on the details."

"Out of sight, out of mind, huh?" Zaire said. "Is it like that with all your homies?" He took a step back.

"Seems so," Khya volunteered. "Seems she leaves us all in the dark."

"Excuse you, Khya," I snapped at her, and then I turned to Zaire and said, "Most of my homies call me."

"Really?" Zaire arched his brow. "So what are you saying?"

Before I could speak Khya interjected, "She's saying that from now on out, she's free er'night, except for when she needs to study for her exams. And don't worry about her saying she has a boyfriend, 'cause we killed him tonight. He's a dead issue."

She has clearly lost her mind! "Khya!"

"What I do?" she said. "I was just trying to help."

"Don't help me, please."

"You're so ungrateful." Khya took Chaz by the hand. "Come on, boo, let's leave the two homies and get us a lil somethin'-somethin' to eat. Bye." She waved as she and Chaz walked away.

Zaire smiled and moved to the side of me and leaned against the brick wall behind us. "So tell me, Love, what was your homegirl talking about?"

"Khya just likes to talk," I said dismissively.

Zaire boldly pulled me in front of him and placed his hands on my waist.

"Here's another bad habit you have," I said. "Putting your hands on me."

"You want me to stop?"

Silence.

"Now," he continued on, "I'ma ask you again, what did Khya mean about you and your boyfriend?"

"Khya was just being Khya. I'm good though."

"What?" he said, confused.

"I'm sayin', I'm straight."

"You straight?"

"Yeah, I'm good."

"A'ight," Zaire said nonchalantly. "Cool, that's wassup. So I tell you what, I'ma go grab me a burger."

"A'ight?" I blinked. "That's it? You don't want to know what happened?"

"Seven, I asked you three times and each time you said some one-word nonsense that meant nothing. So, check it, homie, I'm feeling you and it's clear you're feeling me, but I'm not going to keep beating you in the head with how I feel with you coming back at me with some dryness. Nah, so when you realize that I'ma real dude and I deserve real answers, you let me know." He gave me a pound. "Later."

Wait a minute... what just happened here? Can you say mouth dropped... wide... open? I looked from side to side and said to myself while pointing to my chest, "Did he just... ummm... leave me standing here?" I was stunned. I promise you I had never in my life had a dude do something like that to me.

"Girl, this food is slammin'," Khya said, walking over to me and pointing her burger at me. "You sure you don't want any?" She looked to the side of me. "Where's boyfriend?"

"He left me standing here," I said.

Khya twisted her lips. "Why? Or should I say what did you do?"

"I didn't do anything."

"So then why did he leave?"

"He asked me about what was up with Josiah and I told him I was straight."

Khya blinked. "Straight? After everything Josiah did to you, you so crooked you laid out on the ground. So how can you fix your mouth to tell anybody, and especially a hottie, that you're straight? Why didn't you just tell him the truth?"

"I would've if he had asked again."

Khya looked perplexed. "I'm confused. Why does he have to keep asking you? Why didn't you lay it out to him the first time?"

"Because that would've seemed desperate."

"So you'd rather seem crazy? Oh, and immature?"

"I am not either one of those."

"Well then, let me explain this to you, because dating Josiah for all those years has messed you up." She pointed toward where Zaire stood kicking it with Chaz. "You see that grown, chocolate, hot, and muscle-down cutie over there?"

"Yeah."

"Well, he's a grown N'awlins man. And you can let folks fool you, but it's nothing like a southern honey, and one thing they can't stand is for you not to spell out the truth or tell them how you feel. Okay? Because they will walk away. He doesn't have time to play games with you. Now you better go over there and get your boo, before Gold-digger2damax, who's been peeping him, get up on that."

I hesitated. Tonight was nothing like I expected it to be. I started not to approach Zaire, but then I figured why not. I didn't have anything to lose, and the truth was, I was feeling him and feeling him hard too. "All right," I said to Khya, "I'm going in."

"Work it, girl!" Khya said as I walked over to Zaire and slid in front of him. "Can I speak to you for a moment?"

His eyes roamed all over me. "Yeah," he said with a tinge of reluctance.

"My boyfriend and I broke up tonight."

He paused. "Okay...and how do you feel about that?" he asked me.

"Hurt, pissed...yet relieved," I admitted.

"Why relieved?"

"Because I don't have to pretend anymore that my feelings for him haven't faded away; and I can move on."

"Any regrets."

"Yeah, I should've left him weeks ago."

"Better late than never."

"True."

"So why are you telling me this...homie?" he asked.

"Because..."

"There you go again. Seven, I have no idea what because means. It's simply a conjunction to me."

"It means that maybe we should look into being more than just homies."

25

You must not know 'bout me...

—BEYONCÉ, "IRREPLACEABLE"

I'd sat in the center of my bed, contemplating when I would be the right moment to talk to Shae. Out of everything I'd gone through yesterday, fighting with Shae had to be the worst. I had to make up with her, otherwise what would I do without my best friend.

"Forget it, I'm waking her up," I said to myself; but as soon as my feet hit the floor, Big Country's morning greeting stormed its way into the air by way of Shae's alarm clock radio. "...Big Country bringing you ya mornin' coffee. 'Cause it's not beans-and-cornbread time, it's—"

"Time to wake up." Shae stretched.

I bit the corner of my bottom lip, walked over to Shae's bed, and sat Indian style on the foot of it. She looked at me like I was crazy, but I didn't care. "I'm not leaving until you hear me out. And then after that, I'm not leaving until we make up."

"Well, you'll be sitting there the rest of your life, because I put in for a room transfer."

My heart hit the bottom of my stomach. "You did what?"

Before Shae could answer Khya sat straight up in bed. "What you say, yat?" She blinked. "Didn't I tell y'all about waking me up crazy early?" She stared at Shae. "Now come again."

"I said I put in for a room transfer." Shae shrugged her shoulders.

Tears filled my throat. "Are you serious?"

"Yep."

"Well, it's gon' be a problem then," Khya said. " 'Cause anybody coming up in here will feel the heat of my nunchucks, and besides we're not letting you leave."

"Shae," I said in disbelief, "you're that mad at me?"

"I'm hurt."

"Me too," I said, "but I still love you. You still my girl and I know that you meant well—"

"So then why did you spaz on me?"

"Because you were coming for my neck," I said.

"I was telling you the truth!"

"I know, Shae, and that's what I love about you, but at that moment I just wanted you to fall back. This thing with Josiah had me feeling embarrassed, hurt, and confused and you were just spitting blades at me. I know you did it because we're best friends, but I just needed a minute. That's it and I would've come to my senses."

"I just hate how he treats you."

"I know."

Shae bit the inside of her cheek. "And yeah, maybe... you know I was a little harsh. But I have a lot on my mind too and all I've wanted to do the last few days was share it with you, but you were acting like the world had ended."

"That's how I felt."

"I'm just so pissed that you allow Josiah to treat you like nothing. Ugg, I wanted to slug you and him."

"I know." I chuckled a bit. "You just slugged me with words. But still, I shouldn't have went off like that. The truth is Big Country is a good dude. He's perfect. He loves you, he doesn't act funny towards you, and he doesn't mind telling the world how you're his world. And I guess—" I twisted my index finger into my cheek, like I did when we were kids. "I was a little jealous. And not because I didn't want you to have a good boyfriend. I just wished mine acted the way that yours did."

"I wished Josiah did too, Seven," Shae said. "But he's not treating you right and I can't sit back and watch you take that. I just can't. So I'd rather leave and go to another dorm."

"But, Shae, you don't have to do that—"

"Oh, yes, I do, because if I don't, I'ma end up going to jail for assault, 'cause I'ma cold scrape Josiah."

"We already did that, Shae," Khya said.

"What?" Shae said, surprised. "You beat him up?"

"Not quite," I said.

"Not quite?" Khya blinked. "You're to calm for me, Seven. The answer is heck n'awl we didn't beat him up. Seven wouldn't let me jump him or that trick we caught him with."

"Trick?" Shae frowned. "What trick?"

"You know that girl that would never go away?" I said to Shae. "Well, we went to Josiah's dorm unannounced and she opened the door wearing his jersey and her panties!"

"Oh heck no!" Shae threw the covers off of her. "I'm going to see this dude."

"Shae...Shae." I grabbed her arm, and Khya and I cracked up. "It's cool. I broke up with him."

Shae looked at Khya. "She did?"

"Yes." Khya grinned from ear to ear. "And let me tell you how she did it...." Khya recapped for Shae the entire spiel we put on last night and Shae shot us both a high five and started doing the cabbage patch. "Hey'yay, hoooo!" She waved her hands in the air.

"But, wait a minute, Shae, that ain't the half of it," Khya said. "Tell her, Seven, how you got a fine, chocolate, muscle-bound piece of Bayou candy. Tell her how you and Zaire kicked it all last night.

"Tell her how his Maw-Maw cooked food for you. Tell her how he put you in your place, and said, 'Now, looka here, you gon' have to sattle up, you wanna be with me or not!' Tell her how the sun rose over you two and that he walked you back to the room in the hours of the morning dew. Tell her that Josiah, is what?" Khya took a breath. "Officially black history, bey-be."

Khya stood on top of her bed and said, "I'd like to welcome my girl into the world of moving on to a new boo. Tell her, Seven, tell her what happened to you last night. Girl, Shae"—Khya jumped to the floor. "You ain't even ready for this. Tell her, Seven."

"Khya, you pretty much summed it all up. There's nothing left to really tell her, other than I have a date with Zaire this morning."

"That's wassup." Shae smiled. "So now you officially have a new man."

"You're jumping the gun," I said. "Now I admitted to him that I liked him. But I'm not interested in doing more than just kicking it."

"Kicking it."

"Kicking it. Like homies."

"Oh, Seven, don't get on the made black woman'ish. Now, look, I have something to tell you too."

"Are you about to tell her how your period is late? If so, I already told her," Khya said. "I'm sorry, Shae, I just couldn't hold it in."

Shae shot Khya the evil eye. "Would you be quiet?"

"What?" Khya said. "What I do?"

"Look." Shae shook her head. "I just don't know what to do. My period is two weeks late."

"First of all you should've been using condoms," I said. "I'm real disappointed in you for that one."

Shae agreed, "It was stupid, I know. But it happened."

"Now what?" Khya asked. "Did you tell Big Country?"

"No, I didn't tell him," Shae snapped.

"Well, we have to get dressed and go buy a pregnancy test," I said. "And then we'll figure out the rest from there."

"I already bought one," Shae said.

"And?" Khya and I said, holding our breath.

"I didn't take it yet."

"Why?" I asked.

"Because I wanted you to be here when I did it, just in case I passed out on the floor. I needed someone to catch me."

"You have to go and take that thing now!" I insisted.

Shae hesitated. "You're right." She walked over to her dresser and pulled out an EPT test. She walked toward the bathroom. "Listen out for me hitting the floor."

Khya and I stood behind the closed bathroom door, with our ears pressed to it like a professional pair of eavesdroppers. "Do we really have to stand here and listen to her pee?" Khya frowned.

"Would you hush? This is going to be the longest few minutes of her life."

We waited in silence for about five minutes. Shae opened the door and caused us to stumble and practically fall over one another.

"What?" I said, catching my balance. "Wassup?"

Shae sighed and folded her lips into her mouth. My heart jumped out of my chest and Khya gasped, "O...M...G..."

"It's negative!" Shae jumped up in glee. "It's negative! Thank you, Jesus. Now all we have to do is find my period."

I wiped invisible sweat from my brow. "You know," I said, "sometimes when women all live together their cycles can change and all align with each other."

"Really?" Shae squinted. "I'll run over to the campus clinic today and have a talk with the doctor."

"Yeah, and after that run by Walgreens and hook Big Country up with some Trojans."

"Y'all need to be like me," Khya insisted, "a good Christian girl and wait until you're married. Virgins are wassup!"

"Tell 'em, Khya!" Courtney yelled as he pounded on the wall.

Once we were all dressed for the day, and Shae admitted to us that she didn't really put in for a room transfer, she only had the paperwork, we hunched in the mirror and put our MAC faces on.

"It's so fly that we all have dates this morning before class," Khya said. "This is why I stressed that day we registered for classes that we needed at least one day where our classes started in the afternoon, so we could get our groove on over breakfast. Ain't nothing like seeing a fine man in the morning."

"So true," I said as I turned around toward them and slid back on the counter. "The funny thing is I don't even remember how all of this with Zaire really clicked or how it started. I'm just happy it did."

"Me too," Shae said, "I just want you to enjoy the moment because you deserve it."

"Oh, I plan to," I said as someone knocked on our room door. I looked at my watch. "It's boo lovin' time."

I hopped off the counter and walked toward the door. "Don't hate," I said on my way, "'cause I'ma have Zaire take me to a lil spot in the Ninth Ward, also known as Maw-Maw's." I was a foot away from the door, and then suddenly I stopped in my tracks, and scurried back to the bathroom.

"Listen," I whispered to Shae and Khya, "one of y'all have to go and answer the door. 'Cause if I get it, I might look a lil desperate."

"Yeah, that's true," Shae said.

"I'll get it," Khya volunteered. "You lay in the cut for a minute, Seven."

"All right." Shae and I stayed in the bathroom and I peeked at myself in the mirror one last time to confirm my cuteness. I wore a red and fitted Stiles U T-shirt, glove-fitting jeans, Coach kicks, and fly jewelry. I blew a kiss at myself. How can I say this . . . ? I was, ummm, perfect.

I stepped out the bathroom, prepared to see Zaire's beautiful brown face, only to see Josiah standing there. I was stunned and suddenly the hurt that I didn't want to feel flooded back.

"What are you doing here?" I said, flabbergasted.

"I needed to speak to you." He walked toward me.

"We've already said everything."

Josiah swallowed. "Seven, just give me five minutes. That's it, and I promise after that I'll bounce if you want me too."

"Oh, she will," Khya interjected.

"Can you two just chill and give us a moment?" Josiah snapped at Shae and Khya.

"I wish I would." Shae folded her arms across her breasts.

Khya took a karate stance. "Now try somethin'."

I turned to them. "Can you just give me a minute with him?"

"What?" Shae blinked in disbelief.

"I just need a few minutes."

"Shae, you and Khya can come over here!" Courtney yelled. "I got some extra glasses, we can eat this popcorn and I promise you won't miss a thing."

"That's it, Courtney!" Khya screamed. "I'm calling campus police!"

And of course in true Khya and Courtney fashion an argument ensued, with both of them standing on opposite sides of the wall.

"Khya," Shae said, "look, let's go. You don't have to argue with Courtney."

"True." Khya grabbed her purse. "Yeah, come on, I'll call Chaz and tell him to meet me in the caf."

"Call me if you need anything," Shae said as they walked out of the room.

They closed the door behind them and I turned to Josiah and said, "The clock is ticking. You said five minutes and them getting to the door already took away three of those. So skip to the point."

"Seven, I'm sorry."

"You came here to tell me that?" I frowned. "I knew you

were sorry. Sorry trifflin', inconsiderate, arrogant, turned from sugar to sand. What else? Let's see...hmmm, you lied to me, constantly. Made me look stupid, took advantage of me—"

"Seven, look, I was wrong, I'll admit that, but you had your faults too!"

"I was in love with you! I was trying to recapture your attention, but you were too busy pimpin'!"

"You had my attention. You were my girl. We were in a relationship!"

"That's funny 'cause I don't remember agreeing to you having a sideline ho as a part of the deal."

"Seven, I wanted to be with you, be faithful to you, and I know I was wrong. But I felt like you weren't there for me. You spent more time nagging me than anything else."

"Are you kidding me!" I screamed in disbelief.

"Don't fall for that, Seven!" Courtney pounded on the wall. "That's that whole 'it's you and not me,' spiel, don't do it!"

"Would you shut up?!" I yelled. *God, these walls are too thin!*

"Seven, listen to me." He reached for my hand and I snatched it away. "I'm sorry that I messed up, but we both messed up!"

"Now it's my fault that you were unfaithful?" I screamed at the top of my lungs.

"Seven, sometimes a man needs a woman to back up and understand that he needs his space!"

"Then you should've been straight with me and not run off with another girl! Are you crazy?!"

"You're just as responsible as I am! And after a while you didn't feel like home anymore...."

I knew that Josiah stood in front of me speaking, but all I could hear was my father's voice the day he left my mother. It was as if Josiah had been a fly on the wall, because he pretty much said the same thing to me that my father said to my mother; the only difference is Josiah didn't complain about the kids and the bills. But I promise you everything else was exactly the same. That's when it hit me that I couldn't do this screaming match with him anymore.

"You know what, Josiah?" I said calmly. "I'm glad you came to acknowledge how sorry you are, but you can leave now."

"What?" He blinked in disbelief. "We haven't worked anything out."

"There's nothing to work out," I said as calm as butter. "I'm done—"

"Naw, this isn't over. We'll work through. No relationship is perfect—"

I rolled my eyes to the ceiling. "They may not all be perfect, but I don't want your imperfections anymore. Everything else in your life came before me: basketball, your friends, and now your mistress? Nah, I'm good, you got me twisted."

"Seven, I'm trying to get into the NBA and that's for the both of us. Do you know how upgraded you'll be? People already look at you differently knowing that you're the girl of point guard number twenty-three—"

"And that's the problem. I was the girl of point guard number twenty-three and not Josiah. Josiah would've never done this to me, but you, Mr. Wannabe Kobe or Dying to Be Shaq, whichever fits, are a horrible boyfriend.

So how about this, since I'm not your everything, how about I'll be nothing."

"Seven, I'm not leaving here until you hear me out."

"Can you walk and talk at the same time? Because I have something to do."

"Oh, it's like that?"

"What, did I forget to tell you? If so, then yes, it's like that."

"Seven—"

"Isn't this what you wanted? Now I'm giving it to you, go call up that chick and see if y'all can chill. 'Cause public service announcement: I'm doing me," I said as a soft knock hit against the door. "Come in."

"Seven, I'm not done talking to you."

"Is everything a'ight, Seven?" Zaire looked concerned as he entered from behind the door. "I heard yelling so I didn't know."

"I'm fine and point guard number twenty-three was just leaving."

"Wassup with this?" Josiah turned to Zaire and looked him over.

Zaire looked at Josiah as if he were dismissable.

I walked over to Zaire, stood next to him, and faced Josiah. "I told you I had something to do. Now, if you'll step to the left, Mr. Point Guard, I'll be needing to lock my room up."

"Seven," Josiah said, "are you serious?"

"Dead serious."

Josiah looked at Zaire and said, "You'll see me again."

"You know me, Josiah, so you know it's whatever, whenever."

Josiah didn't respond, instead he stormed out.

"You know Josiah?" I asked Zaire.

"We had a class together," Zaire said a little too quickly. "Now are you sure you're all right?"

"Yeah." My face lit up. "I'm fine." I grabbed Zaire's hand and he kissed me on my forehead.

"So what you wanna eat?"

"Ummm...I was thinking, maybe we need to see what Big-Maw's cooking."

26

"**I**'m not going home for Thanksgiving." I shook my head in disgust, as we sat in the caf eating lunch.

"Why?" Shae asked, completely surprised. "We haven't been home in eons." She sipped her soda.

"My mother would have a fit," Khya spat. "Do you know how much my moms be on my phone with a buncha, 'Khya, whatcha doings?' And I have to tell her, 'The same thing I was doing five minutes ago when you called me.' Geez. So imagine if I don't show up for the holiday? That chick would trip so hard she'd probably start crippin'."

"*Daaaaaang,*" Courtney said. "I see the loco apple don't fall too far from the nut tree, huh?"

Khya squinted her eyes tight and spat, "One day, Courtney, I'ma just steal on you, chop you right in the throat."

"I turn you on, don't I, Khya?" Courtney growled. "One day you're throwing yourself at me, telling me I can be king of the world, and the next day you want to take my head off. I make your wild oats soar, don't I? That's why you want to come for my throat so you can be close to my lips."

"Gagging." Khya stuck her index finger in her mouth.

Courtney blew air kisses at Khya. "One day we should get married just to say we did it." He took the end of his boa and flung it at Khya. "If you want me come to my room tonight and get me."

Shae did all she could not to spit her soda out of her mouth. "You get a little too carried away, Courtney. Anywho, how come you're not going home, Seven?"

"Because, you know my mother's finances aren't what they used to be, so she called and told me this morning that Cousin Shake would be driving here to pick me and Lil Bootsy up and that he and Miss Minnie would be bringing us back. And that ain't going down, round."

"Why not?" Khya frowned.

"Khya, first of all Lil Bootsy needs a booster seat and I am not about to ride all those hours with an angry Midget Mac. And second of all Cousin Shake drives a tricked-out hearse—"

"With leopard upholstery," Shae interjected.

"And baby shoes swinging around the mirror. Don't nobody rock baby shoes around their mirror anymore." I shook my head.

"And," Shae said, "his CD player is stuck on the best of MC Hammer."

"Oh wow, well umm"—Khya blinked in disbelief—"you can always come to Texas with me."

"Awwl, thanks, Khya, but I'll be okay. The Big Easy will take care of me."

"Well, I'll stay with you, Seven," Shae volunteered.

"You know what?" Khya said. "I'll stay too. I'll tell my

mom that I want to be in New Orleans for the Thanks-giving Day Parade. She'll understand."

"Well, don't look at me," Courtney said, "'cause I'm going home. I need to eat some of my mama's hogmawls, pig knuckles, baked chicken gizzards, and sweet potato pie. I like y'all and all, but hmph, it's one thing to put up with you at school but during the holidays? Skip that."

"You are so rude," Khya snapped at Courtney.

"You wanna see me naked, don't you?" Courtney winked at Khya. "Two snaps up and a fruit loop, girl, the things I would do to you."

"Wassup, Seven?" jumped its way over to our table, causing our conversation to come to a halt.

I didn't have to look in the direction of the annoying voice to know that it was Josiah. I cut my eye over at him, flicked him a "Hi" and turned back to my crew. "Maybe for winter break—"

"It's like that, Seven? I can't even hollah at you for a minute? I used to be able to talk to you about anything. We used to be best friends."

I rolled my eyes and turned toward Josiah. "You said hi and I waved. What more do you want?"

"I would like to speak to you for a minute." He paused and when he saw I wasn't moving he said, "Please."

I sighed. "Give me a minute," I said to my friends. Josiah and I stepped to a secluded corner of the room. "What?" I snapped. "What is it?"

He looked me over and smiled. "You look good."

Silence.

"You know I always loved that little crease that ran across your nose when you were mad at me."

"Okay, time's up." I turned back toward my friends.

"Nah, wait," Josiah said. "Just give me a minute."

"I don't have any more minutes to give you."

"Seven, just hear me out."

"What..." I said slowly, "do...you...want?"

"Wassup with you and your new man?"

I stood stunned. "Have you lost all control? You called me over here for this?"

"Yeah, wassup with him?"

"Trust, communication, fidelity, love. Now, big pimpin', wassup with you and your fleet of girlz?"

"I don't have a fleet and I don't have a girl. You're the only one who could ever wear the title of being my girl."

"O...M...G...I'm done." I turned away.

"Seven—"

"What?"

"You need to be careful."

"Of what? You stalking me?"

"Nah, of your boy, I heard he's a rubber-band man."

"What...are you talking about?" I said, clearly annoyed.

"I heard he's living that trap life. You know movin' illegal weight."

I paused and then I spat, "You are such a hater."

"I'm not hatin' on him. Hell, he stole my girl."

"I'm done with this conversation, okay. Now run along"—I flicked my hand—"and go play with your little two-dollar tricks, because Seven is busy."

I know it may have been pouring it on extra thick, but I have to admit that when I glided away from Josiah, I was sure to put a little extra motion in my ocean. "What was that about?" Shae asked when I sat back down.

"Nothing. He's trippin'."

"Oh really?" Courtney said, sliding out of his seat. "Well,

let me see if I can find him, in case he needs somebody to
console him."

"What are we going to do for Thanksgiving if we don't
go home?" Khya asked as we walked back to our dorm
from the caf.

"You'll come with me over to Zaire's grandmother's
house," I said.

"Maw-Maw's?" Khya's face lit up. "She gon' cook?"

"Yeah, and he calls her Big-Maw."

"Honey, Big-Maw, Maw-Maw, just let me in the doe',"
Khya said in an extremely enhanced southern accent. "I
don't even know this lady and I can't wait to eat her food."

"Well, I sure hope it's good," Shae said to Khya, "or it's
obvious you'll be a wreck."

"Chile, a N'awlins grandmamma that can't cook would
tear me apart—hey, Seven." She pointed. "Is that your boo?"

I looked up and Zaire was in the parking lot, leaned
against his truck with some chick dead up in his face. Suddenly I felt stupid and I hated that my mind kept saying,
Not again. Not again.

"Who is that he's talking to?" Khya asked.

"I don't know and I don't care," I said nonchalantly. "So
it's whatever." I turned toward the way of our dorm.

"You're not going to go over there and speak to your
man?" Khya said.

"First off he's not my man, we're just kickin' it. Homies.
And heck no, I'm not going over there." I struggled to play
my hurt feelings off. "For what? I'm not on it like that.
Heck, I just met him yesterday."

"Y'all been kicking it for a month," Shae interjected.
"And just because he's talking to a chick doesn't mean that

she's more than a friend or an acquaintance. Plus, Seven, he's looking over here."

"That's nice." I continued to walk away.

"Seven," Shae called, "he's calling you."

"Girl, bye, do I look crazy? I am so not the one." I walked quickly to the dorm and left them trailing behind me.

"You trippin'," Shae said as she and Khya walked into the room a few minutes after me.

"I'm far from trippin'. I'm just keeping it real."

"Based on what, though?" Khya said, confused. "Josiah?"

"This has nothing to do with Josiah," I said confidently. "This has to do with Seven. And Seven is not about to put up with mess."

"But the boy didn't do anything," Khya said in disbelief.

"He had some chick in his face." My eyes popped out. "He was all in the parking lot kicking it to her, and after what I just went through, you think I'ma ignore that? Nah, not me."

"But true story though, Seven. Zaire put his feelings out there and you said y'all were homies, so like, he really doesn't owe you any explanation about who he talks to."

"Sho' right, Shae," Khya spat. "I bet you you'll be slow about assigning crazy titles from now on out won't you, Seven?"

I flicked my hand. "Whatever," I said as my cell phone rang. I looked at the caller ID. It was Zaire and I nicely pressed IGNORE.

"On that note," Shae said, "who's up for walking down to Bourbon Street?"

"You know I'm down." Khya smiled.

"I'll go too, as long as you two leave the Zaire convo alone," I said as my phone rang again. Of course it was Zaire and I sent his call where? You got it: to voice mail.

"Seven?" Khya asked, "Was that Zaire?"

"Yep."

"Oh, so you have just turned into the mad black woman, huh?"

"Whatever." Zaire called a few more times back to back, and each time I ignored his calls. "Look, can we leave now?" I asked.

"Sure wish I could go to Bourbon Street." Courtney pounded on the wall.

"Oh boy," Shae said, exhausted. "Come on, Courtney!"

"Huh?" Courtney responded and I could only imagine him batting his lashes. "Did somebody call me?"

"Do you wanna come with us?"

"Awwl, that's so sweet, Shae," he said. "Sure, I'll go if you insist."

I chuckled as someone knocked on the door. "Come in," I said.

The door opened and Khya stuttered, "Hey, cutie—I mean strapping—I mean lil daddy. Dang, I keep messing your name up."

"Zaire," he said.

"Yeah, hey, Zaire."

"Wassup, ma?" He nodded at Khya and then to Shae.

"Is Chaz with you?" Khya asked.

"Nah, I think he may still be at practice," Zaire said, never taking his eyes from me. "Seven, I need to speak to you for a minute."

"Yeah," Shae said, "y'all handle that. Come on, Khya and Courtney, it's time to roll." Shae walked past me and whispered, "His name is Zaire, not Josiah."

"So you three are just going to leave me, right?" I asked in disbelief.

"Bye-bye," Shae mouthed to me and blew me a kiss. "Behave."

The door closed behind them, and instead of looking directly at Zaire, I picked up a fashion magazine and thumbed through it. "So wassup?"

"Did you see me standing in the parking lot?" Zaire asked.

"Yep," I said, as I continued to look through the magazine. "Oule, I think I'ma get these shoes." I tapped my index finger on the page.

"Did you hear me calling you?"

"Oule, I like these jeans."

"Seven—"

"Hmm?" I leafed through the pages.

"Are you listening to me?"

"Yeah, I hear you."

"I would like for you to look at me when I'm speaking to you."

I looked up and quickly diverted my eyes from his face. "I'm listening."

He walked over to me, softly placed his hand on my chin, and turned my face in his direction. "I'm Zaire, not Josiah."

"Really?" I blinked twice. " 'Cause the way you had that chick all up in your face, you two surely looked a lot alike to me."

"Check it, if I was kicking it with the chick standing at my truck or anybody else, I would be straight up and tell you—"

I twisted my lips. "You would tell me?"

"Hell, yeah, what I need to lie to my homie for?"

I rolled my eyes.

"Listen, see this whole conversation we're having is not something I'ma keep having with you. That girl I was talking to is someone I have a class with. Period. I missed class the other day; she made me a copy of her notes and gave them to me. That's it. Now if you have a problem with the situation and the label that you gave us, then you clean it up. I already told you how I felt about you too many times to count. But you're holding our life together hostage over something Josiah did."

"That's not true!"

"Then what do you call it?"

"How do you think I felt when I saw you with that girl today?"

"Love, I would never disrespect you by kicking it to some chick on campus of all places. As a matter of fact, you're the only one I'm kicking it to period. I don't think about anybody else but you. So I tell you what, when you get yourself together you call me; 'cause I don't wanna be your homie anymore. I'm done playing with that." He took two steps back.

"Well, then you have to do what you have to do."

"You still acting tough, huh? Even though it's obvious that's not how you feel."

Silence.

"A'ight, if you cool wit' it, then I am too."

"Yup, I'm straight."

"That's wassup." He gave me a pound and turned toward the door.

He placed his hand on the doorknob and I said, "Wait." I swallowed. "Don't go." The sound of my voice was so low it was practically a whisper.

"I'm through with waiting," he said.

"Zaire, it's soooo hard moving past hurt and trusting someone new."

"Seven, have I given you a reason to think I would hurt you? That I would lie to you?"

I shook my head no.

"Then judge me on my own merit, not your ex-boyfriend's."

"How do I do that"—I bit into my bottom lip and walked over to Zaire—"when I'm scared that the same thing is going to happen to me all over again."

"Just let me love you." He pressed his lips against mine. "Dump the homie title, pick up the one that says you're my girl, and we can conquer the world from there."

My heart had said yes right away, but my mind and mouth were stuck on pause and what-ifs. I knew I needed to push past it...but how...?

"Just trust me," he whispered against my lips. "And let me love you."

"Okay," I said as we started to kiss, "I will."

27

I'm more than just an option...
I took a chance with my heart...

—DRAKE, "FIND YOUR LOVE"

"Yo, you cannot talk about the secret bat cave, a'ight?" Zaire said as we lay across his couch, studying for midterms.

"I'm just saying that it's tight."

"You live in a dorm room with two girls and you're complaining that my studio apartment is tight?"

"And hot."

"It's N'awlins, bey-be, what you expect?"

"Not much, just an air conditioner."

"I got your air conditioner." Zaire rolled over and started tickling me.

I cracked up laughing. "All right, all right."

"Now are you gon' talk about my spot again?"

"No." I laughed until I cried. "No."

"A'ight." He stopped tickling me and stood up from the couch. He tossed his textbooks into his backpack and said, "Enough studying for now. Besides, I don't know about you, but I already know I'ma kill my midterms. So I'm good."

I had to laugh. "So what are you trying to say?"

"I'm saying it: if you don't master that chart you gon' have problems. Fa'real."

"You are so whack, to say something like that. Just because I needed you to help me with studying chemistry doesn't mean you're going to get a better grade than me. And besides science is not exactly my thing."

"I know, it's English, which is why I don't know why you won't change your major."

"And do what, teach?"

"You can do more than teaching, but what's wrong with being a teacher?"

"Boy, please."

"Teaching is a beautiful thing. My mother was a teacher."

"She was?" I said, surprised, mainly because Zaire never really talked about his mother. "Tell me about her."

Zaire sat down next to me and started to smile. "She used to teach third grade at a school in the Seventh Ward."

"Did she like it?"

"She loved it."

"What kind of person was she?"

"She was funny, and you could talk to her about anything, but she didn't take any mess."

I laughed. "Sounds like my mother. What do you miss most about your mom?" I asked him.

"I miss hearing her voice and having her kiss me good night." I didn't know what to say to that, so I let him continue talking. "Seven, you have no idea what it is to one day have a family who prayed together, hung out together, laughed all the time, to the next day—the very next day most of your family being dead and the ones left are spread out in places they have never been: Texas, Atlanta, Utah, New York. Yo, most of us, at least from my family, we didn't venture too far from the Big Easy."

"Why not?"

"No money, Love. But mostly because we loved our city. To be from New Orleans or N'awlins, bey-be, is to be from a place so rooted in who you are, so entrenched in your heart that to leave here and to live somewhere else—and especially if it wasn't your choice—is hell."

"So when the city had to be evacuated, where did you stay?"

"In Utah."

"Utah?" I frowned. "Really?"

"Yep, Utah." He nodded his head for confirmation. "Yo, Utah is a beautiful state, filled with orange mountains, but it ain't for me. My grandmother was so depressed living there she was sick. We went from living in our own home in the only place we knew to living someplace we knew nothing about."

"How long did you stay there?"

"About six months or so, then we were allowed to come back to New Orleans. Only to find the home we'd known all of our lives was now a pile of sticks and boards, and broken windows."

"That had to be hard."

"You don't know the half of it. We stayed in a FEMA trailer for at least two and a half, three years, and my grandmother was steadily getting sick. No one knew why and then one day she was in the hospital from an asthma attack and it comes across the news that the FEMA trailers were made with formaldehyde."

"What?!"

"Yep, so now I'm sixteen, it's nobody and it's no other man in my family but me. I need my grandmother, otherwise who I'ma have? My family is dead. We weren't rich and we didn't have any money. The house we owned was nothing, so the way I saw things I had to do what I had to do."

"Which was what?"

He paused. "I had to get a job."

"Doing what?"

He paused again. "Construction. And after a while I saved enough money to have my grandmother's house rebuilt and she was able to move back home."

"Wow..." I said, at a loss for words. "It's hard to imagine you going through that."

"Well, I did, but I'm straight now."

"Are you?" I stared at him long and hard.

"I'm getting there." A moment of silence lingered between us and then he said, "Now come on, get up and let's go get something to eat."

I wanted to talk more about his journey, but it was obvious that he didn't, so when all else failed I said something funny. "All we do is eat. Why are you always feeding me?" I looked at him suspiciously.

"So I guess the movie we caught a few nights back, the bowling, shooting pool, and er'thing else we do doesn't count, 'cause you're too busy counting how many times I feed you. A'ight, so we won't eat."

"Maybe you won't eat, but you gon' feed me." I chuckled.

Zaire smiled, reached for my hand, and pulled me toward him. "You know what I dig the most about you?"

"That I'm cute."

"You a'ight, but you don't look better than me," he teased.

"Whatever."

"Nah, for real, what I'm feeling the most is that we're really friends along with me being your man. Like we really, really chill and I'm feeling that. You're different." He looked at me and our gazes locked.

"Really?"

"Yeah, really." He twirled me around, as if we were making a dance move. "You gon' mess around and I'ma give up everything for you."

"Everything like what?" I smiled.

"Like everything." He held me tightly.

"You love me, don't you?" I gave him a peck on the lips.

"Yeah, too much." He slapped me on the behind. "Now let's go, 'cause I'm starvin'.."

"Oh," I said as we walked toward the door, "that's why we're always eating, because you're always hungry." I cracked up laughing as we stepped outside of the apartment building he lived in. "Let's go to the Gumbo Pot, Zaire, and we can walk there," I said.

"A'ight—"

"Yo, hey man," came from practically nowhere. Zaire and I looked up and it was a tall and extremely skinny man, who scratched the sides of his neck so hard it looked as if he were peeling his skin off. His lips were cracked and chapped. "Yo man," he said to Zaire. "Can I speak to you for a minute?"

Zaire stood stunned, and for the first time since we'd been together the veins on the side of his neck jumped.

"Yo, homie, pot'nah, my man, please I need to see ya

for a minute." The man stuck his hand in his pocket and pulled out a palm full of coins. "Let me talk to you for a minute, playboy."

Zaire turned to me. "Stand there and don't move." Don't ask me why, but suddenly I was scared.

Zaire walked over to the guy, shot him a cold and hard look, and said, "If you ever in your life approach me crazy again, it will be a problem. Now my advice to you is to get the hell on. You understand me?"

The man didn't answer—he just simply took off running.

"What was that about?" I asked Zaire once the man was out of sight.

"Nothing," he said, but I could tell his nothing meant something.

"You told me you wouldn't lie to me," I reminded him.

"And I haven't lied to you. Now are you ready?"

"Zaire—"

"Seven, would you trust me? Damn."

I swallowed. "I never said I didn't trust you. I just want to know what's going on? You can tell me anything."

He paused and stared at me. "Seven," Zaire said, "it's cool, a'ight? Now, I'd like something to eat. Are you hungry or are you going back to the dorm?"

A large part of me wanted to bark at him, "I don't have to stay here and kick it with you." But I didn't and mostly because I could tell that whatever just happened here was bothering Zaire a lot more than it bothered me. "Sure," I said, "let's eat."

28

Thought I'd never fall in love,
And then there was you...

—TREY SONGZ, "ALREADY TAKEN"

"I haven't eaten in two days." Khya held her stomach.

"And why not?" Shae looked at her as if she were crazy.

"Because I've been waiting on Maw-Maw's Thanksgiving dinner, ya heardz me?"

"No," Shae said, "what I hear is an ambulance being called any minute because you have passed out."

"Funny you were eating all day, yesterday, Khya." Courtney pounded on the wall. "I could've sworn that shrimp po-boy was a meal. And if I'm not mistaken, didn't you have a donut this morning?"

"Aren't you supposed to be eating chicken butts by now?" Khya spat. "Oh, wait, I forgot you missed your plane, because you were too busy in my business! You should be a private eye. You would put that job to sleep."

"You think so, Khya?"

"Yup, I'm 'bout to update my page and put that as my status."

"Word?" Courtney said, and I could hear him smiling. "So you really believe in me, huh?"

"Oh...my...God..." I shook my head and said, "Please stop giving him career advice; you know he takes it to heart. Now, Zaire and Chaz are downstairs waiting for us, so come on."

"Sure wish I had somewhere to spend Thanksgiving dinner," Courtney moaned. "But don't nobody care about Courtney!"

"Courtney, just come on!" I barked. "Goodness. But I'ma tell you right now, you better be on your best behavior."

"I'm always well behaved."

"Awl, get it now! Hot Boyz," Courtney sang, as we approached Zaire's truck, "baby, you got what I want, 'cause you be drivin' Lexus jeeps and F-150 trucks. We straight up rollin' in here!" he screamed. "Hey'yay, Zaire!" Courtney slid into the backseat, looked out the window at Shae and Khya, and started throwing up gang signs. "Don't hate, 'cause I'm styling. Don't hate."

"Could you chill wit' all that?" Zaire said to Courtney.

"Opps, two snaps up and a fruit loop, let me fall back, 'cause you look like you gun toting. And the Big Easy is the murder capital, so I'm not trying to piss anybody off down here. Okay?" Courtney slapped the back of his hand and said, "Bad Courtney, bad-bad."

God must hate me.

Zaire's eyes clearly burned a hole through me while Courtney performed in the backseat; and it didn't help any that Courtney was dressed in a tiger cat suit and a feather bandanna.

This was obviously the reason why Shae rode with Chaz and Khya.

"He didn't have anywhere else to go," I mumbled to Zaire. "I couldn't just leave him."

"You owe me big time. Huge," Zaire said as we started to ride.

"Here you go, Zaire." Courtney handed him a CD. "Slide this in."

Zaire cut me the evil eye as he slid in Courtney's CD and suddenly Natalie Cole's "Unforgettable" filled the air.

"Can you turn that up?" Courtney said.

This is going to be a long ride.

By the time we got to Big-Maw's house, the ride with Courtney felt like it took an hour as opposed to twenty minutes.

We parked in front of Big-Maw's house, and once we were out of the truck Courtney whispered to me, "Seven, what in da hell is this?" His eyes scanned the block. "You done brought me over here to Iraq. Have Mercy."

"Would you shut up?" I said, tight-lipped.

"I'm just saying," Courtney continued to whisper, "I have a right to my opinion! What would you think if every other house was on the ground? I'm officially scared now, you could've left me on campus. I had freeze-dried turkey sandwiches."

I didn't even respond to him. I simply walked away.

"I'm so glad y'all came!" Big-Maw met us at the door. "Grandson, you brought home the whole crew, didn't you? Well, I just love it."

"Hey'yay! I'm Courtney." Courtney walked up to Big-Maw and gave her a hug. He looked over at Ling and said, "Look at you, all United Nations up in here."

Should I smack him now or later?

"And I'm Khya!" Khya hugged Big-Maw. "And you look just like this guy I knew named Jamil's grandmother."

"Well, I hope she was a nice lady."

"She was." Khya smiled. "And you know ever since Seven told us she ate your food—although she didn't tell us right away and technically Zaire told me, and I told Shae—but anyway, ever since I heard about how well you cooked I've been dying to be a guest at your table."

"Well," Big-Maw said, "you are welcome anytime." She looked at Chaz. "I take it this is the young lady you were telling me about?"

"Yes, ma'am," Chaz said as he kissed Big-Maw on the cheek.

She looked back at Khya and smiled. "Cute, very cute. And I can tell by her accent, she's from New Orleans. A homegirl, I like that."

"Big-Maw," I said, "you are so cool."

"There's my girl." She smiled at me. "Welcome back, granddaughter-in-law." She winked at Zaire. "It's beautiful to see you again."

"Thank you," I said. "This is my best friend, Shae."

"Hi, Shae," Big-Maw said and then turned to her husband. "And everybody this is my husband, Ling."

"Seven," Courtney whispered to me, "is that Jackie Chan?"

OMG...

We all walked into the house and Big-Maw had completely outdone herself. The dining-room table was covered with all sorts of food: turkey, dressing, ham, gumbo, catfish, rice, greens, macaroni and cheese, yams, potato salad, and pretty much every kind of dessert you can think of.

"I hope everybody came hungry," she said.

"Sho' did." Khya smiled.

"I did too," Courtney volunteered. "That's why I have on this spandex cat suit so it can expand."

Just shoot me.

"Okay, everybody," Big-Maw said, "let's gather around and hold hands."

We each complied and I stood between Zaire and Shae. Zaire held my hand tightly.

"Dear Lord," Big-Maw said, "we thank You for filling this house once again with love, friends, and good spirits. We thank You for allowing us to come home again. Thank You for giving Grandson the strength to not only go to school but to work long hours at his job, in order to help me see New Orleans and my neighborhood again. I don't know what me and Ling would do without him. And I thank You for the special young lady he's brought here today. She has placed a smile on his face that I haven't seen since his mother was alive.

"Thank You for Ling, Lord. Thank You for all the chil'ren that are here at the table this day. Watch over them, guide them, and let them know that no one shall come before You. We ask You to bless the food we are about to receive and have a special blessing upon it. This we pray in Your son Jesus's name. Amen."

"Amen," we all said, as we turned to each other and exchanged hugs.

We sat down and as we passed the food around the table, the room filled with chatter and laughter. Khya and

Courtney didn't argue. Big-Maw and Ling—at my request—shared their love story, and Zaire must've whispered to me about how grateful he was to have me in his life at least a thousand times.

I was convinced that life couldn't get any sweeter than this.

An hour after dinner was done, it was late and time to leave.

"I hate to see y'all go," Big-Maw said.

"We do too," I said. "But thank you so much for having us."

"You sure you don't want to take any food with you guys?"

Courtney grunted. "Well, now that you mentioned it—"

"No, m'am," I said. "Everyone had enough."

"I don't appreciate you cutting me off, Seven," Courtney mumbled, but I ignored him.

"Okay," Big-Maw said, as we each hugged and kissed her on our way out. "I hope to see you all again soon!"

She waved to us as Zaire started to drive.

"I tell you what," Courtney said, "if I had on a pair of pants I'd unbuckle 'em. 'Cause that forth piece of sweet potato pie is sitting right on top of my stomach. I need y'all to hurry up. I think I need to use the bathroom."

"You are so gross," I said in disgust.

"Seven, why are you all in my Kool-Aid trying to figure out if it's sugar-free?" Courtney spat.

"Courtney"—I turned my head toward him—"nothing you have is sugar-free, believe me."

"Hey," Zaire said, cutting across our exchange. "Do you two have your seatbelts on?"

"Yeah, why?" I turned back around and noticed that traffic had slowed down.

"There's a police checkpoint up ahead, and I just want to make sure everything is straight," Zaire said, pointing toward a sign that read PLEASE HAVE YOUR LICENSE AND REGISTRATION READY.

"Do they stop every car?" I asked.

"Nah, only every third car."

I arched my brow. "Well, they just let Chaz and the car in front of him ride by, so it looks as if tag you're it."

Zaire slowed down and pulled the truck to the side of the road. "License and registration, please," the approaching officer said.

"Here you go, officer." Zaire handed his information.

"I'll be right back," the officer said, returning to his cruiser.

Don't ask me why the intensity in Zaire's face caused my heart to race.

"Step out the vehicle please," the officer said as he returned to Zaire's truck.

"What?" Zaire blinked.

"What do they mean, 'step out of the vehicle'?" I asked, confused.

"Ma'am," another officer, who'd just walked to the passenger side of the truck said, "you need to step out of the vehicle." He looked at Courtney and said, "You too, sir."

"Oh Jesus, please don't shoot," Courtney said nervously. "'Cause I'm getting out. I don't know what they're hesitating for, but, officer, the last crime I committed, I was seven and stole a bag of Ranch Doritos. My mother made me take them back and I had to stand before the church and confess. So I have served my time."

"Sir, step out of the vehicle," the officer said. "Slowly."

"Oh, Lawd, I'm going down." Courtney opened the door and immediately fell to the ground. "Two snaps up and a fruit loop, I need my mama."

The officer looked back at me. "You have to get out of the car."

"Why?" I asked, completely in shock.

"Your boyfriend was driving on a suspended license. So I need you to step out of the vehicle and sit over here." He pointed to the curb. My mind raced, but I managed to comply as quickly as I could. I looked over at Zaire and he was handcuffed on the side of the truck. An officer read him his rights and another searched the truck.

I was scared, nervous, and I felt lost... and just when I thought things couldn't get any worse, the officer searched the truck and pulled out four bags of weed clamped between two rubber bands. "Now everybody's under arrest," he said.

I was frozen. Utterly frozen and all I could see was Josiah's face the day he tried to warn me. One officer grabbed me and another grabbed Courtney.

"They didn't do anything!" Zaire screamed. "Officer, it's mine. I promise you it's mine. It's my truck and my drugs. Please, listen to me."

Tears flooded my face, and when I looked at Courtney he was completely passed out.

I had never felt anything as cold as a pair of metal handcuffs, and at this moment I knew that my life had ended. "You have the right to remain silent..." were the last words I remembered hearing.

This was a dream. It had to be, because I didn't remember being brought to the police station; all I remembered was being handcuffed to a wooden bench and connected to a crying Courtney, who wouldn't shut up and told everyone who passed by his life story.

After an hour of sitting on the wrong side of the law, the officer who arrested me walked over to us and said, "We're letting you go. Call your parents, call your friends, just call someone to come and get you."

"I'll walk home," Courtney said. "Just let me go."

"However you get there is fine with me," the officer said. "All I know is that I don't want to see you again. And you two better realize how fortunate you are, because I could've booked you." He uncuffed us. "Now leave."

I was in another world completely. This all happened so quickly that I wasn't sure what was going on. Courtney must've called Shae and Khya because somehow they showed up along with Chaz to pick us up. I was quiet the whole ride, and when we got back to the dorm I climbed into my bed, slid the covers over my head, and cried, until I couldn't cry anymore.

29

It had been a week since everything had jumped off with Zaire, and although he called every day, I sent his calls straight to voice mail. The one time he attempted to show up here without calling, I hid in the bathroom and had Khya tell him I wasn't here.

I mean, what was I supposed to say to him? Thank you for betraying me? Thank you for making me believe that I could love again, that forgiveness was possible, only for you to take my heart, slice it open, and pour piss on the inside of it?

Other than that there was nothing to say...and all I knew is that although I really wanted to cry my heart out, I had to move on. I had to. I couldn't just lie here or roll over and die. I had to bury my love for Zaire and accept the fact that everything about him was a lie...and no, I wasn't being bitter. I was simply keeping it real.

I slung my backpack over my shoulder, and as I opened the door I felt as if I'd tripped and fallen into a wall because Zaire was standing there. Immediately my eyes filled with tears.

"I know you've been avoiding me," he said.

I nervously leaned from one foot to the next, trying my best to calm down my internal screams. "What do you want?"

"Just hear me out, please."

"I don't really have time for this."

"I love you and I'm sorry," he said as if he was in a rush.

"Love me? Is this what the hell love is? Love lies to me? Betrays me? Hmph, well, guess what? You can keep that."

"I didn't mean to hurt you."

"I'm so tired of hearing that." I held my fingers out and started counting on them. "First Josiah—"

"Don't compare me to Josiah."

"Oh, okay, would you like me to compare you to my father, then? Because he was a liar too."

"I'm not your father."

"You're right. I don't know who you are. Are you Zaire the student? Are you Grandson? Are you the construction worker? The rubber-band man? Dope boy? Huh?"

"You know exactly who I am. I'm the man who loves you. Wants to be with you forever. I'm the man that made you face your fears."

"Oh please. 'I'll never lie to you, Seven,'" I mocked him. "'I'm not like this and I'm not like that. Love, you're different.'" I squinted. "What did you mean by that? That I was stupid? Stupid enough to fall for you!"

"No, you weren't stupid to fall for me. We were supposed to be together and we should be together now—"

"But you lied!"

"And I'm sorry, I should've told you the truth." He

grabbed my hand and I hated that I couldn't resist letting him hold it.

"I love everything about you, your smile." He ran his thumb across my lips. "Your sense of humor. I want to be there for you. I want to protect you—"

"Protect me, by having handcuffs slapped on me? Nah, I'm good."

"I'm sorry, Love. Please forgive me."

"You really think it's that simple?"

"I wish it was, but I know it could never be. But we can't just walk away from what we had—we have to start somewhere. All that selling drugs has stopped. Period. And my lawyer's looking at getting me into a program where I don't get convicted and the court will dismiss the charges, if I stay in school and don't commit another crime in the next three years."

"And what happens if you do commit another crime?"

"Then the court resumes those charges."

"Well, then good for you," I said sarcastically. "So like, what do you want, a hand clap? I should be what, impressed? How about you're a day late with that. You should've told me that you had drugs in the car. That every time I was with you I was risking my life!"

"Love—"

"Stop calling me that!"

"I can never stop calling you that."

"You have to." I snatched my hand away. "Because I don't want you to love me. I want you to go away. I'm done, Zaire. Through."

"I need another chance!"

"No." I shook my head feverishly. "I can't give that to you."

"I swear to you I didn't know that I still had weed in my truck. I didn't even know my license was suspended. I promise you, I never ever transported anything when you were around."

"Well, somebody caught you slippin', didn't they?"

"In more than one way," he said more to himself than he did to me.

"Yeah, you're right about that! I mean, seriously do you know how I felt? It's like everybody knew but me. Even Josiah knew!"

"Yeah, he knew," Zaire snapped, "because I was selling to half of his teammates."

"Whatever."

"Seven, I didn't do this to hurt you. I sold drugs because I needed to live; I needed my grandmother to live—"

"So she knows what you do too?" I couldn't believe this.

"No. I told her the same lie that I told you. But I'm realizing that lying to people you love is costly."

"So is that your excuse?"

"Love, I'm not making up excuses for what I did, but sometimes when a person is desperate and they don't have anything else, they turn to what they can get. And slingin' was what I knew I could fall back on."

"So that makes it okay?"

"Nah, and it could never make it okay, and I get that now. I just hope that one day you'll understand that everybody makes mistakes."

Tears streamed down my face, but there was no way I could fold. Zaire kissed the tears from my cheeks and whispered, "I will always love you. But if you want me to go, I'll leave."

"Please leave."

Zaire kissed me on my forehead. "Hey, if nothing else, maybe one day we'll be homies again." And he walked backwards out of my room, closing the door in front of him. All I could do was sit on the edge of the bed, and before I knew anything I was a bumbling mess.

I was crying so hard that it took me a moment to realize that someone was knocking at the door.

I wiped my face and said, "Come in."

"Seven?" It was Josiah and at that moment I knew I'd had enough for one day, and to think it wasn't even noon.

"What is it?"

"I just came to kick it to you for a minute. Were you crying?"

"Look, Josiah," I sniffed, "I really don't have the time to deal with the nonsense. I know you heard what happened, so whatever, it is what it is."

"Yeah, I heard what happened."

"And what? You came to rub it in? Say 'I told you so'?"

"No, I came to see how you were feeling."

"Why?"

"Because I care."

"Josiah, spare me."

"Geez, Seven, when are you going to ease up and stop being so hard all the time?"

"When men who claim they love me stop screwing over me!"

"Look, I know I messed up. I did and if I could do everything all over again I would. But I can't. And for real, you didn't make things any easier. You never let anything go, you harbor everything inside, and I felt like I was paying for your father's mistakes; and I'm sure Zaire felt like he was paying for mine."

"So this is all my fault?"

"No, we're responsible for our own actions."

"So what are you trying to say, Josiah? Because I have to go."

"Look, I just came to check on you, not argue with you. And I know you're going through a lot right now. But maybe if you learn to forgive and the rest of us work on ourselves too, then maybe we'll see that there was a lesson in this for all of us."

I hated that he was right. "Maybe you're right, Josiah."

He smiled. "What? Did you say that I may be right?"

I hated that I was snickering a little, but I was. "Yeah, I said it."

"So if you can admit that, then maybe we could—"

"We can't do anything, Josiah, but go to class."

Josiah laughed and stared at me. "You know, Seven, this is the only time I'll ever say this—"

"And what's that?"

"That not only did Zaire get a good girl, you had a good dude. Don't let my mistakes or his one mistake erase everything that you two shared. A'ight? Because when you were with him, it was the happiest I'd seen you in a long time."

I paused. Josiah had caught me completely off guard. "Yeah..." I bit into my bottom lip. "Maybe...you're right again."

30

Take me as I am...
or have nothing at all...

—MARY J. BLIGE, "TAKE ME AS I AM"

Six months later... the last day of the school year....

"**C**ousin Shake in the hiz'zouse, baby!" A series of pounds beat against our room door. "Now open up, Fat Mama!"

I peeled my eyes open one at a time and shook my head. Cousin Shake was not supposed to be here until this afternoon, yet here he was banging on my door as if he had lost every bit of his senior-citizen mind.

I tossed the covers off of me and stormed over to the door. "Would you stop being so loud?" I snapped at Cousin Shake, who stood wearing a pair of silver metallic pants and a matching vest with no shirt beneath. He jogged in place and his neck full of multicolored Mardi Gras beads slapped up and down against the taco meat on his chest.

Yuck! "Why are you here so early?"

"You opened that door like you wanted to do somethin', Fat Mama? Huh?" He lunged his chest at me and immediately pulled himself back. "If you wanna do some-thin', then busta move."

"Cousin Shake—"

"Ain't nothin' to it, but to do it. I dare ya."

"I am not scared of you," I said. "I fight old people."

"And I beat kids. So what-what."

"Cousin Shake." My mother walked up behind him. "What are you doing?" She placed her hands on her hips.

"I'm giving my Fat Mama my love greeting." Cousin Shake snatched me from the door and started hugging me. "We were 'bout to hug it out."

I looked at my mother and mouthed, "Why did you bring him?"

"Behave," she mouthed back.

"Must be a northern thang." Khya sat up in bed. " 'Cause y'all don't believe in letting me sleep late."

"You don't need to be sleeping late," Cousin Shake growled. "Only wild animals sleep late, 'cause they on the prowl all night."

"Cousin Shake!" my mother said. "Leave these girls alone. Now you go on in Lil Bootsy's room and get him situated."

"Yeah, I'll do that," Cousin Shake said as he walked out. " 'Cause this boy is slow."

"Thanks, Ma," I said, as she walked over to Khya and kissed her on the cheek.

"What is that smell?" we heard Cousin Shake yell, as he walked next door. "Lil Bootsy, is this who you said has been passing rotten gas all year?"

"Two snaps up and a fruit loop!" Courtney screamed. "I know the funk miser didn't put that on me!"

And the next thing I knew a full-fledged argument ensued. "Oh my Lord." My mother shook her head. "I can't
take this old man nowhere, not even to a college campus.
Miss Minnie is the only one who can put him in check. I
wish she was here. I'll be back, Seven. I need to go and
handle this."

"What is going on over there?" Shae said as she walked
out of the bathroom.

I shook my head and all I could say was, "Cousin Shake
is here."

"Oh." She nodded. "That explains everything."

"I see you're dressed and ready to leave us," Khya said
to Shae.

"I couldn't sleep last night." Shae sat Indian style on
her bed. "Like, we have been through a lot this year."

"Yeah, we have," I said, fighting back thoughts of Zaire.
"But I guess that's a part of college life."

"Yeah, maybe," Shae said. "But one thing I never want
to experience again is an M.I.A. period and that's for real.
I was so happy when my period came I didn't know what
to do."

"So what are you going to do to make sure that doesn't
happen again?" I asked.

"Well, we decided to chill for a while—unprotected sex
just wasn't worth the risk."

"I hear that," I said. "I'ma miss being here though."

"We'll be back next year," Khya said. "And y'all promised to come visit me in Texas."

"Yeah, you know we will be there." I smiled. "And I
guess all change is a good thing. I mean, I'm finally an
English major and stopped fighting against it. And I'm single—"

"Any regrets about that?" Shae asked.

"Lots."

"What are you going to do about it?" Khya looked at me.

"I don't know." I hopped off the bed.

"Well whatever you do, you better do it today," Khya said. " 'Cause this is it."

"Yeah, you're right."

As time went on our room was filled with our parents, who were exchanging numbers as we all shed tears and said good-bye. As everyone started moving boxes out of the room, I found myself peeking out the window a little more than usual, I guess hoping to see Zaire...which was crazy considering that I'd sent him away six months ago.

"Seven." My mother walked over to me, as Khya, Shae, and their parents moved boxes out of the room. "Are you okay?"

"Yeah." I hunched my shoulders. "I guess."

"What's wrong?"

"Ma, let me ask you something."

"Anything?"

"Did you ever forgive daddy for what he did to you?"

She smiled at me. "Yes." She nodded. "I did."

"Why did you do that?"

"Because I found myself upset all the time, unable to forgive, harboring things that I needed to just let go. Why?"

"Well...I had a friend—well, he was more than a friend—and, umm, he lied to me."

"Really?"

"Yeah."

"Do you want to tell me what it was? I can push aside being your mama for five minutes."

I playfully twisted my lips.

"Okay," she said, "maybe not. Well, tell me this, is the lie something you can forgive?"

"Yeah, and now that I'm not mad anymore I actually understand why he did it."

"Have you forgiven him?"

"Yes."

"Does he know that?"

"No."

"Well then, you have about thirty minutes to figure out what you want to do." She picked up a box. "Everybody deserves to know they've been given a second chance. Now, I'm going to take this out to the car."

I stood in the center of my empty dorm room and a flood of memories rushed at me, from those that made me smile to those that made me cry and wonder why. I wondered if Zaire would answer his phone—heck was his number even the same? But I guess there was only one way to find out.

I quickly dialed his number before I could think about changing my mind. The phone rang once and I hung up.

"God!" I screamed. "Okay, okay, this is crazy." I dialed his number again and this time he picked up on the first ring.

"Hello?"

I hesitated. "Zaire?"

"Speaking."

"This is—"

"I know who this is," he said, and I could hear a smile in his voice. "How've you been?"

"Okay, I guess."

"The last day on campus, huh?"

"Yeah."

"Cool, so what do you have planned for the summer?"

"Zaire, I forgive you." I know that just came out the blue, but I couldn't hold it in any longer.

"What?" he said, completely caught off guard.

"I forgive you...and I understand why you did what you did. And I know you didn't mean to put me in any danger."

"I really didn't and that's something that I'll always regret."

I couldn't stop smiling. I leaned against the wall and took a long pause, thinking about what I was supposed to say next. "I love you, Zaire."

"Wow, are you sure?"

"I'm more than sure."

"Well, hmph, I've waited so long to hear that again."

"And I guess I've waited just as long to say it."

"Any regrets about that?"

"Yeah," I said.

"What's that?"

"That I'm not able to say it to your face."

"I can arrange that."

"How?"

"Come outside, 'cause I'm standing here."

"What?" I snatched the curtain open and tears raced down my cheeks. *Don't look now, but I think I'm turning into a cry baby.*

I couldn't get outside fast enough. My family and friends looked at me as if I had lost my mind, as I flew past them and into Zaire's arms. I felt like I was melting...actually I know I was.

"So how should we do this?" he whispered against my

hair, as I felt his heartbeat against my breasts. "This is your last day on campus."

"I don't know, but I don't want to let you go."

"I'll come see you," he said.

"When?"

"Next month."

"And until then?"

"I'll call you every day." Zaire hesitated. "Are you sure about this?"

"I'm more than sure. I'm in love with you."

Zaire breathed a sigh and held me closely to his chest. I wanted to be there forever. I never expected my life to be like this or for me to feel that I could ever forgive someone who hurt me, or even love someone besides Josiah... but I guess that's what being upgraded was all about—loving, learning, expecting the unexpected.

Upgrade U

Ni-Ni Simone

ABOUT THIS GUIDE

The following questions are intended to
enhance your group's reading of
Upgrade U.

Discussion Questions

1. Which character did you relate to the most and why?

2. Do you think that Seven should have broken up with Josiah in the beginning of the story? If so, why?

3. If Seven had broken things off with Josiah prior to catching him cheating on her, how do you think the story would've turned out?

4. Do you think Seven should have stayed with Josiah, despite his behavior? If so, why? Does being with someone for a long time mean you have to stay with them forever?

5. What lesson did you learn from Seven and Josiah's relationship? Do you think Seven should have forgiven him?

6. What did you think of the resentment Seven had toward her father? Do you know someone like that?

7. What did you think about most of Zaire's family being killed in Hurricane Katrina? Have you ever experienced anything like that? Do you know someone who has?

8. What did you think of Zaire selling drugs? Do you agree with his reason for doing it?

9. Who do you think Seven should have been with at the end: Josiah or Zaire? Why?

10. If you could change the story in any way, what would you have done differently?